# Tulle Death Do Us Part

TULLE DEATH DO US PART

Book 4 in the Material Witness Mystery Series

A Polyester Press Mystery

e-ISBN: 9781954579835

paperback ISBN: 9781954579842

A MATERIAL WITNESS MYSTERY

# Tulle Death Do Us Part

## DIANE VALLERE

Polyester Press

READING, PENNSYLVANIA

*To Sandy Fields*

# 1

MY TEN-FIFTEEN APPOINTMENT WAS TWENTY MINUTES LATE. I
wouldn't have minded so much if said appointment hadn't
asked me to close my fabric store, Material Girl, to the public
while she browsed the aisles to get ideas for her wedding dress.
It was an unusual request, and I would have politely refused if
she hadn't been referred to me by Adelaide Brooks, general
manager of the historic mansion less than a block away. It was
bridal season, after all, and sending brides my way had become
just one of the many small kindnesses Adelaide had shown me
since I'd reopened my family's business.

It was early October, and the hot summer temperatures
were starting to break. I'd had the store ready to open at ten
and wasted fifteen minutes rearranging a display of delicate
tulle fabric that I'd discovered in the back room just last week.
Someone, presumably my great-aunt Millie, the original owner
of the shop, had wrapped each bolt in quilted cotton to protect
it, which explained why I hadn't found it until recently. It wasn't
unusual for eighty-year-old fabric to exist, but to find several
full bolts, in pristine condition, was like spotting a unicorn in

the frozen foods aisle at the grocery store. Discoveries like this —vintage fabrics that had been preserved by the store, which had been closed for ten years before I inherited it, along with new additions like the proprietary blend of velvet I'd had woven for the store and the end-of-bolt acquisitions I made from my contacts in the wholesale fabric market—helped Material Girl stand out as a place where you could find the fabric of your dreams.

You can only fuss so much with delicate fabric before potentially destroying it, so I forced myself to leave the tulle display, and I moved to the stoop outside my shop. Material Girl was on the bottom floor of a Victorian row house, neighbored on one side by an antique market and the other side by a shop of tiki ephemera. The rest of Bonita Avenue was populated with the kinds of shops, restaurants, and banks that gave San Ladrón its small-town charm. Already, the street parking was filling with cars, and visitors were going into and out of shops, looking for something special.

And my store was still closed.

A young couple came out of Tiki Tom's next door. The woman, a pretty blonde with fair features and wispy hair that framed her cherubic face, pointed at my window. "A fabric store!" She turned to the man next to her. "You don't mind if I go in, do you? I promise I'll be quick."

The man smiled. "Don't make promises you can't keep," he said teasingly. "Go in. Take all the time you want. I'll go across the street and get a cup of coffee."

The woman smiled. They shared a kiss that told me there was no animosity behind his teasing, then she turned toward the shop. That was when she saw me.

"Oh, hi! I didn't see you standing there," she said. She glanced behind me and saw the Closed sign in the window. "Is this shop closed?"

My hours were listed on the window just below the sign, so it wasn't difficult to see that they were in conflict.

I glanced up and down the street. It was a typical Friday morning. By noon, cars would have to circle the block, waiting for a parking space to open. The weather was sunny and seventy-five, one of the first near-perfect days we'd had after the gloom of June and the heat of July, August, and September. Today would bring with it a crowd of day trippers, the best business in a small California town like San Ladrón, and I was at risk of missing them. Adelaide couldn't be blamed for the tardiness of the client she'd referred to me, but I was getting more and more curious about how she'd come to recommend her in the first place.

I pulled my phone out and checked for a message or missed call then made a snap decision. "I was expecting a private, um, consultation this morning, but she's running late. Come on inside." I pulled the door open and stepped back.

At that moment, a small black sports car with tinted windows screeched to a halt in front of Material Girl. The passenger window rolled down, and a blond woman in over-sized black sunglasses and a black beret peered out. "Are you Polyester Monroe?" she called out to me.

"Yes, I'm Poly."

She got out of the car and said something to the driver. She turned back to me. "I've heard a lot about you." She stormed the stairs to my door and cast a dismissive glance at the woman next to me. After an awkward moment, she looked back at me. "My assistant *did* request privacy, didn't she?"

There wasn't a lot I could do in this situation. The woman in the beret was right; the initial request had been for a closed shop for her appointment, and the sign on the door indicated I'd honored her request. Pointing out the woman's tardiness wasn't the best display of service, and Adelaide's referral lingered in the back of my mind.

I turned to the original customer. "She's right. I agreed to close the shop for her appointment. I don't know how long we're going to be, but if you give me a phone number, I can call you when we're done so you can come back."

"That's okay. We only had about an hour before we..." Her voice trailed off as she stared at the woman who'd just arrived.

The woman in the beret and sunglasses smiled at the blonde, and for a moment, I thought she might have a change of heart on her whole privacy thing. She glanced over her shoulder. "I just hope the paparazzi don't track me down here." She gave us a broad smile and swept inside.

It wasn't appropriate for me to make a disparaging comment about a customer, but her attitude was too big to ignore. I glanced at the shy blonde and said, "The paparazzi? That's a little much."

"She's right," the blonde said. "That's Beatriz Rosen. The media love her." She craned her neck, and her gaze followed the woman as she wandered deeper into the store.

I'd heard the name, but it took me a moment to place it. "The ballerina?" I asked.

The blonde nodded.

I turned and looked into my store. "She's on billboards all over Los Angeles."

And with that name, the reason for privacy became clear.

Since moving to San Ladrón, I'd lost touch with the gossip of Hollywood, but Beatriz Rosen's story had come to me before that. She was a prima ballerina who'd first made a name for herself for her bold dance performances and later as a bad-boy magnet, the gossip columns romantically linking her to a steady stream of rock stars, actors, and professional athletes. She'd danced in her first lead over a decade ago, in her late teens, and the internet took notice. Ticket sales boomed as a whole new generation of balletgoers clamored to see her in person.

Someone at the Los Angeles Ballet took her image one step further and plastered it on billboards around the city. I used to see them when I drove to my old job in the fabric district. When I'd moved to San Ladrón, I left those billboards behind. I was more likely to watch movies from the thirties than attend the ballet anyway, and aside from the gossip I'd heard, I didn't know much else about her.

I shared a bittersweet smile with the blonde. "I'm sorry. I did agree to let her shop in private. But seriously, I can call you when she's done or stay open later tonight if you want to come back."

"I can't believe she didn't..." the blonde said, her voice trailing off. "We're on our way north, so we won't be around." She glanced into the shop one last time then turned away and crossed the street. I lingered for a moment to watch her enter the diner. Her cheeks were flushed, and she seemed genuinely excited to share news of her brush with fame with the man she'd arrived with. Their faces turned to the window, and I smiled and waved.

The street filled with more people, so I didn't think much when another woman approached the store. This one was dressed casually in a white T-shirt, jeans, and black-and-white Nike Panda Dunks. Her hair was in a ponytail, and her face was free from makeup.

"I'm sorry," I said. I positioned myself between her and the entrance. "My shop is closed for a private shopping appointment."

"Why don't you take out an ad?" she asked. "When Beatriz finds out you don't know the meaning of the word 'private,' she's going to be furious." She elbowed me out of the way to enter my store.

With a backward glance over my shoulder, I saw the couple watching me from the windows of the diner. Their smiles had faded.

I liked to think of myself as a natural businesswoman, but in the span of fifteen minutes, I'd already turned away one customer and offended another. While the rest of the avenue was bursting with business, I was on my way to ringing up a big, fat goose egg.

I reentered Material Girl and closed the hinged black metal accordion gate across the entrance then locked it. Beatriz and her female companion stood by my bridal area. I'd wanted to maximize the opportunities of wedding season, so I'd pulled every white fabric in the shop into a freestanding display and papered the wall behind with drawings of wedding dresses. My skills were in designing, not sewing, and my imagination coupled well with my ability to sketch a concept. Since moving here, I'd made the acquaintance of a local seamstress who worked for me part-time and could make anything I dreamed up. Most of my customers were capable sewers themselves, but my designs often provided the inspiration.

"Welcome to Material Girl," I said. "I'm the owner, Poly Monroe. Adelaide may have mentioned me when she referred you to the store." I addressed Beatriz, not the other woman, though I sensed she wanted my attention too. Not wanting to insult her if she was someone I should recognize, too, I hoped for an introduction.

"Hello," the original woman said. "I'm Beatriz Rosen."

The introduction was unnecessary, but she had no way of knowing that. She held out her hand, and I shook it. My ex-boyfriend, who studied the art of handshakes in his role as an up-and-coming financial analyst, would have described her handshake as regal—not particularly strong but definitely self-important. She released my hand and gestured toward the other woman. "This is my friend Renee." Her companion held up her hand in a wave.

I smiled and said, "Nice to meet you." I turned back to Beatriz. "Adelaide didn't give me details on your shopping needs. I can give you a tour of the store or make recommendations if you'd like."

"I need to find a wedding dress," Beatriz said.

"You found the right part of the store. Is this for a special performance?"

Renee and Beatriz looked at each other.

"You could say that," Beatriz said. She moved away from us and studied the sketches on the wall.

"She's getting married," Renee said, and added, "She's had a little trouble finding the right dress."

"When's the wedding?"

Beatriz turned back to me. "Saturday."

"Tomorrow?"

"*Next* Saturday."

"That's... soon. Depending on your fabric choices, it will take more time than that to get the required yardage in from a wholesaler."

Beatriz didn't seem to hear what I said. She tapped her finger on one of the sketches. "This one. This is the dress."

I moved to Beatriz's side and looked at the sketch she'd selected. It was one of my quick drawings, a few simple lines on paper to capture the essence of a massive gown comprised of layers of light, airy fabric. It was a fun gown to draw because it was easy to get across the idea of it, but it would be difficult to make and would require a *lot* of tulle—almost everything I'd discovered in the workroom.

Beatriz looked away from the sketch and scanned the bolts

of fabric in my display. "Do you have something more special than what you have on display? I'm not used to wearing inexpensive fabrics."

I bristled at the insinuation. Wedding dresses took far more yards of fabric than most garments, and it made sense to use less expensive ones in the underlayers or hidden parts of a dress's construction.

"For a dress like that, I'd suggest synthetics for the structure and the volume and something more special for the bodice."

"Like what?" Beatriz asked.

"Something light and airy. Netting, voile, something sheer," I said. I pointed at the shelf she'd dismissed. "These are the best."

"What about this one?" Renee asked.

She'd wandered away from us as we spoke, and I already knew she was standing by the vintage fabrics. I turned around all the same. Beatriz crossed the store and ran her hand over the one bolt of vintage tulle I'd placed on display.

"This is beautiful," Beatriz said. For the first time since she'd entered the store, her attitude of self-importance disappeared. She stepped back and exposed about half a yard from the bolt then ran her fingers over it gently. "This is the one. You can make my dress out of this."

It wasn't lost on me that it wasn't a question.

"That's vintage tulle," I said. "It's not the most durable fabric in the shop. My great-aunt, who started this shop, sourced it from Tulle, France."

The two women exchanged a glace.

"That's perfect," Beatriz said, then, as if the time and skills necessary to complete such a preposterous task were of the smallest consideration, she added, "You can do that, right?"

"Actually, I can't," I said, conflicted over the possible loss of business. "It's a near-impossible deadline as it is, and I'm not the most skilled sewer—"

A noise by the front gate hijacked Beatriz's attention. I turned and looked. A man rattled the gate from the stoop outside of my shop. I held up my finger to the two women and said, "Excuse me. He must not have seen the Closed sign."

When I reached the door, I left the retractable gate in place. "I'm closed for a private appointment," I said. "I don't know how much longer we'll be, but I'll probably be open this afternoon."

"Beatriz?" he called past me. He threaded his fingers through the opening of the gate and shook it. "Yo, B. Get over here. I need to talk to you."

I was too shocked by the idea that this rough-around-the-edges man was the fiancé of Beatriz to say anything, so when Beatriz headed my way, I stepped back to give her room. I hovered a few feet away, though, not loving the vibe.

"I told you this was going to take a while," Beatriz said. "We can talk when I'm done. I don't know what else you want."

"For you to answer your phone. I'm not kidding, B. This is serious." He glanced past her at me.

In an attempt to look busy, I reached into the pocket of my black trousers and pulled out my phone. There were two missed-call notifications from a number I didn't recognize. I dismissed the notifications and checked my social media feeds.

"I know this is serious," Beatriz said. "It's the rest of my life. You don't think I would have said yes if I didn't mean it, do you?"

"Hard to say," the man said. "We've known each other a long time, but this whole small-town thing doesn't seem like you."

Something about the conversation sounded more ominous than romantic, and while I wasn't thrilled about Beatriz keeping my shop closed indefinitely, I also wasn't thrilled about this public altercation taking place on my doorstep.

I shoved my phone back into my pocket and approached the couple. "I'm sorry to interrupt," I said. "Beatriz, if you've made your decision, I can ring up the fabric and recommend a few seamstresses who can interpret my sketch."

"I'll be done here when I'm done," she told the man then added, "We'll talk later." She left him by the gate without saying goodbye. I wouldn't bet on the survival of their marriage.

While Beatriz headed back to Renee, I started to close the door. The man turned away from me and stared out at the street. He looked annoyed at the prospect of killing time in a small California town, but if Beatriz was going to be my client, I didn't want to offend her partner-to-be.

"She probably wants you to leave so you don't know anything about her dress," I said. "It's tradition."

"Don't let her fool you," the man said. "Beatriz Rosen doesn't care about tradition. She doesn't care about anything but herself. The sooner you learn that, the better off you'll be." He turned his head, spit on the sidewalk, then jogged down my steps and walked away.

# 2

ALREADY, I REGRETTED HAVING AGREED TO THIS APPOINTMENT.
There had to be a story behind Adelaide's referral, and I
couldn't wait to learn what it was. Adelaide wouldn't have
pushed a celebrity bridezilla on me even if she knew it would
involve a hefty sale and a load of publicity. That wasn't her
style.

My phone buzzed again. I pulled it out and saw the same
unfamiliar number as the other missed calls. I sent the call to
voicemail and tucked the phone away then headed to my wrap
stand to get an index card and a pen. I tucked both into my
apron pocket and joined Beatriz and Renee by the display.

"Like I was saying, I'm not the most skilled sewer. I can
recommend someone if you'd like, but I can't speak for anyone's
schedule. I imagine you'll pay a premium to have someone fit
you into their calendar at this late date, and—"

"Price doesn't matter," Beatriz said. "This is my wedding,
and my fiancé wants me to have whatever I want."

"Yes, but we still need to review the fabric choices, and
there's not a lot of time to order something. And your seam-

stress will need as much time as possible to interpret my sketch, draw up a pattern, and have something ready for a fitting before next Saturday."

Beatriz acted as if I hadn't said anything. "I want the whole thing made of the exclusive tulle."

"You've seen the tulle. It's very sheer. It would take over a hundred yards to build up enough to be discreet."

Renee laughed. "Beatriz Rosen, discreet! As if."

Beatriz shot her a *shut up* glance and addressed me. "I want *over* a hundred yards of tulle." She turned to Renee. "That sounds good, right? For the press release." She turned back to me. "Make sure you use at least that much." She turned to Renee. "Wait until Ursula hears. She's going to love that."

"Is Ursula one of your bridesmaids?" I asked. "You don't need to source their dresses, too, do you?"

Renee snickered, and Beatriz said, "You don't have to worry about the bridesmaids' dresses. They're coming from a boutique in Los Angeles."

I should have been sad that Beatriz hadn't come to me for the fabric for her bridesmaids' dresses, but instead, I felt relief. I knew enough about the world of weddings to know that no matter how far in advance a bride planned, something always fell to the last minute.

Beatriz glanced at the tulle, and her expression softened. "Can you give me a swatch? In case I need to match something."

"Of course." I pulled a pair of shears from my apron and clipped a small piece of tulle from the end of the bolt. "Let me get your number," I said. "I'll reach out to a few of my contacts about making your dress. Between the two of us, we might be able to find someone who can take this job."

"There's no need to spend your time doing that," Beatriz said. Her eyes softened, and she reached out and put her hand on mine. Her entire demeanor changed. "I appreciate everything you've done by closing your store so I can shop in private. And I know what I'm asking for is ridiculous. This is a big moment in my life, and I only want to work with people I can trust. I've heard enough about you to know I can trust you."

She held my gaze and removed her hand from mine but smiled, an endearing smile that had the effect of dissolving the barrier between us and making me feel like a friend.

I felt my resistance weaken, but it wouldn't be fair to lead her on. "I love fabric, and I'm happy to work with someone on the dress I sketched, but my skills aren't in construction. A week is an impossible deadline for even the most skilled seamstresses, and like you said, this is an important moment in your life. I don't think you want to entrust something so important to, well, to someone who isn't a professional. I hope you understand."

I held my phone in my hand while I spoke, and Beatriz's eyes stayed on the screen, not on me. When I finished speaking, she shifted her attention to my face and studied me for a few seconds.

"I'm staying at the San Ladrón Hotel. If you can't reach me there, leave a message with the concierge, and I'll get back to you."

"It would help if I had your direct number," I said.

Beatriz glanced at my phone again and gave me her number. Renee looked surprised. I quickly unlocked my phone and typed it in.

"You should have asked Adelaide to find you rooms at the Waverly House," I said. "They've been newly refurbished using all original antiques. I hear the Jefferson Room is the most exquisite."

Renee sniggered again.

Beatriz cast her a cutting glance and said, "I'll have to ask her about it," in a strained voice.

Beatriz then pointed at Renee's handbag and held out her hand. Renee looked confused for a moment, then opened her large bag and pulled out a pale-pink folder. She extracted a photograph and handed it to Beatriz, who handed it to me. It was a glossy photo of Beatriz in midleap. I flipped it over and scanned her bio, past performances, and measurements.

She tapped the photo. "That has everything you'll need. You should keep that out of sight. We wouldn't want anyone to know I was here."

I forced a smile and slid the glossy photo under my cash register. Most of the stores on Bonita Avenue had switched over to fancy iPads and card readers, far more convenient than the big, clunky register that had been in the store since it opened. And truth be told, I had a digital interface set up, too, but I liked using the vintage register. It connected me to the history of the store, and even if my great-aunt and -uncle were no longer living, it helped me feel that they were with me. I wondered what they would think of Beatriz and her hundred-and-one-yards-of-tulle dress and about whether they would have agreed to close the store for this private consultation in the first place.

The three of us walked to the rear exit. Beatriz waved and climbed into the same black sports car that had dropped them off. Renee took the driver's seat. A few seconds later, they were gone.

I strode through my store to the front door, retracted the black gate, and flipped the Closed sign to Open. I peered through the window at the diner across the street, but the young couple who'd been at my store earlier were gone. It was interesting; of the two potential customers, only one of them had initially appeared to have a love of fabric, but because of the appointment arranged through Adelaide, I'd ended up with the less passionate one. *Too late to regret the decision now*, I thought. I had an impossible wedding dress to create.

After moving the bolts of vintage tulle to the stockroom, I replaced them with a collection of polyester net. I didn't even know if I had one hundred and one yards of vintage tulle for Beatriz's dress or if Beatriz would know if I used a substitution, but that was the least of my problems. I was less concerned with materials than with finding someone to make it, and I knew if there was any way Beatriz's dress was going to be finished by her wedding, I was going to have to beg. And by the time I closed for the day, I had a pretty good idea who I was going to call.

———

"No," Giovanni said definitively.

Once upon a time (six years ago) in a land far, far away (Los Angeles), Giovanni had been my boss. He was a cheap businessman who owned To The Nines, a somewhat tacky dress shop that specialized in inexpensive pageant dresses. It wasn't my first choice of employment after graduating with a design degree from FIDM—the Fashion Institute of Design & Merchandising—but of the one hundred and thirty-nine jobs I'd applied for, it was the one that offered me employment.

Working at To The Nines had been an education in itself. My love of evening wear came from my great-aunt Millie. Long before I was awarded a scholarship to FIDM, she took me shopping for vintage gowns in antique malls and taught me how to deconstruct them and create patterns from the pieces. She taught me about fabric, construction, beads, trim, and feathers —and that a finished dress was more than the sum of its parts.

Giovanni cared about none of that. He cared about making dresses for the lowest possible cost and cutting corners on design to shave off minutes in the construction process. He'd been known to buy damaged bolts of fabric at a steep discount and have me design around the flaw, and in one memorable case where he damaged the fabric himself, I covered the flaw in gemstones three times as costly. We'd stayed in contact since I quit, equal parts me needing help from his workroom and him never doing a favor without asking for an agreed-upon favor in return.

"What do you want, Giovanni?" I asked. Having long since learned what it took to get a yes out of my former boss, I cut to the chase.

"What I want and what I am capable of providing in exchange for what you want don't matter this time."

"Why is that?"

"We're under deadline for a celebrity wedding next weekend. Go ahead and laugh if you want, but I always told you we were more than a pageant dress shop."

"*What* celebrity wedding?" I demanded.

"I can't say. I signed a confidentiality clause. But this celebrity came to *me,* and I'm not one to turn down a lady of the stage—"

"Was it Beatriz Rosen?"

Giovanni was temporarily speechless. "Who told you?" he asked. "I warned the workroom girls not to say anything. It figures they'd call you. Which one of them spilled the beans?"

"Women," I corrected automatically. Along with being a cheapskate, Giovanni was a passive misogynist. He had arguably the most talented workroom of seamstresses in all of Los Angeles, a melting pot of Armenian, Korean, Mexican, and Persian cultures, all skilled in their own right, but to the boss man, they were *girls.* I'd corrected him so often it had become habit.

If he responded, I didn't hear him. It was one thing for

Beatriz to find my shop after having been referred by Adelaide. San Ladrón was only so big, and word of mouth was our best source of advertising. But for Beatriz to have sought out Giovanni's workroom, the home of my previous job, back in Los Angeles? That felt beyond coincidental.

"Nobody violated your confidentiality agreement. I guessed. Did Beatriz say anything when she came in? About me?"

"*Somebody's* become a narcissist since moving to the small town."

"This wedding dress I'm asking for help with? It's for Beatriz Rosen. She was in my shop this morning. She liked one of my sketches and hired me to make it. She said she didn't need bridesmaids' dresses, she was getting them from"—I remembered Beatriz's words and cringed as I repeated them—"a boutique in Los Angeles."

"She called us a boutique? That's fabulous! I wonder if she'd mind if I used that as an endorsement."

"Considering she asked you to sign a confidentiality clause over the dresses, I wouldn't go booking a billboard on Sunset Boulevard."

Giovanni's actions often had me rolling my eyes, but this time I couldn't fault him for being on edge. Depending on when Beatriz had hired him to produce her bridesmaids' dresses, he was under a crazy time constraint of his own.

"I thought you had a staff," he said.

"I have a seamstress who works here part-time. She has her own clients. I can't expect her to drop everything and make this dress on an impossible deadline."

"You should have thought of that before you took the job."

"I didn't take the job. I told her I would make some calls."

"Right. Was it the money or the fame? Maybe you learned something from me after all."

"Goodbye, Giovanni."

I disconnected and set my phone on the counter. It was seven thirty, and I was hungry.

I opened my refrigerator to see what options I had, and two furry beasts charged out of the bedroom and skidded into place beside me. Pins, a gray tabby, looked up at me and meowed. Needles, his brother, similarly marked except in orange, swatted at Pins's head and nosed his way closer to the fridge.

"There's nothing in there for you," I said. I closed the door and prioritized the cats' needs over my own, splitting a can of cat food into two ceramic bowls. I'd made the bowls at a local pottery event, decorating them with each cat's name, but Pins liked the bowl that said Needles and vice versa. Turned out kitten siblings were just like humans—always wanting what the other one had.

I went through the motions of looking for something to eat for another five minutes before picking up my phone and calling my friend Charlie. She owned an automotive garage about half a block down the street, and she never, ever, ever worked past five. I imagined her with her feet up on her desk by now.

"Yo, Polyester. What's up?"

Charlie was one of the few people I didn't correct when she called me Polyester. It was my name, given to me after being born on a bed of polyester in the very store I now ran, but to the rest of the world, I went by Poly. Charlie had a no-nonsense way about her, a tough-girl demeanor she'd actually earned by having a not particularly easy childhood. I respected what she'd built for herself with her auto garage and liked how she didn't automatically bow down to the powerful people in San Ladrón. She had her own thing going, and that was how she liked it.

"I'm hungry. And thirsty. And something happened today that I'd like to talk to someone about."

"Does this have to do with your ex?"

"My who?" I bent down to scratch Needles's head, and he looked up at me and whined. *Don't interrupt my dinner, Mom.*

"Your ex-boyfriend, the finance guy. He brought his car in today for a tire rotation and asked about you. I'm surprised it took you this long to call me."

I lowered myself onto a wooden kitchen chair and stared out the window at the now empty street. "Carson?" I asked. "What's he doing in San Ladrón?"

"Don't know. He said he's been trying to reach you. He asked if you changed your number."

"I've been getting calls from an unfamiliar number, but... hold on."

"I don't do holds. Meet me at the Broadside in half an hour."

"No," I said. "The Waverly House."

"Stalemate."

"Fine, but I'm starved. Make it fifteen minutes."

There were reasons Charlie wouldn't want to meet at the Waverly House, but those weren't my concern at the moment. As soon as we hung up, I checked my call log. The unfamiliar number had a Los Angeles exchange. A voicemail notification popped up, and I tapped the replay icon and heard a voice I'd never expected to hear again.

"Geez, Poly, what did you do, block my number? Call me back when you get this. I have something to tell you. It's important." There was a long pause. "This is Carson Cole."

Carson was, indeed, my ex-boyfriend. We'd met in our college years and dated straight through graduation and into our first jobs, which for him had been a paid internship for a financial management firm and for me had been at To The Nines.

Carson had expected us to marry, and for me to raise our

children and run my boutique on the side while he slayed the world of investment banking. I'd known things were not good long before I inherited the fabric shop, but that event served as the catalyst for our breakup. He never had understood my desire to relocate from the big city to the small town and continue what my family had built.

I was curious. What could be so important that Carson had called me seven times to tell me? I touched the screen and accidentally called him back. And immediately hung up. And then answered the incoming call from his new number.

"This is Poly," I said formally.

"It's Carson."

"Hi. I know you've been trying to reach me, but I'm heading out now and don't have a lot of time to talk. Is everything okay?"

"Sure. Yes. Peachy keen."

"What?"

"Can I see you tomorrow? Take you to lunch or something?"

"Carson, I run the fabric shop. I don't close to eat lunch."

"You haven't hired salespeople yet? That's not a sustainable business model, Poly. You need employees. Is the store failing? Do you need money? You didn't default on your loan, did you?"

My reasons for initiating the breakup came back to me. "Listen. I'm on my way out to meet a friend for dinner, and I don't have a lot of time."

"I can join you—"

"No, you can't. I'll see what I can do about lunch tomorrow."

I grabbed a black leather cross-body bag and slung it over my long-sleeved black T-shirt and wide-legged black trousers. I'd adopted black as my wardrobe choice back when I first started working at To The Nines, a strategy against the assault of glue and grime I picked up in the workroom, and the freedom of not worrying about my clothes had stuck with me after I quit. I slid my feet back into chunky rubber-soled loafers, grabbed my keys, and left.

The sun had dropped, but streetlights illuminated Bonita Avenue. The Broadside Tavern was across the street from the fabric store, and unless Charlie had left the moment she hung up with me, I was going to beat her there. I was standing on the sidewalk, waiting for a break in traffic so I could cross, when I overheard tense voices. I turned to the right and saw a man and a woman on the corner.

The streetlamp closest to them was out, so I couldn't see them clearly, but I recognized them all the same—it was Beatriz and her fiancé. They appeared to be arguing. He leaned forward and pointed his index finger close to her face, and she had her arms crossed over her chest. Her beret was at a cocky angle, shielding most of her face from me. I was caught in the mesmerizing trance of witnessing someone else's personal drama when the man grabbed Beatriz's arms and shook her. She seemed unprepared for his physical assault, and her head bobbled on her neck.

"Hey!" I called out.

The man turned his head toward me but didn't speak.

"Leave her alone!"

The man pushed Beatriz back toward the building and took off down the street.

# 3

I RAN TOWARD BEATRIZ. HER BERET LAY BY HER FEET. SHE LEANED against the brick wall, and her breath came in quick, shallow bursts.

"Are you okay?" I asked her.

She stared at me with wide eyes. Her pupils were dilated, and she seemed unable to speak.

"Beatriz, I'm Poly Monroe from the fabric store. Did your fiancé hurt you?"

"I'm okay," she said in a shaky voice. She looked down the street after him, but he was long gone. She reached up and patted her hair then, realizing her beret had fallen off, scanned the ground for it. I bent down and retrieved the hat then dusted it off and handed it to her.

"I was on my way to have dinner with a friend. Why don't you join us?" I asked spontaneously.

"I can't," she said. She seemed to be very much alone on the street corner, and I waited to hear what she might offer as an excuse. "Too much attention." And, with more conviction, she added, "I'll be fine." She turned and left.

I didn't like the situation one bit. I watched as Beatriz climbed into the driver's seat of the same black car she'd arrived in earlier and drove away. I was a stranger to her, and my invitation might have sounded opportunistic. I'd had enough brushes with celebrity when I lived in Los Angeles to know that these were people just like the rest of us, but I knew in a town like San Ladrón, Beatriz Rosen's presence might turn into a sideshow attraction. I wondered, not for the first time, why she'd chosen here for her wedding. I would have to ask Adelaide tomorrow.

The overseen confrontation between Beatriz and her fiancé stayed with me as I crossed the street on foot, and by the time I entered the Broadside Tavern and located Charlie at the bar, I had to do something. I held up my index figure to her and called Beatriz's number. She didn't answer. The number rang four times, and a voice came on. "You've reached Renee Davis. Leave a message."

This was Renee's number? I remembered how Renee had looked after I asked for Beatriz's private number and how her expression changed when Beatriz gave it to me. Now I understood her reaction. I left a message.

"Renee, hi. This is Poly Monroe from Material Girl. I thought this was Beatriz's number." I paused and thought about how to best phrase my reason for calling Beatriz. "I just saw Beatriz and her fiancé arguing on the corner. I know she doesn't want to bring unwanted attention to herself while she's here, but I was worried about her." What I wanted to say was that Renee needed to intervene and get Beatriz away from this man, but it didn't seem appropriate for a voicemail message. "She seemed like she could use a friend. You can reach me on this number if the store is closed."

I returned my phone to my messenger bag and joined Charlie at the counter. She'd already ordered for both of us, and a bottle of beer sat on the counter in front of the vacant stool to Charlie's left. I hung my bag from a hook under the bar. The owner had lamented the lack of female patrons, and I'd convinced him handbag hooks were a start in wooing them.

It had become something of a post-workday ritual for my friends and I to meet up for drinks and/or dinner when we closed, and that normally included Genevieve Girard, the proprietor of the local French-themed tea shop. Last month, Genevieve had surprised both Charlie and me with the announcement that she was closing her shop for a month and renting a furnished apartment in Paris. Two days after she left, postcards started arriving, and if not for the tea shop, I wouldn't have been surprised if Genevieve had extended her stay indefinitely.

"Yo," Charlie said. "You look less like polyester and more like a rumpled cotton bedsheet. What's up?"

"I've had a day." I took a sip of my beer. "Remember I told you I had an appointment?"

She nodded.

"She was twenty minutes late. Then she waltzed in and asked me to make her a custom wedding dress in eight days. And not just *any* wedding dress. A hundred-and-one-yards-of-tulle wedding dress."

Charlie, to her benefit, didn't ask the obvious questions about my sanity or my sewing abilities. As a fellow business owner, she went a different route. "How much would you make off a job like that?"

"That's irrelevant. I turned the job down. It's an impossible deadline."

"Humor me. How much?"

"Based on the materials alone, it would be a fifteen-thousand-dollar dress. That doesn't account for the surcharge of completing a rush job or the fact that I'm not a seamstress and would have to hire help to make it."

"Aren't you wasting time by sitting here with me?"

"I just told you I turned down the job."

Charlie cocked her head. "And that was okay with the bride?"

I thought back to the conversation with Beatriz. "She didn't say much about it. I felt a little guilty, so I offered to call around to see if I could find someone else to do it."

"But she bought the fabric from you?"

"Yes."

"Did she take it with her?"

"No. She left me with her measurements and told me price was no object. You don't think she still expects me to make it, do you?"

"That's exactly what I think."

"But it's impossible!"

"Right. That doesn't mean she doesn't expect you to do it."

"I said no. More than once. She has to know I meant it." I spun my bottle of beer around in a circle, blurring a wet ring of pooled condensation that had accumulated on the old wooden bar. I took another sip then set the bottle down and pushed it away. If I kept on swigging beer instead of fielding Charlie's questions, I would be drunk in an hour.

Charlie knocked on the counter to get the attention of Sam, the bartender. Sam was a twentysomething who looked fortysomething, the result of living hard in his teens. He fit the Broadside in the way Tiki Tom fit the Hawaiian ephemera shop next to Material Girl, as if working here had been his destiny all along.

"Those burgers coming today or what?" Charlie asked.

"You said well-done," Sam said.

"Right. I said well-done, not hockey puck."

"You're a real pain in the a—"

"Language," said Duke, the owner, rolling his wheelchair out of his office. "I'm trying to class the place up."

"Sorry, Duke," Sam said. He shot Charlie a scowl. "I'll go check on them." Sam draped his towel over the shoulder of his stained white T-shirt and went to the kitchen.

Duke rolled his chair out from behind the bar and made his way to the internet jukebox. A few seconds later, Willie Nelson's voice filled the interior. Sam returned with two red plastic baskets filled with burgers, fries, and small metal condiment cups of ketchup and mayo. He set the baskets in front of each of us and walked away.

Conversation temporarily ceased while I assembled my burger and took a bite. Hot juices dribbled down my chin, and I swiped them away and took another bite before swallowing. I was starving. Charlie bit into her burger with similar gusto. After three bites, I set my burger down and ate two french fries then considered what was bothering me.

"The thing is, I don't think she should get married."

"Who?"

"My bridezilla. I think she's making a mistake. Her fiancé came to the fabric shop this morning, and he wasn't exactly nice to her. And just now, I saw them arguing on the corner."

Charlie leaned back and picked at the label on her bottle of beer. "That's not your problem," she said. "Unless they were arguing about the cost of your fabric."

I rolled my eyes at her jab. "When she was in my shop, she said her fiancé wanted her to have whatever she wanted. She said price was no object. But that's not how he acted. He sounded demanding. And just now, they had a physical altercation on the corner."

"He hurt her?"

"Not exactly. She had her arms crossed, and he grabbed

them. I called out to them, and he pushed her into the wall and left."

"He pushed her, or he let go of her and she leaned back against the building?"

"I don't know. It could have been either, I guess."

"Was she hurt?"

"No. She said she was fine, but I know what I saw—"

"You *don't* know what you saw," Charlie said. "You're making an assumption that he was a bully and she needed help."

"Maybe she did," I said. "Maybe she's in a bad situation and needs someone to help her get out."

"It's not your business, Polyester. You can't change somebody else's life for them if they're not ready for things to be different."

For the next several minutes, conversation lapsed while we finished our burgers and fries. The Broadside was a busy tavern with a steady stream of patrons coming and going. Duke had made changes to the menu and atmosphere to draw a more family-friendly clientele, but the local motorcycle club continued to use it as their meetup location. Somewhere around eight, the crowd shifted from families to bikers. Charlie was more at home in that element, but tonight, she left with me.

"Are you turning into a pumpkin, or do you want to come over and hang?" she asked.

"Actually," I said, checking the time, "I'm going to the Waverly House to see if Adelaide is available."

"That's my cue to leave."

"You can come along if you'd like."

"Not tonight." She stepped back a few feet and added, "Thanks for the invite." She turned around and left.

Charlie had recently learned some details about her biological parents, and I suspected she was still coming to terms with what they meant to the version of herself that existed as an independent woman. I didn't prod around her history, and I was pretty sure that was the basis for our friendship. She had a reputation around San Ladrón for being elusive but was still the go-to mechanic for when your engine made an unexpected noise. I knew Charlie hadn't had the easiest of childhoods, but she was the first to admit that her life wouldn't be close to what it was today if the hard knocks of life weren't behind her.

San Ladrón was the kind of small town that, to outsiders, felt like the setting for a sweet cable-TV rom-com. Streetlights modeled after turn-of-the-previous-century styles provided light for the main stretch of Bonita Avenue. Volunteers from the Senior Patrol, San Ladrón's over-sixty-five crime-observing deterrents, casually strolled through town, inviting window shoppers to stay and patronize the businesses instead of letting the downtown area look like a ghost town after dark.

The city council had voted to keep street parking free, which kept a steady stream of visitors from the greater Los Angeles area coming for day trips. San Ladrón was about a thirty-minute drive east of the metropolis but felt like a different world.

I crossed the street and followed the sidewalk to the corner Circle K then turned left. The Waverly House was the jewel of San Ladrón.

Adelaide wasn't just a fellow resident of San Ladrón; she was also a friend. We were of different generations—her having known my great-aunt and great-uncle, who'd first opened the fabric shop—but we were kindred spirits, and I knew she wouldn't refer a client to me if she didn't think it would be mutually beneficial.

I'd recently helped her with an annual fundraiser that secured her operating budget for the upcoming year, and now the Waverly House was very much in demand. You couldn't drive past the historic Victorian mansion turned museum without seeing a wedding party posing in the luscious gardens. The funds raised had been significant enough that Adelaide had convinced the board to expand, purchasing the property next door and converting it into a nondenominational chapel. The Waverly House had always been a destination spot for rehearsal dinners and wedding receptions, but with the addition of the chapel, they had the space to conduct services as well. Their bookings had doubled overnight, and the guest rooms in the floors above the restaurant and banquet hall were reserved to full capacity through the end of the year.

The tradition of booking the Waverly House for rehearsal dinners and wedding ceremonies on the immaculately landscaped gardens outside had been around for decades, but the chapel had given the property a fresh, new offering. I knew from talking to Adelaide that the chapel calendar had booked up in a weekend, giving her operating budget a boost.

Tonight, the mansion was decorated like a gingerbread house. Tiny white lights lined the eaves, windows, and turrets of the blue-and-white exterior. The porch had wooden swings on either side of the front entrance, and an employee dressed in the uniform of white shirt and black trousers stood next to the swing on the left, punching up the cushions.

A wedding party spilled out from the entrance, laughing among themselves. The bride wore a traditional white gown, and the group of women behind her wore identical dresses in vibrant magenta taffeta. Men in black tuxedos accented with purple satin bow ties and cummerbunds followed. I should have known it was a bad time for a pop-in visit. I stayed on the sidewalk and passed the main entrance. The door to the chapel was propped open, and light leaked onto the path leading up to the entrance. Faint music trickled out, vaguely familiar but not immediately identifiable. I headed toward it, welcoming the opportunity to poke my head in and see what tomorrow's bride had selected as her color palette and floral display.

But when I reached the entrance, I stopped short. Pale-blue-ribbon bows sat in a pile on the floor. White roses, which appeared to have been bound in the center of the bows, were likewise discarded in piles, and some of the blooms had turned brown. It looked as if someone had intentionally destroyed the decorations.

I entered the chapel to get a better look at the mess. The music, initially pleasant, now felt ominous, like the soundtrack for a creepy fun house.

"Hello?" I called. "Is anyone in here?"

I went farther inside and heard a *thump*. The music skipped and replayed the last second or so on repeat. It was a record with a scratch. I strode down the center aisle to the sound system, with the intention of switching the record player off, when I found something more disturbing than the music.

Lying on the floor by the first row of chairs was the body of the man who'd been arguing with Beatriz Rosen earlier today, on the ground with a pool of blood forming on the ivory carpet underneath him.

# 4

THE MAN'S EYES WERE GLASSY AND STARING UP AT THE CEILING OF
the chapel. I pushed any squeamish feelings aside and checked
his wrist for a pulse. There was none. I pulled out my phone,
dismissed the latest notification of a missed call from Carson,
and called 911. I provided the necessary information and stayed
on the line until help arrived. The sheriff's office was directly
across the street, and San Ladrón's resident crime fighter,
Sheriff Clark, would be here soon.

Sheriff Ryan Clark was a competent investigator who'd
managed his way around more than one homicide since I
moved to San Ladrón. He was in his mid-thirties and had a
solid build and ruddy coloring not to mention relatively
unreadable body language.

"What happened here?" Clark asked as he approached me.
I sat in a ghost chair in the second row of the chapel, far
enough away from the body to keep it out of sight but close
enough to know it was there.

"I don't know," I said. "I came to the Waverly House to talk to Adelaide, but when I saw the chapel door was open, I came here instead."

"Why?"

"I wanted to see the decorations."

Sheriff Clark nodded. He looked around the interior, taking in the same details I had, then looked at the body on the ground. The carpet around the man's head was stained an unfortunate color that, among other things, didn't match the wedding theme.

In the short amount of time that I'd lived in San Ladrón, there had been a couple of murders, and while Clark hadn't been correct about the murderer every time, he'd proven himself to be a friend, not a foe. Instead of automatically dismissing what I had to say, he listened. He pulled a pair of latex gloves out of his pocket and stooped down to the body, shifting the man and removing his wallet.

"Mr. Laird Harden from Los Angeles," he said. He looked up at me. "You're from Los Angeles. Do you know him?"

"It's a big city," I said. "I don't know everybody who lives there." My reply came out more sarcastically than I'd intended, but Clark didn't seem to notice. He nodded and put Laird's wallet into his pocket.

"You're taking his identification?" I asked.

He looked up at me.

"I mean, I don't mean to imply that he'll need it, but is that standard procedure?"

"He's visiting our town, and he was murdered in one of our most famous city-owned buildings. I'm going to need to ask around to find out why he was here. Having his identification will help."

In the background, the record continued to skip, playing the same few measures over and over, slowly driving me mad. I wanted to go find it and turn it off, but now it wasn't just an annoyingly irregular rhythm anymore. It was part of a crime scene.

"He's engaged to Beatriz Rosen," I said. "She's a prima ballerina from the touring Los Angeles Ballet."

"I thought you said you didn't know him."

"I didn't. I don't. Beatriz had an appointment with me this morning, and he came to my shop. They argued, then later—" I stopped talking when I realized Clark was giving me his full attention.

"Then later what?"

"I saw them arguing on the street corner too."

"Do you know what this argument was about?"

"No. He looked like he was threatening her, and I interrupted them."

It was the second time I'd relayed what I'd seen earlier tonight, but this time, with a dead body only a few feet away from us, the very same account meant something entirely different. Especially to the cop now investigating the crime.

"When's the last time you saw Ms. Beatriz Rosen?"

"After I interrupted their argument. He left first. On foot. I think she drove away."

"Do you know how to reach her?"

"She's staying at the San Ladrón Hotel."

Clark nodded again. He didn't write down any of what I said, but he knew where to find me if he needed to follow up with my information.

"Poly, I'm going to have to ask you to leave while I secure the chapel."

"But what about the wedding tomorrow?"

"There won't be any weddings tomorrow. Besides, I doubt any bride and groom will want to say their vows in here until the carpets are replaced."

He was right. "I'll go find Adelaide and let her know."

I left Clark and this time ignored the indications that the Waverly House was closed for a private event. Twice, employees tried to stop me, but each time, I told them it was an emergency, and something about my expression must have sold them on the urgency of my request. I finally found Adelaide in the restaurant with a well-dressed, older man. He wore a gray suit that coordinated with his wavy steel-gray hair, and a mint-green shirt open at the collar. The two of them appeared to be sampling a variety of cakes that sat on mismatched plates on their table.

"Poly," she exclaimed. "Lovely to see you, as always, but you have caught me during a cake testing. Are you okay, dear?"

"No," I said. I pointed over my shoulder. "There's been a—" I looked at her face and that of the man with her and then back at her. "Can I talk to you alone for a moment? It's urgent."

"Of course." She turned to the man. "I do apologize, Evan. We can reschedule our tasting for another time."

Adelaide led me through the kitchen and out into the hallway that led to her office. She didn't sit. She closed the door behind me and kept her hand on the knob. "Something bad has happened," she guessed.

"Yes," I said. "There's been a murder in the chapel. The victim is Laird Harden." Adelaide didn't seem to recognize his name. "Sheriff Clark is there now. He said the chapel is off limits for the foreseeable future, which means you're going to have to cancel tomorrow's nuptials."

Adelaide was a seventy-year-old with the mind of a far younger woman. She oversaw everything that happened at the Waverly House, and the idea that someone had used the chapel without her knowledge was like a slap in the face. She went to the back of her desk and pulled a set of keys out of her desk drawer then came back around the desk and opened the door. "First things first. I need to talk to the sheriff. Is he still there?"

"I imagine he'll be there for a while."

She led the way out of her office, and I followed. We paused for a moment while she addressed her hostess. "Evan Grant is sampling the menu in the restaurant. Please wrap up anything he'd like and reschedule him for another time." The hostess nodded and left. Adelaide led us out the front entrance.

The door to the chapel was now closed, and when we went inside, it was quiet. Clark must have turned off the record player.

"Sheriff Clark," Adelaide said. "Poly has informed me about what happened here. How can I help?"

"I'll need to know anything you can tell me about the victim. I understand from Poly that he was going to be married here next week."

Adelaide appeared to be confused. "No, I don't believe there's a Harden wedding party."

"It might have been listed under Rosen," I said.

Both Adelaide and Clark turned to me.

"Beatriz Rosen. He was engaged to her."

"No, Poly, you're mistaken," Adelaide said.

"I don't think I am. Beatriz was at Material Girl earlier today for the appointment you set up, and Laird came to see her. They argued about—" I glanced at Clark, who was making no pretense about listening to my account of earlier today. "I don't think he liked that she came to my store for her wedding dress. He said something about them knowing each other for a long time and how that decision didn't seem like her."

"You're correct that Beatriz Rosen is one of our brides, but Mr. Harden wasn't her fiancé." She put her hand on my arm to comfort me. "You don't know?"

"Know what?" I asked. Something about her tone put me on alert.

"Beatriz Rosen is marrying your ex-boyfriend, Carson Cole."

———

I LEFT Adelaide and Sheriff Clark inside the wedding chapel and stepped outside to return Carson's latest call. Now that I had an inkling about what he wanted to tell me over lunch, I took the rip-the-Band-Aid-off approach.

"Carson Cole," he said upon answering, which seemed a little silly since he must have recognized my number.

"Hi, Carson," I said.

"Finally," he said. "Geez, Poly, I thought we were friends."

"We weren't friends, Carson. We were a couple, and we broke up."

"Right, but there's no hard feelings, right? At least not on my part. Unless you have second thoughts—"

"Nope, I'm fine," I said quickly. The tone of the conversation felt off considering what I'd just dealt with, but talking to Carson was preferable to talking to Sheriff Clark. And I couldn't help thinking that Carson, through his engagement to Beatriz, was going to be drawn into whatever had happened in the chapel earlier tonight.

"Listen," he said. "I'm coming to San Ladrón tomorrow, and there's something I need to tell you."

"I thought you already were in San Ladrón," I said, remembering what Charlie had said about his car.

"Where'd you hear that?"

"Doesn't matter. Whatever you have to tell me, you can tell me now."

"I'd rather talk to you in person."

"Carson, does this have to do with your engagement to a notorious prima ballerina?"

Carson didn't say anything at first. I gave the conversation the space it required. Part of me was happy that Carson had found someone after we broke up, but I was having a hard time reconciling the bridezilla I'd met earlier today with the Carson I'd dated for most of my twenties. His only interest in fame had been in famous peoples' investment portfolios, and he'd never once indicated an interest in the performing arts.

"I told her not to say anything."

"Who?"

"Trixie."

"Who?" I asked again.

"Beatriz. Trixie. My fiancée. I told her to see you about having her dress made, but I said not to say anything about me. I wanted to be the one to tell you."

"It's true," I said.

"Which part?"

"You're engaged to Beatriz Rosen."

"I'm sorry, Poly. I didn't realize you were hoping we'd get back together."

Carson had always been a bit delusional, but now wasn't the time to address his mental leap. "Who is Laird Harden?"

"He's her old dance partner. She doesn't want anything to do with him anymore. Why?"

Points of information converged into a bright pinprick of light behind my eyeballs. I felt a splitting headache at the spot and closed my eyes, pretending for a moment that I didn't have to do what I knew I had to do.

"Pack an overnight bag, Carson, and come to San Ladrón. Laird Harden has been murdered, and I'm pretty sure your fiancée is going to emerge as the main suspect."

"Why would the police suspect her?"

"Because I told them to. See you tomorrow, Carson."

# 5

I WASN'T ENTIRELY HAPPY ABOUT THE WAY MY SCHEDULE WAS
unfolding, but that seemed a petty thought in light of the
murder a few yards away. I didn't know anything about Laird
Harden save for what I'd observed earlier today, and while he
hadn't shown himself to be a calm, caring person, he was a
person nonetheless. He didn't deserve to be murdered.

Probably.

I reentered the wedding chapel and found Sheriff Clark and
Adelaide standing by the back row of seating. Adelaide, who
was calm, cool, and collected in any situation involving the
Waverly House, was slightly more ashen than usual. She wore a
mauve sweater over a long floral dress, and the only other indi-
cation that she was troubled by what she'd seen was her
fidgeting hands.

My reentry gave them reason to pause their conversation
and look at me. "I didn't know if I should come back or not," I
said.

"I was just leaving," Adelaide said. "I'll walk you out." She
turned back to Sheriff Clark. "I and my staff remain at your

disposal. Do keep me apprised of the investigation as it unfolds."

The look on his face reflected my thoughts: It wasn't police procedure for him to report to the manager of the crime scene. But to Clark's credit, he simply said, "Yes, ma'am."

Once Adelaide and I were outside, she took my hand. "There is much here to unpack. You're coming with me to my office."

And like Clark, I said the first thing that sprang to mind. "Yes, ma'am."

The Waverly House was quiet. Earlier, the dining parties had brought merriment, and with merriment came noise. Now, the restaurant was empty, the kitchen crew was minimal, and the rest of the staff was skeletal. Even the interior lights had been turned down to a subdued level, providing atmosphere but not much illumination.

When we reached Adelaide's office, I sat in a tufted chair across from her desk. Adelaide was an efficient manager, and her office reflected her ability to juggle the day-to-day needs of the historic property. Today, her desk was covered in folders, Post-its, and menu suggestions. A white nosegay lay next to a pale-blue envelope. She slipped a card out of the envelope and read it, smiled, and slid it back inside.

"Join me in a drink?" she asked.

I nodded. She opened an antique wooden cabinet and removed a bottle of Sauternes and two cordial glasses. Without asking me if I wanted one, she filled both glasses and set one in front of each of our seats. She did not return the bottle to the cabinet.

"It doesn't seem the time for a toast, does it?" she asked.

"No, it doesn't."

"Then we'll simply have a moment for the victim. May he

rest in peace." She raised her glass to mine and swallowed the contents.

The last time Adelaide and I had sat in this office while sharing a glass of Sauternes, the circumstances had been very different. I hadn't even known how to drink it, and it had been her lead, sipping the sweet but strong beverage, that had taught me. But that had been a more social visit than this one, and I felt Adelaide's anxiety. I picked up my glass and tossed it down the hatch too. I felt it travel down my throat and warm my chest. Seconds later, my arms felt heavy, as if I'd slipped on wrist weights before starting an aerobic workout.

"I'm contemplating a refill," Adelaide said. "I haven't yet decided if that's my best course of action."

Something about Adelaide suggesting that we sit in her office getting tipsy on a rare French vintage after discovering a body in the wedding chapel outside struck me as funny, even though it very much was not. I giggled then covered my mouth with my hand. She refilled our glasses, but neither of us drank. I felt the energy in the room shift as the reality of what had happened outside settled on our shoulders.

"Did you really not know?" Adelaide asked.

"About Carson?" I clarified. When she nodded, I said, "I really didn't know. He's been trying to reach me, but he must have changed his number. I didn't recognize it, so I didn't answer."

"Have you spoken to him tonight?"

"Yes. He coming to San Ladrón tomorrow."

Adelaide adjusted herself in her chair. "Why did you think Ms. Rosen was engaged to Mr. Harden?" She waved toward the side of the room, which I knew was meant to indicate the chapel outside the property.

"Beatriz was at my fabric shop earlier today for her private shopping appointment, and Laird showed up halfway through."

"How did her appointment go?" she asked.

"Honestly? She was twenty minutes late, and when she arrived, she had a bit of an attitude. She liked one of my wedding dress sketches and demanded that I make her dress even though I told her repeatedly that I'm not a seamstress. She said she's getting married in a week, which I told her was a near-impossible deadline. I don't think she's used to people telling her no. I expected someone sweet. Not someone like her."

"Sometimes, the most demanding brides are the ones who need their weddings the most," she said. "A wedding can be an end as much as it is a beginning."

"An end to what?"

"To a life one is ready to leave."

I sipped my drink and considered what Adelaide had said. "Carson said Laird was Beatriz's old dance partner. I got the feeling Laird wanted something from her that she didn't want to give. After they argued, he said something to me. He said she doesn't care about tradition. She doesn't care about anything but herself."

"And you thought this man was her fiancé?"

I shrugged. "It's hard to understand affairs of the heart."

"Speaking of which, how is your heart?"

If I hadn't been on my second glass of Sauternes, I might have expected the question. Adelaide wasn't just my friend. She was also the mother of Vaughn McMichael, the man I'd occasionally dated since breaking up with Carson and moving to San Ladrón. Adelaide, who tried her hardest to stay neutral about most topics, didn't do a particularly good job of hiding her hopeful feelings about this one.

"My heart is fine," I said. "I'm just focused on my business, and there hasn't been a lot of time for anything else."

"Your shift in priorities wouldn't have anything to do with my ex-husband's financial stake in your store, would it?"

"I'm just concentrating on one thing at a time."

"Well," she said. "If you decide to multitask, I'm certain my son would love to hear from you."

I wasn't ready to say too much about that.

The night had taken a tragic turn, and another drink wasn't going to improve it—not on top of the beer I'd had with Charlie earlier. I said good night to Adelaide, and she walked me to the front door. I was halfway down the sidewalk when something struck me.

I turned back around and asked, "Are your guest rooms fully booked?"

"No. Why do you ask?"

"Beatriz said she was staying at the San Ladrón Hotel. It seemed unusual that someone of her position would stay there instead of here, especially if she was going to have her wedding here next week."

"The San Ladrón Hotel?" Adelaide repeated. "No, I'm sure that's not right. Her bridal party may be there, but she told me she was staying with a friend in town."

"I wonder why she lied. Did she say who this friend was?"

"The same friend who referred her to me in the first place. Her fourth-grade teacher."

"Where is she now?"

"About to retire so she can live a comfortable life on the outskirts of town." Her eyes strayed from me to the now-dark wedding chapel. Several orange cones had been set up around the front door, and yellow-and-black Caution tape had been applied to the door frame to keep people from entering. "Maybe it's time I followed her lead."

"And give up all this?" I asked, waving to encompass the building and grounds behind her.

"Nah," we said in unison.

———

MATERIAL GIRL WAS LESS than a block from the Waverly House, closer if I took the path that led to my rear exit, which I did tonight. It was after ten, and the streetlights had switched off. I wasn't thrilled about walking home alone after having discovered a murder victim, so I practically ran, covering the distance in half the time it would normally take. I had my back door unlocked and relocked behind me less than five minutes after leaving Adelaide.

I went upstairs and met the kitties on the other side of my door. "It's been a day," I said. "Starting with a tardy bride and ending with a dead man in the wedding chapel, and that's not the worst of it."

Pins rubbed up against my leg, and Needles meowed. From the day I'd found them in the dumpster in my parking lot, they hadn't strayed far from each other, almost as if they'd learned at an early age that if they had each other, they wouldn't be alone. I scooped Needles up and held him to my chest and led the way into my bedroom. Pins hopped up onto the bed and nosed Needles when I set him down. I sat next to them and kicked off my loafers.

"Remember Carson?" I asked. "He didn't like the fact that I adopted you." I ran my hand over Needles's head and Pins's next. "That might have been the straw that broke the camel's back. Just think. If you hadn't come along, I might have gone back to Los Angeles. *I* could have been on the verge of being Mrs. Carson Cole instead of Beatriz." As the weight of that sank in, I bent down and kissed each cat on his head. "Lifesavers, the both of you."

The cats settled in on the middle of the bed and promptly fell asleep, leaving me either the right or the left side of them, because every cat owner knows you don't disrupt cats when they look adorable. I changed out of my black clothes and into a vintage white cotton nightgown, washed my face and brushed my teeth, and stared at my reflection in the mirror. The events of the day had left me tired, and my skin was sallow. My short auburn hair provided a contrast that, tonight, was less than flattering. I pinched my cheeks à la Scarlett O'Hara. Instead of creating a healthy-looking bloom, I was left with two sharp red marks on either cheek.

Oh well. Tomorrow was another day.

I was in the process of calculating which side of the bed had more space when my phone rang. Only one person would think it was okay to call at this hour: Carson. I let the call go to voicemail. Immediately, it rang again. I'd left my bedroom to retrieve my phone, if only to turn off the ringer, when I saw the caller's name: Vaughn.

"Hello?" I answered.

"Poly," Vaughn said. His voice was edged with a note of concern. "I'm sorry to call so late."

"Did something happen to Adelaide?"

"No. My mother is fine. She told me what happened at the Waverly House, and she suggested I check to make sure you got home safely."

I smiled to myself. Leave it to Adelaide to find a way to play Cupid. "It's a short walk. I'm already here."

"Until Sheriff Clark finds out who killed Laird Harden, you might want to travel with a companion."

Instead of returning to the bedroom, I sat on my sofa and stretched out my legs under the colorful quilt that my great-aunt Millie had sewn. Patches of vintage lace, cotton, wool, and silk, all remnants from fabrics she'd collected to sell in the store down below, intermixed beautifully. I pulled the quilt up to my chest and snuggled under it.

"Do you know anybody suited for the job?" I asked playfully.

"Maybe. Where should I tell people to apply?"

There wasn't much not to like about Vaughn McMichael. He was San Ladrón's most eligible bachelor, which strangers might attribute to his dad's vast accumulated wealth as a successful venture capitalist and Vaughn's ultimate inheritance of it. I knew Vaughn had mixed feelings about working for his dad. Vaughn had attended a college in Virginia and interned at a financial firm in the same area after graduation to gain experience and referrals. His dad had a heart attack, and that brought Vaughn back to the West Coast. Little by little, he took on clients at McMichael Investments, but his dad had yet to hand over the reins and retire.

His dad had also swooped in and cosigned my bank loan application, a fact that neither I nor Vaughn knew at the time. I needed the loan but had never expected to owe the same man who'd wanted to buy the store out from under me. Maybe he wanted to see me succeed. Or maybe he wanted to be first in line if I failed so he could snap up my property for pennies on the dollar.

Technically, it was Vaughn who'd found the kittens in the dumpster, not me. It might have been the first time we had something to focus on other than our animosity toward each other. I'd been battling the ghosts of San Ladrón from the moment I'd arrived, and that included Vaughn coming uninvited into the fabric store and being present when I first happened upon the site of my great-aunt's murder. That was also the day I learned that Vaughn had ghosts of his own.

"You know," I said, "this is the kind of position that will go to the person who best demonstrates his or her ability to fulfill the job expectations. If memory serves, you've shown yourself to be a competent companion, haven't you?"

"Competent? Wow. You're tough."

It felt good to be sitting in the dark talking to Vaughn after the day I'd had, and I would have liked nothing more than to keep our light flirtation going well into the night, but a second call beeped through the phone. I pulled it away from my head. It was Carson.

"Can you hold on? I have another call."

"This late?"

"What can I say? I'm trying to fill a very important job, and the applicant pool is bigger than I expected. Hold, please." I clicked over. "What do you want now, Carson?"

"I want you to let me in. There's a murderer on the loose, and I'd rather not spend the night in your parking lot."

# 6

OH NO. NO, NO, NO, NO, NO.

"You're in my parking lot?" I asked Carson.

"Unlock your door. This isn't funny, Poly."

"I agree." I sat up and put my feet on the hardwood floor. It was cool under my bare soles. I tossed off the quilt and stood then said, "I'll be there in a sec. I'm on the other line."

"Poly—"

I clicked back over to Vaughn. "Hey," I said. "Where were we?"

"I was about to express interest in the position of being your regular companion for the foreseeable future."

"Right." I flipped on the light and made my way down the stairs, carefully gripping the banister to keep from falling. I was something of a klutz, and the last thing I wanted was to trip down the stairs while on the phone with Vaughn. "I hate to be a buzzkill, but can we pick this back up tomorrow? Carson just showed up, and I need to let him in."

"Your ex-boyfriend?"

"Yes. I called him to let him know what happened. I thought he was going to come here tomorrow, but, well, surprise."

"Sure. Right. Surprise. Well, keep my application on file if something opens up." He hung up abruptly.

I stared at my phone. That conversation had been going so well before Carson crashed my night.

I checked the camera over the back door and recognized Carson standing by himself with a designer duffel bag over his shoulder. He wore a trench coat buttoned up to his chin with the collar flipped up. A light rain sprinkled on him, nothing anybody else would be bothered by, but from the look on his face, to Carson, it was like being caught in a monsoon. I flipped the dead bolt and opened the door. He barged in and dumped his bag on the floor.

"What took you so long?" he asked. He immediately unbuttoned his trench coat and shook it off, revealing a suit and tie underneath.

"Let's see. It's after ten, and I was upstairs on the phone. What are you doing here?"

"My fiancée won't answer her phone. Her former dance partner is dead. My ex-girlfriend is the one who told me about the murder, and the police have left two messages on my voicemail. I've got a six-figure deposit riding on this wedding, and I stand to lose half if we don't make it to the altar. Where do you think I should be?"

"Let's start with Beatriz. If she hasn't answered her phone, have you tried to reach her at her hotel?"

Carson laughed.

"Or through her friend Renee?"

Carson wasn't looking at me. He was scanning the interior of the fabric shop. "Renee isn't Trixie's friend. She's her PA." He turned to face me. "Personal assistant," he clarified.

"I thought Renee was a bridesmaid."

"She is."

I remembered another name. "What about Ursula? Beatriz mentioned her, too, and when I asked if she was a bridesmaid, Renee laughed."

"Ursula is Beatriz's press agent."

"But she's also a bridesmaid?"

"Yes."

I got the feeling Carson was going to stand in the fabric store and discuss Beatriz and her staff all night if I didn't do something, so I grabbed the handles of his bag and led the way to the stairs. "Does Beatriz have any bridesmaids who don't work for her?"

"I told her to ask you, but I guess she didn't."

I dropped his bag and turned around. "You told your fiancée to ask me, a perfect stranger—*your ex-girlfriend*—to be one of her bridesmaids? Do you not know *anything* about how the female mind works?"

"Ursula said three bridesmaids was the best for the wedding photos. Trixie doesn't have a lot of female friends, and I didn't want her to be jealous of you. I thought if you two got to know each other, you might get along. You have a lot in common."

A middle-class fabric store owner and a wealthy prima ballerina? I couldn't wait to hear this.

"Like what?"

He beamed. "Me, for starters."

It was so ridiculous that I couldn't help but laugh. I pointed at his bag. "Carry that yourself and follow me. And if you're mean to my cats, you're out in the street."

The day had left me with very little fight. I trudged up the stairs to my apartment with Carson a few feet behind me. After we entered, I left him in the living room and got a fresh set of sheets and a spare pillow out of the antique linen hutch in the hallway. By the time I was back in the living room, Carson had removed his suit jacket and tie and loosened the top button on his dress shirt. The initials CC were monogrammed onto his left cuff in navy blue. "Help yourself to whatever you need. I'm barely standing at this point. We'll talk in the morning."

I paused before turning off the overhead light and caught a glimpse of Carson's face. He looked like a child lost in a department store. Carson was a planner, someone who thrived on knowing the variables of any situation, and mere hours ago, he'd thought he knew what his future held. My news had obliterated his security blanket. Now he was in my living room, in a small town he'd sworn he would never visit again, with his upcoming nuptials in question thanks to his fiancée's connection to a murder victim. Everything he thought he knew had been tossed in the air, and the pieces were falling around him in a pattern that was the opposite of neat.

In an impulsive move, I hugged him. "It's going to be okay," I said. "I'll help you get through this."

For the first time since I'd met Carson in a college bar in downtown Los Angeles, he didn't have anything to say.

———

THE NEXT MORNING, I woke to the scent of coffee. Somewhere in the night, the cats had shifted to the bottom corner of the bed, giving me ample space to find a comfortable position. I got up and pulled on my robe then found Carson in the kitchen. Since he wasn't wearing his baseball hat, I could see that he'd buzzed his hair to little more than a half an inch. He wore his suit pants and a white T-shirt under a navy-blue cashmere sweater.

"Good morning," he said. "There's fresh coffee and fresh orange juice."

"I know," I said. "I mean, I can smell the coffee, and I have a pitcher of fresh OJ in my fridge."

"If it's in a pitcher already, then it's not fresh." He picked up a glass and handed it to me. "This is fresh."

I took the glass and drank. One of the benefits of living in San Ladrón was being surrounded by citrus. There were trees bearing oranges, lemons, limes, and grapefruits all around us, and most residents didn't mind sharing their yield as long as you left something on the tree for them. I regularly swapped bundles of fat quarters to the local quilting guild in exchange for fruit from various members' properties.

"We could have gone out for breakfast," I said. "Or I could get doughnuts."

"Breakfast is the most important meal of the day." The microwave beeped, and he removed a round bowl of scrambled eggs. They were light and fluffy but deflated in front of my eyes. He used a small rubber spatula to free the eggs from the bowl and set them on a plate next to slices of avocado and diagonally cut pieces of rye toast. He handed me the plate.

"What about you?" I asked. "Where's yours?"

"I already ate."

"When? It's not even seven."

"I eat at five thirty every morning. It's better for your body to have a schedule."

I carried my plate to the table and sat, then I assembled my eggs and avocado on top of the toast and took a bite. The avocado and egg slid off the toast and landed in a messy pile on my plate. Carson rolled his eyes. "You still eat like a ten-year-old."

"We used to have that in common."

"Things change." He didn't look directly at me, but I felt an undercurrent to his words.

I ate the rest of my meal with a knife and fork like an adult.

Carson surprised me by cleaning up the kitchen while I
finished. He took my cleaned plate and put it into my
dishwasher.

"Where are your dishwashing tabs?"

"It's not full."

"You'll save water by running your dishwasher every day."

"Yes, but I'll spend any money I save on dishwasher tabs."

"Suit yourself." He sat in the chair opposite me. "So, what
should we do today? After I follow up with the sheriff, you can
introduce me around town."

"You're joking, right?"

"What's wrong with my suggestion?"

"I have to run the store," I said. "Remember? I own a fabric
store now? The same one you walked through when you
showed up unexpectedly last night?"

"Right. Okay, I'll help you today."

"Help me how?"

"I'll be your employee."

It wasn't the worst idea. Carson had put himself through
college by working part-time at a sporting goods store. He was
still annoying around the edges, but he understood the tenets
of customer service, and he knew his way around a cash
register.

"Okay, but if you get any questions about fabric, don't
pretend you know anything. Direct them to me."

"Give me some credit, Poly. I wear custom suits made from
super one hundred wool, and I buy made-to-measure shirts
from Turnbull & Asser. Plus, I lived with you for close to a
decade, didn't I?"

"That's all well and good, but it's bridal season, not finance-
guy season."

"You're the boss."

The beauty of running my store was that I couldn't just

clear my schedule and start nosing around Clark's investigation. The unfortunate thing about running my store was the very same thing.

Carson and I made a decent team. It was Saturday, and with the weekend came droves of visitors. With him covering the register, I was free to greet customers and discuss their fabric needs, talking up the inventory that made Material Girl different from other fabric stores in the area. I showed off vintage bolts that I'd discovered when I took over the store and told stories about having worked here in my teenage years. I'd been correct about it being bridal season, and I met with three different brides about patterns and yardage and exceeded my daily sales quota before lunch. More than once, I watched Carson chat with a customer while he rang up her purchases, often adding pins, thread, scissors, and other items I kept stocked at the register for that very reason. I caught his eye from across the room and gave him a thumbs-up.

The mail arrived in the afternoon. In addition to the usual bills, credit offers, and coupon packs, there was a postcard with a picture of the Eiffel Tower on it and a black document mailer with neither a stamp nor a return address. I didn't have time to read any of it, so I carried the pile to my apartment upstairs during a shopping lull and set it on the kitchen table. I let Pins and Needles follow me back downstairs, providing a new source of entertainment for the waning customers.

Five o'clock arrived faster than usual. I joined Carson behind the register and ran a tally of sales for the day. "That can't be right," I said.

He peered over my shoulder. "That's right," he said. "I checked half an hour ago and rang up three people since then."

I stared at him. "But this is three times the business I usually do on a Saturday."

"I told you I'd be an asset," he said. "We make a good team, Poly. Or did you already forget that?"

I nodded, not wanting to admit he was right. I walked to the front door and pulled the accordion gate into place then flipped the sign to Closed and locked the door behind it. The cats chased a felt mouse around the floor. I headed toward the back exit, but it opened before I could reach it. Sheriff Clark let himself in.

"Poly," he said with a nod. He looked at Carson. "Did you finally hire some help?" he asked me.

I didn't know if Carson had returned Sheriff Clark's messages, and it was with divided loyalty that I made the introductions. "Sheriff Clark, this is Carson Cole. Carson, this is Sheriff Clark."

The two men shook hands.

"Mr. Cole," Clark said. "I've been trying to reach you."

I narrowed my eyes at Carson. His reasons for volunteering to help me in the store all day became clear.

"We're just closing up here, Officer," Carson said.

"He's the sheriff," I corrected.

"Right. Sheriff. I asked Poly to take me to the sheriff's office earlier today, but when I heard she needed help running the store, I figured we could do it later." He grinned his I'm-a-charming-guy smile and made a show of checking his watch. "I guess now is later. Let's talk upstairs."

"Excuse me?" I asked. "I didn't give you permission to commandeer my apartment."

"Poly, I do need to talk to Mr. Cole," Clark said.

"Fine. *I'll* go upstairs. You two can stay here."

I blew kisses to the cats, and they came charging at me. The three of us went upstairs. I held the door open, they entered, and I closed the door behind them. If either of the men in the store below were listening, they would likely assume I'd followed the cats into the apartment. I quietly lowered myself onto the top step and listened in on the conversation below.

"Mr. Cole," Clark said. "Did Ms. Monroe tell you about what happened last night?"

"She told me she found the body of my fiancée's former dance partner in the wedding chapel where she and I are to be married next Saturday. That's correct, right?"

"What is this former dance partner's name?"

"Laird Harden," Carson said.

"Did you know Mr. Harden?"

"I've met him, but I didn't know him well."

"And your fiancée? How does she feel about him?"

I felt Clark fishing for something, and I admired the way Carson handled the conversation. "Her career as a ballerina was established before she and I met. If you want to know how she feels about her former colleagues, you'll have to ask her."

"I'd love to ask her. You wouldn't happen to have a lead on her whereabouts, would you? She's told several people she's staying at the San Ladrón Hotel, but there's no record of a Beatriz Rosen ever checking in."

# 7

I WANTED TO STAND UP AND PEER OVER THE BANISTER TO SEE what expression Carson wore now, but if either of the men saw me, they would know I'd been eavesdropping. I'd told Sheriff Clark where to find Beatriz based on what she'd told me. If what she'd told me turned out to be a lie, Clark would have to figure out which one of us had lied and why. And Carson, engaged to Beatriz as he was, should be the one person to know the truth.

"Beatriz isn't a regular person like you and me," Carson said. "She's famous in circles most people don't know exist. When we go on a trip, I've known her to make reservations at up to five different hotels to confuse any reporters who got wind of her travel plans. If someone told you she's at the San Ladrón Hotel and you've determined she's not, then I'd say Beatriz didn't trust the person she gave that information."

It was a chilling breakdown of what had probably happened. In short, Beatriz had lied to me. And I, being the trusting person that I was, had never once doubted her. I'd told Charlie and Adelaide and Clark the same misinformation. If

Beatriz was trying to protect her privacy in San Ladrón, then she'd been right to lie to me. That thought didn't make me feel any better.

"For the purposes of this investigation, I need to talk to Ms. Rosen. Can you provide any information about her whereabouts?"

The silence following Clark's question stretched uncomfortably, feeling even longer than it was because I couldn't see either half of the conversation. When Carson finally spoke, it wasn't the answer I'd expected.

"We agreed that it's better she doesn't tell me where she's staying when she travels. She has my mobile number and will call me when she can."

Even though this explanation wasn't for me, I had a million questions. What kind of arrangement was that? Didn't Carson see how one-sided it was? Why would he have agreed to it?

Sheriff Clark seemed to have the same questions. "You agreed to that?" he asked.

"Trixie's travel schedule is grueling, and she doesn't always sleep and eat when the rest of us sleep and eat. There's practice, rehearsals, press junkets, costume fittings, and public appearances. If I call at a bad time, she has to ignore the call, but it pulls her out of whatever it is she's supposed to be doing. She's performing at a high level, and we both understand it's best to let her focus on that when she's away. She always finds time to fit me in when she can."

Wow. Just... wow.

I couldn't help feeling a tinge of jealousy at Carson's understanding of the demands of Beatriz's life. He sounded like he respected what she did for a living. It was different from the constant put-downs he'd made about me working for Giovanni at To The Nines. Carson's whole vision of our future was for him to manage his portfolio of clients, me to leave To The

Nines and open a boutique in Los Angeles, and us to get married and start a family. But for his future with Beatriz, he'd pushed all that aside.

"When's the last time you spoke to Ms. Rosen?" Clark asked.

"Yesterday."

This time, Clark allowed the silence to blossom to an uncomfortable point. Finally, he said, "When you speak to her again, ask her to call me. My mobile number is on this card."

I didn't miss Sheriff Clark's use of the phrase "mobile number," a phrase most people didn't use but Carson just had. It sounded like a jab at Carson's pretentiousness. I smiled to myself, picturing Carson in his made-to-measure suit and custom shirt facing off against Clark in his dusty khaki sheriff's uniform that probably had a jelly doughnut stain on it. That was not a dig against cops; it was a dig against Clark. It was a well-known fact around San Ladrón that the way to the sheriff's heart was with boysenberry-jelly-filled doughnuts. He always bought two because one usually squirted onto his uniform.

After the awkward pause, I heard Carson say, "I'll give her the message." It was the one reply that would take the onus off Carson. If he did speak to Beatriz, he wasn't responsible for whether she followed up on the request or not.

"Will you be in San Ladrón for a few days?" Clark asked.

"Yes," Carson said.

"Where will you be staying?"

"Here."

*What?*

"I'll be in touch."

Carson crashing on my sofa for one night was one thing. Carson staying indefinitely was another. I stood quickly, and the blood rushed to my head. I grabbed the banister to help me keep my balance and turned the doorknob and went into my apartment. I looked at the sofa where Carson had slept. The sheets were still draped over the cushions like a makeshift bed, and a copy of *The Art of War* sat on the coffee table nearby. A few of the pages had been dog-eared at the corners, keeping the book from closing properly. Neither of the two cats were in the room.

"Hey," Carson said from the doorway.

I hadn't heard him climb the stairs, and his sudden presence gave me a start. I waited for him to say something about his conversation with Clark, but he didn't.

"Do you have anything to drink?"

"Water and tea," I offered.

He crossed the room and unzipped his overnight bag then pulled out a bottle of something amber. I knew nothing about whiskey, rye, or bourbon, but I did know something about Carson. If he traveled with a bottle, it would be expensive.

And it meant, despite what he would have liked for me to believe, that his life was less than charmed.

"I'll get glasses," I said.

I took the bottle to the kitchen. The mail I'd carried up earlier sat in the center of the table. I flipped over the postcard with a picture of the Eiffel Tower on it and read: *Bonjour, Poly! C'est le jolie vie! xo, Genevieve.* Pins slinked into the room and meowed. He went to his food bowl and swatted at it.

The bottle was scotch. I set it on the counter and filled the kitties' food bowls then gave them fresh water. Once my immediate family was fed, I pulled two crystal tumblers out of my cabinet and pulled the strip around the opening of the bottle. I poured a tiny amount into one glass and about an inch of liquid into the other then recapped the bottle and carried the glasses back out to the living room. I handed Carson the fuller one, and he clinked it with mine.

"Here's to old times," he said. He took a sip and leaned back against the sofa.

I sat in the armchair. "So," I started tentatively, "how've you been?"

On the surface, I already knew how Carson had been. Since our breakup, he'd continued to climb the venture capital ladder. The last I'd heard, he'd hit his stride. He'd backed the development of a predictive algorithm that forecast environmental changes based on tech advancements. The algorithm hit big when it went public. Carson had made enough to leave his firm and start his own company, making him young, successful, and rich—everything he'd ever wanted.

"I'm okay," he said, swirling the contents of his glass. He took another sip. He set it down again. "You?"

I gestured around the interior of my apartment. It was the same apartment that had belonged to my great-aunt and -uncle when they moved to San Ladrón and started the fabric shop. "I'm great," I said. "The fabric store is turning a profit, and I've got a solid circle of friends in San Ladrón. I love running the store, but I have enough free time to enjoy my life too."

"And your love life?"

I flushed as I thought back to my conversation with Vaughn. "My love life is off-limits."

Carson nodded and stared at the amber liquid in his glass but didn't take another sip. He set the glass down next to his book and ran his hand over his closely shorn hair.

"I thought all of this would feel different," he said.

"All of what?"

"Work. Success. Money. Love."

Yep, that was pretty much all of it. I could go any number of directions with this conversation, but one stood out. "How did you and Beatriz meet?"

"Tit for tat, Poly. If you want to talk about my love life, you have to talk about yours."

"So, how about those Lakers?" I asked.

Carson chuckled. He put his feet up on the coffee table and his hands behind his head. "I met Beatriz at a coffee shop on the west side. She was in this pink wraparound top and faded 501s that hung low on her hips. Her hair was in a ponytail, and she didn't have on any makeup. She was the prettiest woman I'd ever seen. She looked soft and vulnerable but strong too. When I paid, I gave the cashier a fifty-dollar bill and told her to ring up the order behind me with the change and keep what was left as her tip."

"Smooth."

"I thought so. Beatriz chased me down in the parking lot to thank me, and I asked her out."

"And the rest is history?"

"More or less."

I waited for him to elaborate, to tell me more details about their meet-cute or their blossoming romance, but he didn't. Maybe it was because I was an ex-girlfriend. I didn't flatter myself by thinking Carson saw me as the one who got away, but we'd shared that crucial time in our lives when we were becoming who we were meant to be. I wondered how many people who met at that time went on to have fulfilling relationships with each other or if we'd been destined to be each other's stepping stones all along.

I'd poured myself the tiniest amount of scotch, and even though I hadn't had any yet, my glass looked close to empty. Carson had been nursing his, a fact I found reassuring. He was just unwinding at the end of the day like he always had.

He seemed to notice my empty glass. "Help yourself to a refill if you want. I know you gave yourself about a tablespoon."

"I'm not much of a drinker."

"You've never had this scotch."

I picked up my glass and sniffed. Carson snickered and shook his head at my trepidation. I poured the contents into my mouth. The heat from the alcohol burned the back of my throat, and I coughed. The lingering aftertaste was sweet and supple with hints of oak, honey, and fruit.

"You get used to the burn," Carson said. He picked up his glass and finished the contents then set it on the floor next to the sofa. He lay back against the pillow and closed his eyes. Within seconds, he was snoring gently.

It was too early to go to bed, but Carson's nap gave me some much-needed alone time. I left him in the living room and went to the kitchen. The last thing I'd eaten had been Carson's breakfast, and the scotch now sat in my empty stomach. My options were as thin as they'd been yesterday: frozen pizza, two apples, and a four-day-old banana. I picked up my phone and called Charlie.

"Hey," she said instead of hello. "I've been waiting for you to call. I'm already holding our table."

"How'd you hear?"

"Clark."

"Are you two...?"

"No. He came in asking if I'd seen the ballerina."

"Have you?"

"Did you not hear me say I'm holding our table? If you don't get here soon, I'm pretty sure Duke's going to revoke my dining privileges."

"I can't leave. My ex-boyfriend is here."

"Are you two...?"

"No. He helped me at the store today and fell asleep on my sofa after a glass of scotch."

"Where'd you get scotch?"

"He brought it with him."

"Your ex probably has expensive scotch. Scratch the Broadside. Dinner's coming to you."

"I was hoping you'd say that. Bring two club sandwiches and an order of fries."

"No burger?"

"I don't know how long Carson's going to sleep. The club will hold up better."

The pile of mail I'd carried up earlier sat on my place mat, so after I hung up, I set the stack of envelopes aside and picked up the black mailer. I turned it over and tore it open. Inside was a résumé with a note paper clipped to the edge that read, *At the bare minimum, you owe me an interview. —V.*

I removed the note and scanned the résumé. At the top, it said Vaughn McMichael. A timeline of work experience indicated his ability to perform the job of my regular companion: regular coffee drinker, willingness and ability to pick me up after I stumbled over my feet, owner of a car with excellent gas mileage, proximity to where I lived, overlapping circle of friends. He'd left off his education and added, under special skills: *sense of humor, understanding, good kisser.** At the bottom of the résumé, next to an asterisk, it said, **references available upon request.*

# 8

I CARRIED MY PHONE DOWNSTAIRS AND STOOD INSIDE MY FRONT gate, waiting for Charlie to arrive. Charlie was Vaughn's sister, a fact most people in San Ladrón either didn't know or kept to themselves. The secrecy had more to do with the circumstances of Charlie's childhood than anything else. She valued her privacy, and if you didn't respect it, you were dead to her.

While I waited, I called Vaughn. "Hi," I said when he answered. "I'm confirming receipt of your résumé."

"Will you be conducting interviews anytime soon? I may need to clear my calendar."

"Hmm. That may be a problem. I'm looking for a candidate with a wide-open schedule."

"In that case, you should talk to the guy who feeds the pigeons by the town gazebo. I can send him your way if you'd like."

"That won't be necessary," I said, laughing. "I wouldn't want the pigeons to get hungry."

It felt good to hear Vaughn's voice. I pictured him lounging on his dark-gray velvet sofa in his art deco apartment on the outskirts of town. I'd been there once, while he was in the middle of renovations, and had been surprised at how closely Vaughn's decorating style mirrored my own. We came from vastly different backgrounds, but during the times when we forgot about that, we were highly compatible.

When our laughter subsided, I changed the subject. "Did you talk to your mother today?"

"I spent the day with her," he said. "The events calendar is a mess."

I looked across the street and watched Charlie exit the Broadside Tavern. She wore a cropped black sweater, baggy jeans that had been belted to fit her waist, and black steel-toed boots. Her thick, dark hair was held back from her face with a purple bandanna. She glanced at oncoming traffic and crossed the street as if daring the oncoming traffic not to stop.

Who was I kidding? This was a small town in California. Of course they would stop.

I unlocked the gate and retracted it so she could enter. "Your sister just showed up with my dinner, so I have to go."

"Good night, Poly." Vaughn hesitated. "I'll wait to hear from you about that interview." He disconnected.

Charlie barged into the fabric store. She held a large brown paper takeout bag with twine handles. "Let's get this party started," she said.

I held my finger up to my lips. "Shh. Carson's sleeping."

"Who falls asleep at seven o'clock?" She thrust the bag at me and clomped up the stairs as if her livelihood depended on her ability to make noise. If Carson didn't wake up at the sound of the hinges on my gate, he was sure to by the sound of Charlie being Charlie.

I followed more slowly. I might not have told Vaughn any details about the murder, but his mother would. And the knowledge of Carson sleeping on my sofa for a second night would find its way to Vaughn too. It didn't matter that Carson was engaged to someone else. Not if we couldn't find her. I had a bad feeling about Beatriz Rosen and the impact she was having on my life.

———

CARSON SLEPT through Charlie's visit. She'd done her best to wake him, flipping pages of his copy of *The Art of War* and looking for highlights. She helped herself to a glass of his scotch and brought up her conversation with Clark about the murder. It was this last subject that interested me the most, so after covering Carson with my heirloom quilt and watching it rise and fall with his even breathing, I signaled for Charlie to follow me downstairs, where we could talk freely.

"That was no fun," she said. "Guys like him give me an outlet for my anti-capitalist nature."

"You're as much of a capitalist as he is."

"I'm not a capitalist, I'm a Charlie-est. Your ex cares about money. I care about me."

"Yeah, well, Carson's life seems to have gotten more complicated since we broke up." I repeated what I'd overheard him tell Sheriff Clark. "He said he doesn't know how to reach his fiancée."

"And you believe him?" Charlie asked. "People lie to the cops all the time."

"I don't know if he was lying or not," I said truthfully. "I can read Carson's body language, but I couldn't see him when he talked to Clark."

"Where were you?'

"On the stairs, listening in."

"What was Clark's response?"

"There were some awkward pauses to the conversation,

almost like Clark was giving Carson a chance to trip up or offer more information."

"People don't like awkward silences, especially around strangers. Clark was counting on that."

"He didn't get much. Carson explained that Beatriz's life on the road is demanding, and he and she agreed that it was better for her to contact him when she was available instead of him interrupting her schedule. It all made sense, except it's an odd way to exist in a relationship. Don't you think?"

Charlie shrugged. "Sounds perfect if you're Beatriz."

I thought about the résumé Vaughn had sent. He'd taken some time to create it, to specifically target my daily needs. He added the note and delivered it while I was working so I would have something to brighten my day and take my mind off last night.

"It doesn't sound perfect to me," I said. "I don't want a one-sided relationship. It all sounds a little 'seen but not heard.'"

"Have *you* asked Carson about her?"

"He told me how they met, and he told me he suggested she come here for her dress. He seems to be smitten with her. But..." My voice trailed off.

"But what?"

"But Beatriz's former dance partner, who I saw her arguing with *twice*, has turned up dead, and Carson's phone hasn't rung once."

———

CARSON'S brief snooze turned out to be a deep slumber. After finishing my club sandwich and keeping Charlie company while she had another glass of Carson's scotch, I went to bed. The cats were hunkered down in my closet. I left the doors open wide enough for them to get out if they needed to and fell asleep in the middle of the bed.

The next day, I woke to classical music. A beam of early morning sunlight filtered through my sheer voile curtains, highlighting Pins and Needles on my reading chair. I got up and pulled on a robe then found Carson in my kitchen. My blender was on the counter, and it was full of something green.

"Good morning," I said.

"Is it? Still morning?"

"It's quarter after nine," I said. "That counts as morning."

"I've been up since four thirty."

"That's your problem, not mine." I went straight to my coffee maker, positioned a mug underneath it, and inserted a pod. The machine heated up, and seconds later, hot, dark coffee dripped out. "What's that?" I asked, pointing at the blender.

"Microgreen smoothie."

"Where did you get microgreens?"

"The farmer's market. I was there when they opened."

"How did you get back in?"

"I took your keys. You were dead to the world."

"Sounds familiar. Like you at seven o'clock last night."

Carson filled a glass with green stuff and handed it to me. I held it up and sniffed it.

"What's with smelling your drinks?"

"I'm checking for the scent of bitter almonds."

It was a joke, and I assumed Carson would get it, but some unrecognizable emotion flashed across his face. He recovered quickly and said, "It's got the nutrients you need to get through the day. Drink this every morning and you'll give up your daily coffee."

"Never." I tentatively took a sip. It surprised me with a crisp lemony flavor. I drank half of the contents then carried the glass to the table. My mail had been tidied up, with Vaughn's résumé on the bottom of the pile. I glanced up at Carson to see if he was going to say anything. He turned his back on me and poured the remaining contents of the blender into his glass then placed the blender in the sink and filled it with soapy water. He left it there and sat across from me.

"I need your help, Poly. You're right about my life. I'm one week out from my wedding day, and I don't know where my fiancée is. I don't know if she's busy making last-minute plans or if she's hiding from the police."

"The only reason for her to hide from the police would be if she's guilty."

"No," he said. "She could be scared. She might know who killed Laird."

"If she knows, then wouldn't she go to the police? That's what I would do."

"Everybody's not like you. Some people don't want to get involved."

I wondered what that would be like. Going about my business and letting other people do the same. Not forging connections through questions and a quest for the truth.

Carson's eyes were wide. He searched my face, and I felt his fear.

"People are going to start talking soon, and it won't be long until Trixie's name makes the papers. A story like this takes on a life of its own. I want to protect her from all that."

"Beatriz might not need protecting."

"Reporters will dig up her past with Laird, and nobody will care about her dancing. They'll only think of her as the ballerina who might have murdered her partner. Her performances will become sideshow attractions, and it'll affect the touring company. The caliber of the dancers will change. That world is cutthroat enough. She doesn't need this too."

"Cutthroat how?"

Carson stood and turned his back to me while he attended to the appliance in the sink. He cleaned everything before rinsing it and leaving it all on a tea towel to dry. I didn't ask how long it had taken him to go through my cabinets to find my blender, towels, or glasses, because the rules of offering up your sofa for someone who needed to crash included the freedom to go through your kitchen cabinets for whatever they needed.

Either Carson was being thoughtful, or he was avoiding the question. Just to be sure he heard me, I repeated it. "Cutthroat how?"

"I heard you the first time," he said over his shoulder. He dried his hands on a second towel and hung it from the oven then turned back and leaned against the sink. "Beatriz wasn't always the principal dancer in her ballet company. She was part of the troupe. But the lead ballerina was injured during a dress rehearsal, and Beatriz got her big break. After she moved in with me, I found an article in her bedroom that hinted at a scandal around the time she took the lead."

"What happened?"

"Technically? The company said they hold auditions every once in a while to shake things up."

"Okay, not technically. What did the article surmise?"

"The reporter suggested that Laird miscalculated the catch on purpose. He wanted to dance with Beatriz. And after that, the lead was out, and Beatriz stepped in. She's been the principal ballerina ever since."

# 9

"THOSE ARE WILDLY DIFFERENT STORIES," I SAID.

"That's why Trixie keeps a publicist on her payroll. A story like that could have tarnished her reputation before she danced her first lead, but Ursula was able to put the spotlight on Trixie's talent. Everybody knew it was her time."

Whether or not that was true, the rumor didn't paint either Laird or Beatriz in a positive light. It was unclear whether Carson saw that or if he was so in love with his bride-to-be that he'd accepted her version of events.

But everything else he'd said made sense. Beatriz was a prima ballerina with a few years left before her body would demand she retire. She was at the top of her game, and it would be tragic for something like this to cut her dance career short. I also understood Carson's desire to protect her from the possible scandal, yet I couldn't help but remember what Charlie had said when we first talked about Beatriz's visit to Material Girl. *You can't change somebody else's life for them if they're not ready for things to be different.* Maybe Beatriz had wanted out of a bad situation. Maybe we were looking at the aftermath of her trying to make a change herself.

Sunday hours at Material Girl—and all the shops on Bonita Avenue—were noon to four. It was a short day, but even before I opened for business, I was anxious about being confined to the store and not able to hear the town gossip. I glanced at the clock in the kitchen.

"I've got an errand to run before I open today," I said. "When are you heading back to Los Angeles?"

"I can't go back now. Besides, I'm getting married in a week. The office doesn't expect to see me until I get back from my honeymoon."

"If you need some recommendations for where to stay, let me know."

Carson stared at me with a blank face.

"Or," I said, regretting what I was about to say but unable to stop the words from coming out of my mouth, "you can crash on my sofa if you want."

"Thanks, Poly. I knew you'd understand." He stood and cleared the glasses from the table. "What time do we open today?"

*We?* "Noon. We're busiest between twelve thirty and three thirty. It can feel like a madhouse in those three hours, but the last half hour is best left for cleaning up."

"What do we do until then?"

"Most Sundays, we feed the cats, go to Lopez Donuts for breakfast, check our email, and come back here in time to flip the Closed sign to Open." I wasn't entirely disappointed in Carson's green juice concoction, but I would be lying if I said I didn't still want my Sunday cruller.

"Speaking of the store, how's it going?"

I'd been waiting for this. Actually, I'd been waiting for this yesterday, but Carson's vulnerable side had lulled me into a false sense of confidence that he wasn't going to criticize my business acumen.

"It's fine," I said. "You worked with me yesterday. Didn't you see how busy we were?"

"I did. And I feel bad that I couldn't help you more."

I braced myself for the inevitable suggestion that I hire staff or the observation that running the store by myself was an unsustainable business proposition. I secretly made a bet that Carson's next sentence would use the phrase "paradigm shift."

"Since we have a couple of hours before you open the doors, how about you give me a tour? I'd like to be better informed so I can help with customers."

And not for the first time in the past twenty-four hours, Carson left me speechless.

———

THE CATS HAD BEEN NOTICEABLY absent from the kitchen while we ate—or drank—our breakfasts, so while Carson tidied up the sofa, I refilled the water bowls and doled out food. I went into my bedroom and changed into a black turtleneck, black flare-bottom pants, and black square-toed booties. I squirted a handful of mousse into my palm and scrunched it through my hair then finger styled it around my face. After a swipe of plum lipstick, I went downstairs.

Carson stood by the bridal display, staring at my sketches. I hadn't had a chance to replace the design Beatriz had originally requested, and now there was a blank space in its place.

"Did you come up with all of these designs?" he asked.

"Yes."

"Have you made any of them?"

"No."

He turned to me. "You still don't know how to sew?"

"I know how to sew. I'm just not at this level." He took a breath as if to say something, and I held up my hand to silence him. "I already know what you're thinking. A fabric store owner should know how to sew."

"Not necessarily," he said, surprising me. "You're the boss. You need to oversee everything. If you're stuck behind a sewing machine, you won't be available for everything else the business requires."

"That's what I thought."

"It's nice to see you picked up something from our time together."

"I did manage a workroom in Los Angeles for seven years," I said.

"Yes, but I don't think you picked up a lot of business habits from Giovanni," he said with a smile.

"Speaking of Giovanni, did you know Beatriz hired him to make her bridesmaids' dresses?"

"Of course. I told her to."

"Why?"

He shrugged. "Giovanni is a cheapskate, but his team works well under pressure, and I knew that based on the publicity alone, he wouldn't turn her away."

"What publicity?"

Carson turned to me. "Trixie has a press agent. Her team was supposed to leak our engagement to the tabloids and tease the idea that we might have a big public ceremony."

"How come I didn't hear about this?" My mom, who lived in a town that was Los Angeles adjacent, would surely have called me about Carson's engagement even if my friends in LA did not.

"Trixie wanted to get her plans in place before the story

broke. She said once the public knew about it, it wouldn't be her life anymore."

I couldn't tell if Carson recognized what a change marriage to him would mean to Beatriz's life. She may have said yes to his proposal, but that yes came with a lot of additional pressure for her. Saying yes and making it to the altar were two very different things.

"If the two of you were planning a big public wedding, then why did she book the Waverly House? Why come to a small town thirty miles east of where you live instead of having the ceremony on her family's estate?"

"Trixie doesn't have family. Her parents are both deceased. She was born here but moved to Los Angeles when she was fourteen. Her mother enrolled her in the Encino School of Ballet. She was homeschooled while she trained, and her career kept her from going to college. As far as I know, she's kept in touch with one person from her childhood—her fourth-grade teacher."

Adelaide had mentioned a teacher last night. "That teacher still lives here, doesn't she?"

Carson nodded. "When we talked about where to get married, Beatriz suggested here because it's where she grew up. She said her teacher could pull some strings and get us a date at the Waverly House. I asked her to set up an appointment with you for her dress." He shrugged. "It's a lot of money. I thought it might help you with your loan payments."

It was funny how our initial observations could be so far from the truth. I'd taken Beatriz's appointment because Adelaide had recommended her, and I respected Adelaide's opinion. And when I'd learned about Beatriz's engagement to Carson, I'd gotten a different idea: that Carson wanted to flaunt his success and famous fiancée in my face.

But none of that was true. Adelaide had taken Beatriz's

appointment on the referral of a local elementary school teacher, and Carson had been trying to help me by referring his fiancée's business. He didn't know what she'd selected or how impossible it would have been to make. He was the groom, and the details of the dress would have been kept secret.

I pointed at the empty space on the wall. "That was the dress she picked. It was the most elaborate one, and I told her I couldn't do it in a week. She said her fiancé wanted her to have whatever she wanted. She selected vintage fabric that Millie acquired back when she was still alive."

"Where is it?"

"The dress? I haven't had time to start on it, and now—"

"The fabric."

I walked Carson to the climate-controlled stockroom, and he followed me inside. Tables filled with bolts of fabric covered the middle of the room, and a wall of cream-colored floor-to-ceiling bookcases, filled with bins of notions, trim, buttons, and thread, lined the far wall. This was the heart of the fabric store. It was where my great-aunt had been murdered over ten years ago, and it was where I'd almost fallen victim to a similar crime. And now, it was where I stored the most valuable fabrics when they weren't on sale in the store.

The three bolts of vintage tulle that I'd set aside for Beatriz's dress sat on an otherwise empty card table where I'd left them. Two of them were still bound by quilting cotton tied off with light-blue ribbon and tagged with the original sales information. The third, the one that I'd placed on display in the store, had been hastily rerolled after Beatriz first discovered it. I unrolled it and held the fabric out so Carson could see it.

"This is what she chose."

Carson had never shown any real interest in fabric or fashion. He wanted me to dress like the wife of a CEO would dress, a style he was never able to define, and he often balked when I leaned into the thirties style I loved. He knew I occasionally acquired damaged vintage dresses from the prewar era, but he'd never once asked why they hung at the back of my closet instead of being worn on one of our nights out.

Once, early in our relationship, he'd gifted me a vintage headpiece he found at a costume shop on his way home from a business trip to Las Vegas. He'd found it in a costume shop in Proper City, Nevada, while heading home from Las Vegas. The shop, Disguise DeLimit, had specialized in costumes and vintage clothing, and Carson's luck at the blackjack table had left him feeling generous. He'd purchased the headpiece, a fully beaded and fringed flapper cap that he'd said was part of a Great Gatsby costume they had available for rental. He'd bragged about how he had the store break the costume into parts so he could buy the headpiece. I'd always wondered about his impulse to buy me a vintage hat when I collected vintage dresses, but I accepted the gesture as Carson trying to bend toward me, to respect my interests. At the time, I thought it was touching. I'd thanked him and tissued the cap and stored it in a velvet bag then hung the cap in the back of my closet with the rest of my heirloom garments.

"I don't know anything about fabric, but this is beautiful," he said of the tulle. "It reminds me of Trixie's dance costumes."

Carson stood over the fabric, running the rough texture between his thumb and forefinger, for a few seconds. I studied his sloped shoulders and dejected stance, and my heart went out to him. This was a side of him I'd never seen. With me, he'd wanted to be in control. He'd planned everything down to Monday meatballs and Tuesday tacos. He negotiated our lease fourteen months at a time to get us a discount, and he took his car in for regularly scheduled maintenance as recommended.

Carson wanted security. He believed if he played by the rules and followed the path established by those ahead of him, he would get everything he'd ever wanted out of life.

And maybe, to the rest of the world, it looked as if he had.

"Hey," I said. "You're going to hear from her soon. She's probably busy interviewing hair salons for her bridal party. She might not even know about Laird's murder."

"You think?" he asked hopefully.

I didn't have the heart to say, *No, I don't think. In fact, that's just about the most preposterous thing anybody could think right now,* so I said nothing.

"It's possible," I said. I put my arm around him and steered him back to the main shopping area.

I had about an hour before I opened for business, and once I flipped my sign, I would have no chances to leave until the shop closed at four. I handed Carson my opening checklist and made up an excuse on the spot. "I like to take a walk before we open on Sundays. Say hello to any early tourists, get a read on the day. Are you okay by yourself?"

"You're going to the doughnut shop, aren't you?"

"Bye, Carson."

I left out the back door and strode to the corner before Carson could suggest he tag along. It wasn't so much that I needed that Sunday morning doughnut as it was that I needed some distance from Carson. Ever since he arrived, he'd shown me a side of himself that I hadn't seen since the early days when we first started dating. The part of him that worried about the future.

This was the fundamental chink in the romantic armor of Carson and me. He wanted his life to be set in stone. "Avoid decision fatigue," he'd said. "If you always know what you're supposed to do, your mind is freed from minutia to think about loftier concepts." It sounded like hogwash to me, but then again, while my mind had been clouded with thoughts about how to make my loan payments in the early days of reopening the store, Carson's had been free to identify the possibilities of the environmental algorithm that had exploded when it went public and made him a self-made millionaire overnight. Maybe he was right about decision fatigue.

But there was something more than the uncertainty of his life. Beatriz had told me that the wedding was this upcoming Saturday. That left six days between then and now. Why the rush? If it was all about a quickie wedding with no publicity, then why not make the four-hour drive to Las Vegas and elope? Why pretend it was a secret while booking a historic property for the nuptials? Why order an impossible-to-make dress out of irreplaceable vintage tulle from your fiancé's ex-girlfriend when there were far fancier wedding dress shops in your Beverly Hills backyard?

Something about Beatriz's actions didn't make sense. Maybe Carson was blind to it, but I wasn't.

Lopez Donuts was at the end of the block on the opposite side of the street. I rounded the corner and crossed the street. The lobby of the popular doughnut shop was full of customers. Almost all the booths were full too, mostly with couples, but one contained two young children hopped up on sugar. One of the boys, probably about five, pulled on the ponytail of the woman in the booth next to them. The woman wore dark sunglasses and a baseball hat worn low over her forehead. She reached behind her head and smoothed her ponytail, then scooted out of the booth and went to the restroom. She left two cups of coffee on her table, along with two doughnuts, neither one having been touched. The line advanced quickly, so I moved past her and found myself at the counter facing Maria Lopez.

Maria was a five-foot five Mexican woman who helped her

husband run the place when she wasn't attending to the cleaning service she co-owned with her sisters. Together they had two boys who regularly broke labor laws by helping them when the shop got busy. Today, the boys were nowhere to be seen.

"I didn't expect to see you in here today," Maria said to me.

"Why not? I always buy a dozen glazed on Sunday."

She looked out the window and jutted her chin toward the street. "I noticed a strange car parked in front of Material Girl yesterday. Still there overnight. Did your parents buy a vintage Mercedes?"

"No. That's my ex-boyfriend's car," I said. Seeing Maria's expression, I shook my head. "It's not like that. He's getting married next Saturday, and I'm making the wedding dress for his bride."

Maria's forehead creased. "It's bad luck for the groom to see the wedding dress before the wedding."

"He didn't see the sketch she chose. He didn't get here until yesterday."

"Is that what he told you?" she asked. She pulled a pink bakery box out from under the counter and set it next to the register. She opened the lid, and I peered inside, seeing my usual Sunday morning order.

I nodded to confirm that the order was correct. "He came to my store on Friday night. He got there after—" I narrowed my eyes and studied Maria's face. Her expression was unreadable. "What aren't you telling me?"

"Just that your ex has been in San Ladrón since Friday morning too. He's been walking around in a Dodgers hat." She punched a few keys on the register, and the cash drawer popped open. She lifted the black plastic tray that held the money and pulled out a business card. She held it out to me between her first two fingers. "He asked Big Joe if he was interested in franchising the doughnut shop."

"You're sure?"

"I don't forget faces, Poly. If he lied to you, you might want to find out why."

# 10

I TOOK THE CARD. IT WAS EMBOSSED: *CARSON COLE, INVENTIVE Business Solutions,* followed by Carson's contact information. I pulled my cell phone out and checked the number he'd been calling me from against the card. They were a match.

"Can I keep this?" I asked, holding up the business card.

"Sure," she said. "Big Joe wasn't going to call him, but if we were to expand, we'd go with someone local." Her eyes twinkled at the reference to Vaughn. I averted my eyes from her face to the doughnut box and slid Carson's card into my back pocket.

"Would you look at the time," I said. I held out a twenty-dollar bill. "Can you ring me up for the doughnuts?"

She waved my cash away. "We ran out of change. Credit cards only."

"My card is back at my shop. Can you spot me until tomorrow?"

"I already charged you," she said. "I keep your card on file."

In the short amount of time I'd conversed with Maria, the line at the counter had doubled. I picked up the box and carried it out. Booths had turned over as soon as they'd been vacated, and Big Joe cleared tables and wiped them down as soon as they were available. The family with the rambunctious kids was still there, but the woman in the baseball hat next to them wasn't. Her table still held two full cups of coffee and two untouched crullers, and a blue rabbit's-foot key chain with a couple of keys on it sat next to one of the coffee cups. It seemed almost rude for two people to occupy a booth that fit four when business was this busy, but there would have been no way for the couple to know how busy the doughnut shop would get in a short time. I glanced around, but the woman wasn't there.

Sundays were a compressed day of business. The four hours of foot traffic left our registers full and our employees exhausted. I would have liked to say the dozen doughnuts were for early customers, but I already knew I would eat a few throughout the day, relying on sugar to keep me going until dinner. I carried the box of doughnuts back to the shop and set them up on a table in the stockroom. When I came out, I found Carson counting the cash in my register. I thought about what Maria had told me, and instead of hiding the box, I leveraged the information to get the truth.

"You were right about the doughnuts," I told him. "There's a box in the stockroom. Help yourself. But do *not* bring sticky fingers into the store. There's a jug of hand sanitizer on the table, and at the back of the stockroom, there's a sink and faucet."

Carson shook his head. "You're going soft, Poly. Those doughnuts aren't going to do anything for you that my green juice can't."

"Those doughnuts represent community, business, and friendship," I said defensively. "Isn't that why you approached the Lopez family about franchising their shop?"

I'd hoped to catch him off guard, but his only response was

to snigger. "Franchising a small-town doughnut shop? Sounds more like something your buddy McMichael would say to impress you." He shook his head with a smile still on his face and closed the register drawer. "Are you going to open or what?"

I stared at him, and I felt myself go cold. If Maria had been right about seeing Carson on Friday, then Carson had gotten very, very, *very* good at lying. But I knew Maria well enough to know she wouldn't have said something if she wasn't sure, and she had Carson's business card as proof.

A new, alternate timeline of recent history cropped up in my imagination: Carson following Beatriz to San Ladrón on Friday morning, observing her encounters with Laird, and confronting Laird at the chapel on Friday night. Maybe that confrontation hadn't gone well.

"What?" Carson asked. "Why are you staring at me like that?"

"You have something on your face," I lied. I left him checking his reflection in his phone and went to the front of the store to officially open for business.

———

WHATEVER DOUBTS I had about Carson's story were temporarily silenced while we worked in tandem for the next four hours. The copresidents of an out-of-town quilting group were impressed enough with my inventory of novelty cottons to buy several yards to take back to their chapter for a quilting challenge. I'd already swapped out my summer inventory with a display of Halloween and Thanksgiving prints, but when I learned the women were from Philadelphia and their quilts would be raffled off at a charity event to raise money for the Betsy Ross museum, I went to the stockroom and retrieved several end-of-bolts of Independence Day fabrics. They bought them all and took two bolts of novelty fabric printed with pretzels as well. This was my favorite thing about out-of-town customers—you could never predict what might light someone up. I mean, pretzels!

In addition to the quilters, I consulted with two bridal parties who had hired Jun Wong, a local seamstress, to make their bridesmaids' dresses. Jun was a petite Chinese woman who had a dressmaking shop in town. She occasionally picked up part-time hours from me when her schedule permitted, but wedding season was her busy time, and she'd already told me she might not be available to work for me until late November. The first maid of honor told me Jun had spoken highly of me and recommended I advise them on their color selection. They settled on a taupe-and-lilac palette and bought thirty yards of silk in each color for the dresses. The second party resisted every one of my suggestions, leaving the store empty-handed. They came back an hour later and bought a bolt of bright cobalt blue that I'd stocked because it matched San Ladrón High's colors. To save them from what might be cringeworthy photos, I offered them a discount on a complementary shade of blush pink that would eliminate any possibility of them unconsciously displaying their school spirit.

The day passed quickly, and the crowd thinned somewhere around quarter to four. I leaned back against the cutting table and surveyed the store. Prior to opening every day, I adjusted every bolt to the same one-inch hang so the fabric wouldn't overlap with each other. Now, the fabrics had been pulled off the rolls, hanging anywhere from several inches to a few feet from the bolt, hiding the fabrics displayed underneath them. One by one, I picked up the bolts left by the cutting table and returned them to their displays while I chatted with the few remaining customers.

Across the store, Carson stood talking to a man and a woman. I recognized them immediately as the couple who'd wanted to shop the day I was closed for Beatriz's appointment. I hadn't thought I would see them again, and I was happy that this time when they came in, I was open. I left the task of restocking the store for after I closed for the day, and I approached them.

"Hi," I said brightly. "You came back. Is there something I can help you find? Or would you prefer to look around?"

The woman looked uncomfortable. "Your associate said you're closing in a few minutes."

I glanced at Carson. He neither confirmed nor denied what she'd said. "Take your time and shop as long as you like. I still regret turning you away on Friday when I had a private appointment." This time, I had to fight from looking at Carson to gauge his response.

"I was telling—asking—" She turned to the man with her. "Honey, can you give me a couple of minutes? I don't want you to hear me."

"Of course," he said. He wandered over to the display of sewing machines.

The woman hesitated. I had a feeling something had transpired before I got to her, so I turned to Carson and handed him my keys. "Can you go lock up the stockroom?" I asked. "Take any remaining doughnuts out to the dumpster in the parking lot outside and empty the rest of the trash bins."

Carson took my keys and left me alone with the woman. "He's new," I said after he was out of earshot.

"Oh. Maybe that's why he said what he said."

"What did he say?"

"I told him I heard you carry vintage fabric and that I was looking for something for my wedding dress. He said I must have heard wrong."

I turned away from the woman to stare at the back door. Carson had gone into the stockroom to get the box of doughnuts like I'd instructed, but the vintage tulle that Beatriz had selected for her wedding dress was back there too. He knew about it because I'd told him. What was he playing at?

"I'm Poly," I said. "I own the store. I didn't catch your name the other day."

"Katie," she said, pointing at herself. "I didn't expect to be back in San Ladrón so soon, and I took a chance that you might still be open."

"I am, and I'll stay open as long as you want. And you heard correctly. I do carry vintage fabric. Follow me." I led her to the bridal display, where cream, ivory, white, and blush shades of silk and lace hung. I'd replaced the vintage tulle that Beatriz had wanted with a vintage reproduction that had come in last week. "The silk and lace are both limited quantities, so they're a bit pricier, but I can order reproductions of any of them if you prefer. The vintage fabrics are delicate and might not wear as well as the new ones, but I understand why you might prefer them."

"Which do you like better?" Katie asked.

I smiled. "It's hard not to love the original ones." I reached out and gently tugged the edge of a bolt of vintage marquisette. I stepped back a few feet and extended the sheer, delicate fabric from the roll. It had yellowed slightly with age but was otherwise intact. "This one was commonly used for wedding dresses in the early twentieth century. By the twenties, it was so popular it was used for curtains."

"Curtains!" she exclaimed. "It's too pretty to use for curtains."

"By the thirties, it was everywhere. This one is silk, but manufacturers started producing it in nylon, which is much stiffer. It all but disappeared during World War II, but it came back in the fifties."

"That makes sense," she said. "All of those crinolines and Betty Draper dresses." She smiled shyly. "*Mad Men* is still my favorite show."

"If it's the fifties and sixties you like, then you'll love the reproduction of the lace used for Grace Kelly's wedding dress in 1956," I said with a smile. I turned to my left and rerolled a shopworn bolt of duchess satin to expose an exact replica of the turn-of-the-century Brussels lace that had been used on the most famous wedding dress in the world. When I'd first learned that a small fabric shop in Los Angeles's shopping district had reproduced the fabric, I called the bank and requested an increase to my line of credit. The princess's dress took upwards of four hundred yards, an obscene amount of fabric to most people, and if someone wanted a reproduction, it wouldn't do me much good if all I had in stock was one bolt!

Once upon a time, Material Girl had been Land of a Thousand Fabrics. It was the brainchild and life passion of my relatives. When my great-uncle passed away and left the store to me, I'd spent a week in San Ladrón to understand what it was that I'd inherited. Despite a lucrative offer to buy the place from the small town's resident investment banker, Vaughn's father, I learned during that week that life doesn't have to follow an expected path and that every day, we are granted opportunities to create a divergent future from the one we'd grown to expect.

What I'd come to learn in that week was that Land of a Thousand Fabrics would never be what it was, and trying to force a closed-for-ten-years business to reopen and succeed in modern times was a failing proposition. But between the knowledge I'd gained from my degree at FIDM and my time working at To The Nines, I had a vision for what the fabric shop could be. I'd met with advisors and the bank, signed the requisite paperwork, and reopened as Material Girl, named in part after the song my relatives used to sing to me when I was a baby.

Material Girl might have been experiencing new life, but the past infused almost everything about the place, and my favorite part of running the business was connecting with like-minded folks who loved fabric too. That was why I lost track of time while discussing mid-century wedding dresses with Katie and why it was only after she and her boyfriend left that I realized Carson had never come back to the store.

# 11

I DIDN'T MIND THAT KATIE SAID SHE WANTED TO THINK ABOUT her fabric choices before choosing one. In fact, I understood that response more than Beatriz's sudden interest in a sketch that was more fantasy than fashion. Katie signed up for my mailing list, and I made a mental note to follow up with links to my favorite historical wedding dress blogs. Katie's boyfriend was waiting for her on the sidewalk out front. I gave her a business card and asked her to call me when she decided what she wanted, then I closed the gate behind her and bolted the door into place.

It was quarter to five, and Carson was still missing in action. Under normal circumstances, I would have gone upstairs to let the kitties have their run of the store while I tidied things up and made plans for dinner, but nothing about the past two days felt normal. I walked through the store and opened the back door, half-expecting to find Carson in my parking lot. He wasn't there; his car wasn't there. I peered into the dumpster and spotted the pink bakery box on top of yesterday's trash. So, he'd made it this far before being abducted by aliens.

I went back into the store and locked the door behind me. If Carson showed up, he was going to have to request permission to enter, and I would grant it only after asking him some very pointed questions. There was something suspicious about his behavior, and I was starting to have a very bad feeling about that too.

Once the doors were locked, I went upstairs and let out the cats. They both charged down the stairs as if they'd been held against their will in my upstairs apartment. Instead of immediately following them downstairs, I entered the living room. Carson had folded the sheets and blanket and set his pillow on top of them in a neat pile on the arm of the sofa. His copy of *The Art of War* sat on the coffee table, and his bag sat on the floor, zipped shut.

I knew it was wrong to go through Carson's bag. I also knew he'd shown up, invaded my life, and lied to me, and if that duffel bag held the clues to his motivation, I needed to know what they were.

I unzipped the bag and peered inside. Carson had wanted me to think his arrival in San Ladrón was spontaneous, but the contents of his bag belied that assumption. He'd packed two sweaters and two pairs of socks. A plastic bag held two pairs of white boxers. A pair of loafers was nestled under his Dopp kit, and a small pouch holding an array of power cords was inside a hidden pocket. The only thing he hadn't packed was a pair of pajamas, a discovery that was equal parts surprising and presumptuous.

Having gone on more than one road trip with Carson in our time together, I found nothing suspicious about the contents of his bag. That alone should have comforted me, but it didn't. I wasn't looking for proof of his innocence; I was looking for answers. I was already too deep into my violation of Carson's privacy to stop now, so I pulled out his Dopp kit and opened that next.

On top was a crushed Dodgers baseball hat.

I pulled out the hat and set it next to me. Any remaining doubts about what Maria had told me vanished. Carson had been here in San Ladrón on Friday. That didn't have to be a big deal, not if his fiancée had made an appointment to meet with me at his suggestion, but he'd lied about it, and that bothered me more. Carson was hiding something.

Under the baseball hat was the expected assortment of overnight supplies: toothbrush, toothpaste, comb, refillable razor, replacement blades, and a tube of shaving cream. A bottle of aspirin and a jug of daily vitamins. I didn't know what I wanted to find, but nothing about the contents left me any more informed about why he'd shown up on my doorstep or why he'd suddenly left.

I zipped Carson's bag closed and pushed it back in place at the end of my sofa. Carson's actions were part of a bigger mystery that appeared to tie into Laird Harden's murder, and the only thing connecting those two men was Beatriz Rosen. Now two of the three of them were missing while an investigation into the third one's murder was ensuing. Nothing suspicious about *that*.

I picked up my phone to call Charlie and had another idea. I flipped to my recent calls and hit Giovanni's name.

———

"No," Giovanni said conclusively. "I can't believe you'd even ask me that."

"She's a client of both of us," I said, "and I need to talk to her. She must have given you contact information."

"She gave me the names and numbers of her bridesmaids and told me to contact them directly with questions."

"You forget that I worked for you for six years. I know how you run things. You would no more have agreed to contact several different women than you would have agreed to take this job without a deposit."

Giovanni was quiet.

"I'm right, right? Which means you have her number."

He mumbled something into the phone.

"What?" I asked. "I didn't hear you."

"She gave me the number of her wedding planner."

"Renee Davis?"

"No, Renee's one of the bridesmaids. Her wedding planner is Evan Grant."

I felt a chill wash over me. This name shouldn't have meant anything to me, but it did. This was the gentleman who'd been sampling the menu with Adelaide at the Waverly House the night I'd found Laird's body. I fought to keep my voice even and said, "Right. Evan. Can you give me his number?"

"If you didn't know he was her wedding planner, then I hardly think you have reason to contact him."

"Giovanni, listen to me. There was a murder here in San Ladrón—"

"Another one? If I were you, I'd stop drinking the water."

"—and the victim knew Beatriz," I finished, pretending I hadn't heard him. Yes, he was correct—this wasn't the first murder since I'd moved back. I didn't love how crime had crept into the community I'd once thought of as charming and safe. "She hasn't called me back. She may have given you a deposit, but she didn't give one to me, and I'm not going to start on this wedding dress until I confirm a few things with her."

"That's your business, not mine."

I turned around and leaned against my kitchen counter. "How do you think Beatriz will respond when she hears she doesn't have a wedding dress?"

"She's going to be furious."

"Right. She might even postpone her wedding."

"That would serve you right."

"It won't serve me anything I don't already have, but it might affect the business of the person making her brides-maids' dresses."

I could practically hear the gears turning in Giovanni's brain, calculating the known potential loss of the deposit he would have to refund and the less measurable potential loss of publicity. Giovanni was a cheapskate, but he was no dummy.

"I'll have Evan contact you at his earliest convenience."

"Thank you."

He hesitated for a moment. "And if you send me your design, I'll have Beatriz's dress made by my workroom."

I narrowed my eyes in suspicion. It was too big of an offer. This went beyond Giovanni's fear of losing business *or* public-ity. "You want to take credit," I guessed.

"It's a legitimate proposal," he amended. "Just think about it."

I thanked him and hung up before he could propose anything else.

Before I lost my nerve, I called the number Beatriz had given me, this time knowing the number belonged to Renee. I left her a message and followed it up with a text that said pretty much the same thing: *This is Poly Monroe from Material Girl. I need to speak to Beatriz about her dress. Please give her the message. It's urgent. Thank you.*

My battery was low, but I wanted my phone nearby so as not to miss any incoming calls. I carried it downstairs and plugged it into an outlet then resumed the routine of returning the store to its previously organized state. I put away three bolts of fabric and decided to leave the rest for later. Tomorrow was Monday, and all the shops on Bonita Avenue would be closed. I'd been cooped up inside for most of the day, and I was curious to see how news of Laird's murder had trickled out and spread through San Ladrón.

I found Pins and Needles hiding inside the cutting table and on a pile of mohair, their latest favorite nesting spot. I might never have known they were there if Pins hadn't reached out to swat my leg. I chastised them briefly but silently gave thanks that they'd chosen to play inside a fixture and not try to climb vintage fabrics. Kitty claws could do irreparable damage, and some days, giving them run of the store was like playing Russian roulette.

"Come on out, you two. It's time to go back upstairs," I said. I reached in and helped Pins out. Needles jumped out on his own and meowed up at me. I grabbed a plastic measuring tape from the cutting table and trailed it behind me while I headed toward the stairs. The cats took turns pouncing on it as I moved. The game got them back upstairs, where I fed them, collected my keys and handbag, and left out the back door.

On any given Sunday, proprietors of businesses on Bonita Avenue could be found dining at the Waverly House. It was a win-win situation. At the time when the rest of us were available, the Waverly House experienced a lull. Adelaide had the kitchen organize what had become known as the Beggar's Buffet: a spread of various foods left over from the weekend's events menu. It had become a challenge for the chef to create inventive dishes out of a hodgepodge of foods, and based on our feedback, a few of the dishes he came up with had gone on to become part of the regular restaurant offerings.

Tiki Tom was lugging his trash bin to the corner. He wore a

tan-and-red Hawaiian print shirt over a long-sleeved white T-shirt. "Hey, Poly," he said. "Good day?"

"I haven't checked the sales tally, but it felt like we were busy. You?"

"Nonstop. I found a good home for the Witco wall hanging behind my register, among other things. Did your bride have a chance to talk to you?"

"My bride?"

"Yes, she was in my store earlier today. Cute girl. She said she met you the other day to talk about her wedding dress."

"She came in right around closing, but I think we found something for her."

"Good. She seemed a little nervous when she was in my store, but I figured it was pre-wedding jitters." He leaned back and positioned the metal bin by the alley, where the trash collectors would empty it tomorrow morning. "I told her to wait until you closed if she wanted to talk to you alone."

"She was a little shy at first, but she opened up pretty quickly. Maybe it's because she didn't want her fiancé to over-hear what she wanted."

Tiki Tom perked up. "He finally showed up? I'm sorry I missed him. She said he was a big baseball fan, and I wanted to show him my collection of Dodgers tiki totems."

I put my hand on Tiki Tom's arm and made him look at me. "Can you describe this bride?"

"Pretty girl but a plain Jane. She had her hair in a ponytail under a baseball hat."

"Was she wearing a pink wraparound sweater? And sunglasses?"

"Yes. She said she left her prescription glasses in her car. What's with the twenty questions?"

I stood in the alley and faced Tiki Tom, but my mind was at the doughnut shop. Because the person Tiki Tom had described wasn't the bride who wanted a Grace Kelly wedding dress. It was a different bride, and her description matched that of the person I'd seen in a booth earlier today. And I could think of one good reason that particular bride would need to skulk around in a disguise, and it had nothing to do with her vision.

# 12

"THIS BRIDE DIDN'T LEAVE ANY CONTACT INFORMATION WITH YOU, did she?" I asked.

"No. Why? Don't you already have it?"

I chewed off the last of my lipstick. I didn't want to be responsible for spreading rumors about an acclaimed ballerina, but I felt like this information, on top of Carson's suspicious actions, was somehow relevant to Laird Harden's murder.

"I forgot to get one of her measurements," I said.

"You can still catch her if you want," Tiki Tom said. He pointed at the end of the alley. "I just saw her go into the Circle K on the corner."

I didn't realize I'd still had a grip on Tiki Tom's arm, but I let go and took off, calling a quick thank-you over my shoulder.

The Circle K was at the end of the block. It sat across the street from Charlie's auto shop and was often a last stop for day trippers thanks to the cheap gas and the assortment of road-trip-appropriate snack foods. I hurried to the entrance and scanned the interior. There were several people inside the minimarket, but none of them was familiar. I waited until the line at the register had dwindled and plunked a pack of gum onto the counter. Bruce, a teenager who worked part-time at the gas station, scanned the barcode on the gum and waited for me to pay. I used the twenty-dollar bill I'd tried to use at Lopez Donuts, earning a belabored sigh at forcing him to count out change.

"You didn't happen to see a woman come in here?" I asked. "About this tall," I said, holding my hand around my eye level, "with a ponytail and sunglasses. She was wearing—"

"Restroom," Bruce said.

"—a pink sweater."

"She's in the restroom."

I twisted halfway and scanned the interior. "Where are your restrooms?"

"Outside." He pointed at the wall.

"How do you know she's still there?"

"She didn't bring back the key."

"Thanks," I said.

I made it to the door before he called out to me. "Don't you want your gum?"

"Keep it."

I rounded the building and located a nondescript door on the outside of the building. It had been repainted a few times, the paint bubbling under the hot, California sun, revealing shades of blue and gray and red that it had been from time to time. I yanked on the door, but it was locked. I knocked and said, "Beatriz, it's Poly Monroe from the fabric store. I need to talk to you." I gave her a few seconds to unlock the door, but when she didn't, I added, "It's about Carson."

I stood outside the door. The longer I waited for it to open, the surer I was that Beatriz wasn't inside. I pressed my ear to the heavy metal, but it would have taken supersonic hearing to detect movement on the other side.

"There's a restroom at the Waverly House," said a male voice. I turned around and saw Sheriff Clark striding toward me.

"Hi, Sheriff," I said lightly. I considered stepping back and forth from foot to foot to make it appear as though I couldn't make the short walk to the historic mansion, but that bordered on ridiculous. "I think one of my customers is in here," I said, "and I need to ask her a question."

Clark, no dummy, stepped closer and rapped his knuckles on the metal door. "How long have you been waiting for her to come out?"

"Not long."

"Stay here." He left me outside the restroom and rounded the corner to the front of the store. Seconds later, he returned with Bruce. The teen held a long wooden stick with a key on the end.

"I thought she had the key," I said.

"This is the master," Bruce said. "I'm not supposed to unlock the door when there might be someone inside. We could get sued."

"Ms. Monroe here is concerned about her customer," Clark said. He glanced at me then back at the teen. "Unlock the door."

Bruce fitted the key into the lock. I might not have seen his hand shaking if not for the wooden block attached to the key. He looked at Clark before turning it, and Clark nodded to him. He turned the key and stepped back.

"I'm not going to be the one to open the door," Bruce said with a trace of defiance. I had to applaud his courage in the face of Clark's intimidating police presence. Clark nodded to him and grabbed the handle. I was taller than Clark, and even though I was behind him, I could easily see over his shoulder. The problem was, there wasn't anything to see. The toilet stall door swung on its hinges, and the small, dirty room was otherwise empty.

Clark turned to me. "I thought you said your customer was in here," he said.

I turned to Bruce. "That's what you told me."

He scratched his head. "She asked for the key and left. Great. Now I'm going to have to explain to my boss how I lost another bathroom key."

Before Clark could stop me, I entered the bathroom and looked around. The trash can overflowed with used brown paper towels, despite the air dryer mounted on the wall. Pieces of toilet paper were scattered around the floor, and dampness around the base of the commode seemed to indicate either a plumbing leak or poor aim. It would take a desperate person to use this restroom instead of going to one of the many restaurants on the street.

I wasn't eager to soil the soles of my loafers with the unknown substance on the floor, so I backed away from the stall and rejoined Clark outside the Circle K. Bruce had left us to return to his shift.

"Who was this customer?" Clark asked.

I didn't see the point of lying. "Beatriz Rosen," I said. "She's getting married at the Waverly House next Saturday, so her dress is a rush job."

He nodded. "Your ex-boyfriend is the groom, isn't he?"

"Yes."

"And that doesn't bother you?"

"We broke up when I moved to San Ladrón," I said defensively. I'd been the one to break off the relationship with Carson, and I didn't like the inference that him moving on so quickly troubled me. "He's free to live his life."

Clark nodded again. "Is Mr. Cole still in San Ladrón?"

"I don't know." Clark studied me, and I added, "Material

Girl is closed tomorrow, but Carson has a job back in Los Angeles."

"You just said he's getting married here on Saturday."

"We never discussed his plans."

"But he's staying with you?"

Even though Clark had sunglasses on, there was no mistaking the way he turned his full attention on me. I'd been on the receiving end of Clark's suspicions before, and I'd thought my actions from that time would have earned me some trust. Apparently not.

"He slept on my sofa last night but we never talked about anything more than that." I pointed over his shoulder. "He took his car in to Charlie's shop. Why don't you ask her about his actions?"

Clark didn't turn around. He and Charlie had a history, though it had never been clear whether it was anything more than the occasional booty call. Whatever had happened with them had stopped as suddenly as it had started, and neither one of them was talking.

"Call me if you hear from either Beatriz Rosen or Carson Cole."

Maybe it was because I didn't like the way Clark treated me, or maybe it was because I was hungry, but without giving it too much thought, I said, "What about Renee, Ursula, or Evan?"

He pulled off his sunglasses and rubbed his eyes. "Who are they?"

"Renee is Beatriz's personal assistant, Ursula is her publicity agent, and Evan is her wedding planner." *According to Giovanni.* "Renee and Evan are here in San Ladrón. I don't know Ursula's schedule, but if you want to talk to Beatriz or Carson, you might want to talk to them too. Or have you already taken each of their statements?"

Clark pulled out his phone and recorded a note. "Follow up

with Ms. Rosen's wedding party as related to the Harden investigation." He held the phone down. "Is there anything else you've dug up that you'd like to share?"

"I haven't 'dug up' anything," I said sweetly. "I came across those names while assisting a bride with her wedding plans."

"Be that as it may," he said, "I'd appreciate a heads-up if you come across anything else."

# 13

THE LAST THING I WANTED WAS TO SIT AROUND THE BEGGAR'S Buffet while casually discussing business with my fellow shop owners, but in second place was the idea of returning to my shop and finding Carson waiting for me in my parking lot. I left Clark and crossed the Waverly House lawn to the main entrance, went inside, and waited for my eyes to adjust to the dark interior. The restaurant seemed unusually quiet for a Sunday night after a busy day of retailing, but since there was no firm time for the buffet to start, people often trickled in late.

"Poly," Vaughn said, sticking his head out of the kitchen. "You're here."

"You're very astute. You should add that to your résumé."

Vaughn tucked his chin and grinned. His blond hair fell over his forehead. When he looked up at me, the light caught in the gold flecks of his otherwise green eyes, and I felt a tingle through my arms that traveled to my fingertips.

He came closer. "That's not the only special skill I left off," he said in a hushed voice. "I also make an excellent cup of coffee."

I wanted to keep up the friendly, flirtatious banter, but a loud *ka-chunk* sounded, and the lights in the kitchen behind him went out. I tried to look past him over his shoulder, more difficult than it had been with Clark since Vaughn was over six feet tall.

"Why is the kitchen dark?" I asked. I turned the other way and leaned forward to peer inside the restaurant. "Where is everybody?"

"They're at Lopez Donuts," he said. "Didn't Big Joe call you?"

"If he did, I didn't get the message. Did something happen?" I glanced around. "Where's your mother?"

"She went out to dinner," he said. He gave me a funny look. "Clark shut down the Waverly House while he conducts his investigation."

"He can't do that."

"Yes, he can." Vaughn put his hand on my back and steered me into the restaurant. Exterior lights from the building provided an ambient glow that highlighted the neat white tablecloths on the tables around us. He pulled out a chair next to a window, and I sat. He took the seat opposite me.

"I just spoke to Clark," I said. "Why didn't he tell me?"

"Did he know you were coming here?"

"I don't know. I just assumed he did."

"Where was this?"

"Outside the Circle K restroom."

Two creases appeared between Vaughn's eyebrows. "Why would you use a public restroom when you live less than a block away?"

"It's complicated."

"Complicated is my middle name."

It was my turn to smile, but even I knew the smile didn't reach my eyes. I tipped my head back and studied Vaughn.

He'd gotten his degree from the College of William & Mary, and preppy collegiate style had stuck with him. Tonight, he was dressed in a white oxford under a navy-blue sweater, paired with khaki trousers and white leather Stan Smiths. "Are you sure you want to hear this? It involves my ex-boyfriend." Vaughn's smile faltered. "And his fiancée."

"An investment banker and a prima ballerina in a gas station restroom? Maybe you should save this story and sell it to a tabloid."

"See, that's the thing. I can't tell if they want me to talk about them or if they want me to keep quiet."

"Okay, that's it. You need a sounding board, and barring the presence of a more qualified audience, you get me." My stomach let off a loud rumble. "And you get dinner."

I followed Vaughn out of the dining room and into the kitchen. The room was dim. Squeaky-clean metal surfaces reflected the minimal emergency lights. A wall of shelves held milky-white plastic containers, each labeled with a strip of tape and a date, some with a time as well. The trash bins were empty, and the floor still showed traces of damp tile as if it had recently been mopped. A digital clock on the wall read 5:57.

Vaughn opened the refrigerator and pulled out a tray of deviled eggs and half of an angel food cake topped with colorful sprinkles. "Which one?"

"It's been a long day. Why not both?"

"I like the way you think."

Instead of carrying the food back to the dining room, Vaughn set it on the counter. He removed an already open bottle of deep-red wine from a shelf and poured the contents into a decanter then swirled it around several times and set it between us, along with two stemless wineglasses.

"I don't think I've ever had wine and deviled eggs before."

"It's a classic combination. Like peanut butter and popcorn."

It turned out wine and deviled eggs *was* like peanut butter and popcorn: a combination best sampled once and never revisited. I ignored my wine in favor of the cake, and I wasn't ashamed to admit I had a second slice after I finished the first.

After I sated my hunger, I brought Vaughn up to speed. "Beatriz and her personal assistant came to my fabric store on Friday morning. I found out this morning that Carson was in town, too, but I didn't find out from him."

"Who told you?"

"Maria. She said Carson was skulking around in a baseball hat."

"I know I haven't spent as much time around your ex as you have, but that doesn't sound like him."

"I found the baseball hat in his overnight bag."

"When did you have the opportunity to see the contents of his overnight bag?"

"I'll thank you not to draw mundane conclusions. He slept on my sofa."

"That's what I assumed."

"Naturally." I sipped my wine. "He didn't tell me he was here on Friday, and Beatriz didn't mention it either. But Laird was definitely here on Friday. He came to my store and argued with Beatriz. After I closed for the day, I saw him accost her on the corner of Bonita."

"Did you tell Clark?"

I thought back to that first conversation with Clark after finding Laird's body. "More or less."

"Which is it? More? Or less?"

"It was right after I found Laird's body. At the time, I thought Laird was Beatriz's fiancé. Your mother was the one to tell me Beatriz was engaged to Carson."

"You didn't know?"

"I'd been getting calls from an unknown number. Turns out they were him. After Adelaide told me, I checked my voicemail messages and called him back. He said he wanted to tell me in person, then he showed up at my shop."

"Later that night?"

"No. While you and I were on the phone."

I pressed my index finger onto the crumbs and colored sprinkles on the plate and stuck my finger in my mouth. The ridiculous sweetness forced my mouth to pucker. Vaughn leaned over the counter and kissed me unexpectedly. His lips lingered on mine for a moment, soft and gentle, like a promise to be fulfilled at a later date. When our mouths separated, he didn't pull completely away, and I felt the puff of his breath on my face and the smell of his recent swig of wine.

"You taste like my tenth birthday," he said softly.

"You had sprinkles and wine on your tenth birthday?"

"I was a curious kid."

I laughed at the unexpected response, and he caught my chin between his thumb and index finger and raised my face so I was looking directly at him. "I know you think your ex is happily engaged to Beatriz, but I want to be clear," he said in the same tender voice. "I don't trust his motives for showing up on your doorstep, and I don't plan to give him the chance to win you back."

My heart pounded in my chest, so strong that I feared Vaughn would see it through my turtleneck.

Adelaide Brooks's voice ruined the mood. "Vaughn? Where are you?" she called into the dining room.

Vaughn straightened, but his hand lingered on my face. This wasn't the first time we'd kissed, and I hoped it wouldn't be the last. But for now, we both silently agreed to act like friends.

"I'm in the kitchen, Mom," Vaughn answered.

Adelaide rounded the corner and flipped on the overhead light. I squeezed my eyes shut to block out the sudden brightness.

Vaughn pulled away from me and covered his eyes. "Mom!" he said.

She turned the lights off, leaving white spots dancing in front of my vision. "Poly!" she exclaimed. "What are you doing here?"

"I came for the Beggar's Buffet," I said, blinking rapidly. "I never got the message that you canceled it."

As my eyes adjusted to the darkness, I could see that Adelaide was dressed more formally than usual. Tonight, she wore a long-sleeved pink dress that landed below her knees, along with low-heeled nude pumps with sparkly rhinestones on the toes. Her gray hair was pinned to the back of her head, and tasteful diamond studs glistened from her ears. A silvery wrap was draped around her shoulders, and she held a pale-pink clutch that matched her dress.

"I trust my son found you something to eat?" she asked and glanced at the spread between us. One blue sprinkle sat on the plate. Her eyes moved to the decanter of wine. She shook her head after drawing the obvious conclusion. "Oh dear," she said. "It's your tenth birthday all over again."

Vaughn grinned and stood then kissed her on the cheek. "The only thing missing is the bounce house."

"You had a bounce house?" I asked Vaughn. "After cake and wine?"

"There was a very important lesson to be learned at ten years old. Wine and anti-gravitational activities don't mix."

I held up my hand. "Save it for NASA."

Adelaide pulled a delicate blown glass goblet from a shelf and poured herself a glass of wine from the abandoned decanter. She held the glass up to her nose, sniffed the bouquet, and held it up to the dim emergency lights to check the color. She took a sip then made a face. "Did you take this bottle from the cellar?"

"No. I took it from the shelf." Vaughn pointed over his shoulder.

"It's on the verge of corking," she said. "The decanter has helped but not enough to save it."

"Then I guess we'll have to finish it," he said. He pulled two fresh glasses from the shelf and filled them then topped off hers.

Adelaide watched the wine pour into the glasses. She took the empty decanter and carried it to the sink. "Next time, offer Poly her choice of wines. We don't want her to think we only serve her food and drink that's on the verge of spoiling."

"To be fair, I did come here for the Beggar's Buffet," I said. "And beggars, I've heard, can't be choosers."

Spending time with Adelaide had always been easy. Vaughn, well, our time together had had its ups and downs. But little by little, we were getting more comfortable around each other, almost like dancers who were learning to trust their partners.

As soon as the thought entered my mind, a new thought followed on its heels, and I felt a tingle of adrenaline arrive with my sudden clarity. Beatriz and Laird had been dance partners. In order to dance together at the level they did, they would had to have trusted each other. Maybe I had seen them arguing, but that couldn't be the only aspect of their relationship, not if they were able to perform in tandem and wow educated audiences.

When I saw Laird and Beatriz together, my first assumption was that he was trying to strong-arm her into doing something she didn't want to do. But what if Beatriz was the one with the power? What if her decision to marry Carson had left *Laird's* trust broken? It was then I remembered what Laird had said to me: *Don't let her fool you. Beatriz Rosen doesn't care about anything but herself. The sooner you learn that, the better off you'll be.*

At the time, I'd thought Laird was the fiancé, but now I knew better. Laird was Beatriz's partner, but Beatriz's choice to marry Carson had left Laird with nothing. The confrontations at Material Girl and on the corner of Bonita? Those weren't the overbearing actions of her lover; they were shows of escalating desperation. I'd wanted to see Beatriz as the victim, as the poor ballerina being bullied in public. I'd even rushed to her defense to break up their argument.

But Laird was the victim here, not Beatriz. Any number of people might have been upset that Beatriz was leaving the world of ballet, but Laird stood to lose more than the others if she retired.

I was starting to suspect my ex-boyfriend was engaged to a killer. Maybe Laird had tried one last time to convince Beatriz to change her mind, and maybe her only way forward was if Laird was no longer in the picture.

# 14

I suddenly didn't feel very well. I put my hand on my forehead to cool it down.

"Are you okay?" Vaughn asked. He glanced at the wine and cake then back at me. "You don't look great."

"I'm fine," I said as the wave of nausea subsided. "I'm probably just tired. I didn't sleep well last night."

Vaughn scowled, and too late, I remembered I'd told him that Carson spent the night on my sofa. I'd already told him it was innocent, and Vaughn had no reason to doubt me.

Adelaide, who didn't know the details of last night's sleepover, said, "It's no wonder you don't feel well." She turned to Vaughn. "Walk Poly back to the fabric shop. It's the least you can do after giving her a dinner of cake, deviled eggs, and wine."

"I'm fine," I said again, embarrassed by the suggestion that I wasn't but also aware that my protests weren't particularly smart. "Really, I am."

"Still," Adelaide said, "it's getting dark, and I'd like to lock up and retire for the night."

"Plus, there's a murderer on the loose," Vaughn said. "Let's not take any unnecessary chances."

I glanced at the clock on the wall. We'd squandered over an hour in the kitchen, and until my mind had tripped on thoughts about Laird and Beatriz, that hour had been a welcome reprieve. I didn't know what—or who—I might find back at Material Girl, and I wasn't in a hurry to find out.

"Give me a couple of minutes to clean up," Vaughn said. He covered the deviled eggs with a fresh piece of plastic wrap and resecured the lid onto the cake plate then put both back into the refrigerator. He ran fresh water over a rag from a nearby shelf and wiped down the counter. Adelaide stood by the door, watching him with a critical eye, and I suppressed a smile. Mothers were the same everywhere. Never quite believing their kids could handle a task without being observed.

"Adelaide, before we leave, I wanted to ask you about the elementary school teacher who referred the Rosen-Cole wedding to the Waverly House."

"That would be Janet Demeulemeister," Adelaide said.

"Janet De-who?"

"Mrs. D. to her students," Adelaide said.

"Do you have her contact information?" Even though I wasn't looking at Vaughn, I felt him pause his cleaning routine. "Carson told me how instrumental she was in Beatriz becoming the ballerina she is today, and I thought it would be fun to talk to her. Maybe put together a special memory book for Beatriz for her wedding."

"That's nice," Adelaide said. "She'll be at the elementary school tomorrow. It's a minimal school day, so the students are let out at nine thirty. I'm sure she'd clear time for you if you call her in advance. Follow me to my office. I have her number there."

I glanced at Vaughn. "Be right back," I said.

He nodded and resumed cleaning.

The halls of the Waverly House were dim, lit by Victorian-era sconces on the walls. Renovations to the Waverly House had been done to modernize the wiring and ventilation system while maintaining the appearance, and the painstaking tasks had been worth it. Very few people knew a control panel with dimmer switches had been installed in Adelaide's office or that with the flip of a breaker, the entire building would be bathed in light that rivaled the local football field during a nighttime game.

Adelaide sat behind her desk and tapped the space bar on her computer. She clicked her mouse a few times, typed something in, and looked confused. "That's funny," she said.

"What?"

"I was sure I had her personal contact information, but the only thing here is the number of the elementary school."

"And if it's a minimal school day, she'll probably leave after the students do."

"It's likely," Adelaide said. "Janet and I became friends when Vaughn was in her class. We stayed in touch. If you'd like to speak to her, I'm sure you can leave a message for her at the school." She looked up at the doorway behind me. "Will I see you tomorrow morning?" she asked, but the question was not aimed at me.

I turned around and saw Vaughn leaning against the doorframe.

"That depends on Poly," he said.

"Oh?" she asked. Her voice gave away a note of hope.

"I heard you talking about Ms. D." He looked at me. "If you're going to San Ladrón High, I'd love to tag along. Show you my old locker."

"Sure. Right. Of course that's what you meant." I felt my temperature climb up my neck, like alcohol rising in a thermometer. I was thankful that my black turtleneck hid whatever shade of red my skin was turning.

"Sheriff Clark has requested we keep the chapel closed for an additional day, so if you do plan to come here afterward, call first. I don't know what the day will bring."

"Good night, Mom," Vaughn said.

The cool October air was welcome against my flushed skin. Together, Vaughn and I walked out of the front door and down the path to the sidewalk. A breeze tossed my auburn hair around my face, and I reached up and held it back while we walked. I tripped over a crack in the sidewalk and lurched forward. Vaughn caught me by my elbow and steadied me while I regained my balance. I held my index finger up and pointed at him. "Don't you say a word," I cautioned.

"What?" he asked with a look of feigned innocence. "I was going to say it's time my mom had the sidewalk cracks fixed."

"Of course you were," I said, not believing him.

I pulled out my phone and switched on the flashlight, illuminating the path in front of me to minimize the possibility of me tripping again. Klutziness was among my less desirable habits, and nothing killed a romantic walk home like a faceplant.

We slowed our pace and stayed on the sidewalk even though the walk would have been shorter if we'd cut across the lawn. "Are you going to tell me the real reason you want to talk to Mrs. D.?" Vaughn asked.

"What makes you think I lied to your mom?"

"I don't think you lied, per se, but I *do* think you have an ulterior motive."

"If you must know..." My voice trailed off, and I pretended to be conflicted. "Fourth graders are ten years old, which means she might be able to shed some light on your curious years."

"Ten was third grade," he said. "I'd settled down by the time she got me in her class."

"That's too bad. I would have liked to know you in your bad boy years." I was about to add a comment about the positive influence of the public school system when I saw some movement outside the Circle K.

I stopped walking. Vaughn seemed to have noticed it too. He put his arm out in front of me as if to protect me. We were about fifty feet from the minimart, and whatever it was that had caught my attention seemed to have vanished.

"Did you see something?" I whispered.

"I think I did, but I don't know what. You?"

"Same."

I grabbed Vaughn's hand and threaded my fingers through his then crept forward slowly. When we got closer to the exterior of the building, I aimed my phone's flashlight down the alley. It looked a little creepier than usual thanks to the irregularity of the lights coming off the back of the shops along the street. I moved my flashlight back toward the Circle K, this time spotting a row of trash bins along the outside of the building. The one on the end lay on its side, and something furry was half in and half out.

"We might have seen an animal," Vaughn said.

I didn't reply. I held my flashlight up and pulled Vaughn along with me as I crept closer. My heart pounded again but not because I felt any danger. The gas station/mini mart was open twenty-four hours, and even though it was dark, a steady stream of cars jockeyed for position at the pumps. Bruce, the teen who'd been working earlier, rounded the corner and set another trash bin at the end of the row. He jumped when he spotted us.

"Hey, Vaughn," he called out.

"Hi, Bruce," Vaughn called back. "Everything okay?"

"Yeah. Just getting the trash out for tomorrow's pickup." A customer yelled his name, and he looked over his shoulder. "One of the pumps is stuck." He turned around and jogged to the pump.

While Vaughn talked to Bruce, I watched the furry animal in the tipped-over bin. Except what I'd originally thought was an animal had started to look like something else. It lay flat, like hair from a discarded doll. I stepped closer to the bin, and when I was a few feet away, I reached into the bin and pulled out a hank of long hair bound by a rubber band.

"Is that someone's hair?" Vaughn asked.

I gripped the severed ponytail and nodded. I'd seen this very ponytail on a woman at Lopez Donuts this morning, along with a baseball hat and dark glasses. I handed the hair to Vaughn—who looked less than thrilled about holding a clump of hair I'd found in a public trash can—and I dumped the rest of the bin's contents onto the gravel. Under the hair was a baseball hat, a pair of dark glasses, a pink mohair sweater, and an empty bottle of peroxide. And under that was a sketch of a wedding dress—*my* sketch of a wedding dress, the dress Beatriz Rosen had asked me to make for her wedding to Carson. The edges of the drawing paper were smudged with something dark and red that looked very much like blood.

# 15

"THIS ALL CAME FROM BEATRIZ," I SAID. I POINTED AT THE ITEMS on the ground as if taking an inventory. "Her hat. Her glasses. Her sweater." I stood straight and pointed at the ponytail. "Her hair."

"Her blood?" he asked, pointing at the sketch.

"I don't know," I said. "I hope not."

Now that I'd dumped the bin of clues onto the ground, it wouldn't be long before a four-footed critter carried them off, so it was with a sense of responsibility that Vaughn and I went not to Material Girl but to the Sheriff's Mobile Unit conveniently located across the street from the Waverly House.

"We have to tell him," I said to Vaughn as much as to myself. "I mean, I know we have to tell him, but there's no way around it, right?"

"You're sure this is Beatriz's hair?" he asked, brandishing the hank of hair like a spectator at a Fourth of July parade might brandish a miniature flag.

"I'm not sure, but I'm almost sure. And 'almost' seems like obstructing-justice territory."

"Come on," Vaughn said. "Let's let Clark be the judge."

I'd come to learn that during a homicide investigation, Sheriff Clark kept odd hours. We found him inside watering the plants. He seemed as surprised to see us as I was to see him, evidenced by the fact that he shifted his aim and dumped a stream of water from his green plastic pitcher directly onto the floor.

He recovered quickly and set the pitcher on his desk. "Poly, Vaughn." He nodded at each of us, and his sight moved to the hair in Vaughn's hands. "This isn't a social call, is it?"

"No," Vaughn said. He looked at me and nodded.

"We found something," I said. "You should come with us."

Clark held up his hands. "Is this in regard to the murder of Laird Harden?" he asked.

"I think so," I said.

Clark went to his desk and sat down. He motioned to the two chairs that faced his desk. I didn't sit right away, but when Clark showed no signs of getting back up to follow us, I looked at Vaughn, and he nodded. We each sat down.

I pointed at the hair in Vaughn's hands. "I think that hair belonged to Beatriz Rosen. I found it in the trash outside of the Circle K." I pointed over my shoulder. "There's other stuff there too—her sweater, a pair of sunglasses, and a baseball hat. When I met her yesterday, she was wearing the sweater. I saw her at Lopez Donuts earlier today, and she was wearing the hat and sunglasses. I didn't know it was her at the time, but I'm sure of it now."

Clark listened while I spoke. He leaned back in his chair and picked up a pen, but he didn't write anything down. When I finished speaking, I looked at Vaughn to see if he'd found Clark's behavior as odd as I did. He held the hank of hair as if it were now fused to his hands. I gently took it out of his grip and set it on the center of Clark's desk blotter.

Clark used the end of his pen to push the hair away from him.

"That's not Beatriz Rosen's hair," he said.

"How do you know?"

"Ms. Rosen was here earlier today. She wanted to cooperate with my investigation into her dance partner's murder. She provided a detailed timeline of her stay in San Ladrón from Friday when she arrived to this evening. She also provided critical information about Mr. Harden's recent activities that broadened the scope of my investigation."

"Like what?"

"I'm not at liberty to discuss the case with you."

"But you are going to collect the trash from outside the Circle K, right? It's just sitting there on the parking lot."

"Why isn't it in the trash bin?" he asked with narrowed eyes.

"I dumped the bin on the ground to see what was inside."

He tapped his pen on his desk and looked at Vaughn. "Did you see her dump the contents of the trash bin on the parking lot outside of the Circle K?"

"No."

I felt my eyes widen, and I gripped the armrests of the worn wooden chair tightly. Vaughn's face was stoic. He didn't look at me despite the way my eyes bugged out at him from my seat.

"Then it's possible she didn't just admit to violating California Penal Code 374.3, correct?" Clark asked. "Because I would hate to have to detain her while I wrote up the paperwork, and I'm sure she would prefer not to pay the fine associated with that criminal act."

Vaughn said, "Yes, that's possible."

"Good," Clark said, nodding. "I'll add the rest of your statement to my case file. Is there anything else?"

I sat in the chair, looking back and forth between Vaughn's and Clark's faces, unsure if I should say anything else. "You said

Beatriz cooperated with your investigation," I said after a long pause. "Does that mean you have a suspect?"

"I do," he said jovially. He didn't offer any additional information.

"Then we should be on our way," Vaughn said after another awkward pause. "Poly? Are you ready?"

I was *not* ready, not by a long shot. I needed a distraction while I rooted through Clark's inbox for the Harden file and checked to see who he considered a suspect and why he didn't believe me. But then it occurred to me that if Clark didn't feel the need to collect the evidence I'd found in the trash outside of the Circle K, the evidence was mine for the taking.

"Ready as I'll ever be." I stood up and reached across Clark's desk for the hair.

He flipped his pen over and placed it on the back of my hand. "Leave it," he said.

"But I thought you said—"

"Thank you for your cooperation with the sheriff's department."

Vaughn and I didn't speak until we were across the street. A number of questions were filling my brain, but I asked the obvious one first. "What's Penal Code 374.3?"

"The unauthorized dumping of garbage, waste, and other matter on public or private property."

"How do you know that?"

"It's the most common crime perpetrated at the Waverly House."

"But it wasn't my garbage."

"Considering the circumstances, I don't think that mattered to Clark."

Our walk led us back to the gas station. Bruce had on yellow rubber gloves and was in the process of emptying the row of trash bins into a large, filthy dumpster. The row of trash that had lined the wall of the minimart earlier was gone, replaced by empty bins, some upright and some lying on their sides.

"What are you doing?" I asked, rushing forward.

"Standard procedure. The last part of my shift is to consolidate the trash into the dumpster so it gets picked up in the morning. Why? You didn't throw something out by accident, did you?"

"No," Vaughn said at the same time I said, "Yes." We looked at each other, and I turned to Bruce. "I dropped a pink sweater."

Bruce looked embarrassed. "Is this it?" he asked, pulling a wad of pale-pink cashmere from inside his jacket. I questioned the motives of someone who would take a sweater from the garbage and hide it inside his coat, but my interest in the sweater trumped my judgment of Bruce's actions.

"Yes!" I said then narrowed my eyes. "Why did you have it in your coat?"

"I was going to wash it and"—he glanced over both shoulders—"use it to line my cat's bed."

I snatched the sweater from his hand. Despite having been balled up and discarded in a public trash can, it was soft and luxurious, and I could easily imagine how Pins and Needles would love to curl up on top of it. "Come see me at the fabric store when you get some free time," I said gently. "I'll give you a yard of mohair. Your cat will love it."

Vaughn and I walked back to Material Girl in silence. When we'd left the Waverly House around seven, the night had felt young and full of possibility. Between the garbage, the trip to the sheriff's office, and the interaction with Bruce behind the Circle K, over an hour had passed. I was starting to feel the effects of last night's lack of sleep and today's long day. Vaughn's and my flirtatious energy had given way to something more somber.

We trudged through the alley and reached my store. The parking lot was empty save for my yellow VW Bug, covered in dust after not being moved from the space where I'd parked it last week.

"You got me home safely," I said. "Now let me return the favor." I pulled my car keys out of my pocket.

"That's not necessary. My car's at the Waverly House."

"There's a murderer on the loose. Let's not take any unnecessary chances." We got into my Bug, and I drove the short distance back to where we'd started our night. "Thanks for keeping me from getting arrested," I said lightly. "I owe you one."

"If Clark ever catches me in a penal code infraction, you'll be my first phone call." He unclipped his seat belt and got out of the car then leaned back down and said, "Call me tomorrow if you want company at the school."

"Don't you have to work?"

"I could use a day off," he said. "Plus, I don't want to miss an opportunity to see Mrs. D."

"Good night, Vaughn," I said. "See you tomorrow."

Vaughn got into his small silver BMW. He buckled up and turned over the engine, and seconds later, he backed out of his space and pulled out of the lot.

I swung my car into a semicircle and followed, turning right when he turned left. I rolled down my window and waved even though I doubted he could see my hand in the darkness. I left my window down and angled my face toward the cool breeze to keep my hair from blowing directly into my face.

Bonita Avenue was tranquil. Even the Broadside Tavern, usually the home of raucous late-night activity, was quieter than usual. I passed Material Girl and turned right at the end of the block then turned right again before returning my car to the space it had occupied minutes earlier.

It was a short walk from the car to my back door. I carried Beatriz's soiled pink sweater with me and tucked it under my elbow while I flipped through my keys and unlocked the back door. I was tired and happy for this day to have ended and not paying as much attention to my surroundings as I should have been.

I stepped inside the store, and as I was closing the door behind me, a hand reached out and caught the door. The hand was connected to an arm in a hooded blue sweatshirt, and the arm was connected to Beatriz Rosen.

Beatriz had her hood pulled up over her head, but I recognized her face. The refreshed, confident woman I'd met days ago had been replaced by one with dark-purple circles under her eyes. Her skin, free from makeup, was covered in red bumps and breakouts.

"I'm not here to hurt you," she said. "I just want to talk."

"You have my number. You could have called."

"I lost my phone. Please, Poly. I'm scared, and I need to talk to you. It's about Carson."

I closed the door in her face and pulled out my phone. My finger hovered over Vaughn's name then Clark's. It was the sheriff's confident dismissal of my Beatriz-as-killer evidence that gave me pause. He hadn't given my theory a thought—like he knew something I didn't that took her out of the suspect pool without question.

There was a knock on my back door, and I checked the camera overhead to make sure it was still just Beatriz. I reopened the door. "I just came from the sheriff's mobile unit," I said. "You may have fooled him, but I don't trust you."

"I'm scared for my life, Poly. I think Carson may have killed my dance partner, and I think he might be coming for me next."

# 16

OF ALL THE ACCUSATIONS BEATRIZ COULD HAVE SAID, NAMING Carson was the least expected, and it had the effect of temporarily stunning me.

"You think Carson is a killer?" I asked.

She glanced over her shoulder into the parking lot and back at me. "Please, Poly. I can explain."

The longer we stood by my door, the more I wanted to trust her. She'd been waiting for me to return, and she could have jumped me, or pushed me inside, or committed any number of violent acts before I knew she was there. But before I dismissed the last of my doubts, a white Camaro rounded the corner and parked in my lot. It was Charlie. She got out of the car and slammed the door shut, not seeming to care who heard.

"Hear her out," Charlie said. "She didn't do it."

Beatriz turned to Charlie, and Charlie nodded at her. If strange things had been afoot at the Circle K, then stranger things were afoot in my parking lot.

Charlie shouldered her way past Beatriz and entered my store. She knew she was always welcome, but tonight, I wouldn't have minded the courtesy of a heads-up. She turned around and gestured for Beatriz to follow. I glared at Charlie. She was impervious to my silent hostility.

Once Beatriz was inside, Charlie closed the door and threw the dead bolt. Beatriz removed her hood, revealing a pixie cut that appeared to have been done quickly. Not only had her hair been cropped close to her head, but it had also been dyed a dark-auburn shade not all that far from my own.

"I cut off my hair in the restroom of the gas station on the corner," she said. "I dyed it with a box of dye I stole from the dollar store at the other end of this street."

"Save it," Charlie said, holding up her hand. "Poly gets the truth."

"Which is what?" I demanded.

Charlie and Beatriz looked at each other. Charlie crossed her arms over her chest and raised one of her eyebrows. Her long, thick hair was bound behind her head with an elastic band. Underneath her tough-girl exterior, she was stunning, but she'd long ago prioritized self-sufficiency over beauty. It was refreshing to be friends with someone who expected nothing from me. When Charlie asked me for something, it was because she needed it, not because she saw our friendship as transactional.

"Okay, I'll start." Charlie pointed at Beatriz's head. "Beatriz didn't cut her hair. I did."

"Why?"

"So I wouldn't look like myself," Beatriz said.

"Right," I said. "Because you murdered your dance partner, or maybe you helped Carson murder your dance partner, and now you're turning on him. I found your hair in the trash can outside of the Circle K restrooms. I've already gone to the police."

Charlie and Beatriz looked at each other again, and this time, both of their faces registered surprise.

"Say that again," Charlie said.

"Which part?" I asked, turning my attention to Charlie. She of all people should have known I would find out whatever it was the two of them were hiding, and I didn't understand why she'd been conspiring with Beatriz in the first place. "The kid who was working told me she"—I pointed at Beatriz—"took the key to the restrooms. On my way home from the Waverly House, I found her stuff in the trash."

"What stuff?" Beatriz asked.

"The baseball hat and glasses you were wearing at the doughnut shop this morning," I said. "Your hair," I said, pointing at her head. I held out her sweater. "Your sweater. And the wedding dress sketch I gave you on Friday."

Beatriz's face drained of color. She reached out for support and put her hand on the edge of the wrap stand. Her posture was rigid, and her feet were in ballet position number three. I recognized it because it was the one that provided maximum stability, and as a person who often tripped over her feet, I'd defaulted to it on more than one occasion. Beatriz held out her free arm, dropped into a plié, then stood and held her foot out in front of her and slowly moved it to the side then behind her. She dropped her foot so her toe rested on the floor, then she bent her knee and brought her foot back to the front and repeated the exercise. I was waiting for answers, for an explanation, and she was warming up for a performance.

I pointed at her and looked at Charlie. "Is she kidding with this? You're both about ten seconds from being kicked out of my store, and she's wasting my time."

Beatriz turned to me. "What do you do to eliminate stress?" The question was simple, direct. There was no animosity behind it. I remembered a night when I'd been inside this very fabric store, stressed beyond the ability to do anything practical, just needing to clear my mind. The store's electricity had been out at the time, but I'd used a treadle machine and cranked out an entire fabric makeover for Genevieve's tea shop because I'd needed something to do with my anxious energy.

"I sew," I said.

"You said you're not a very good sewer."

"Not when it comes to complex construction, but my skills are passable. There's a mindlessness that comes with sewing, at least for me. Cutting out pattern pieces and sewing them together requires enough concentration to distract me from other, bigger issues."

"I'm a trained ballerina," Beatriz said. "It's what I do. When I get stressed, I warm up. It serves the same purpose."

Not only was it plausible, but it also gave me a window into Beatriz the person. From the moment I'd met her, she'd held the upper hand. She'd swept in, twenty minutes late, and demanded an impossible dress on an impossible deadline, and I'd been scrambling to handle her business ever since. Learning that she was engaged to Carson hadn't humanized her. It had simply made her more of an oddity.

But now, I saw something else. She was a woman who thrived in the world of ballet. This wedding—this *marriage*—was unfamiliar territory, and she was out of her element. Add in the complications of her former partner's murder, and she probably felt like she was fighting to breathe. I didn't know if I trusted Beatriz yet, but I trusted Charlie. Not quite enough to take our party upstairs, but we were getting there.

Beatriz finished a few more pliés and asked, "Can I use your restroom?"

"What are you going to do this time? Pierce your nose? Apply self-tanner?"

"Poly," Charlie admonished.

I pointed at the back corner of the store. "Next to the denim. The door is open."

Charlie and I stared at Beatriz's back while she walked across the store. She entered the small powder room and closed the door behind her. I didn't give Charlie an opportunity to control the conversation.

"Something shady is going on," I said. "How did you get mixed up with her?"

"Clark called me from the police station. He said he needed a favor."

"I didn't know you and Clark were talking."

"We're not." She shrugged. "We weren't. I was curious."

Not long ago, a murder investigation had led Clark to turn up information about Charlie's past, information she'd fought hard to keep quiet. Charlie was a private person by nature, and the fact that she hadn't held the upper hand had soured her on him. Until now, I never knew if she'd forgiven him or even accepted that his job of town sheriff gave him access to the otherwise secret histories of the San Ladrón residents.

"What did he want?" I asked.

"She was there. She knew he wanted to talk to her, and she went in of her own volition. When he asked if there was anybody in San Ladrón who could vouch for her, she said me."

"Why you?"

Charlie leaned against a fixture and shrugged. "She went to school with me."

"I thought you went to school in Encino."

"I did. And when Beatriz got accepted into the Grand Academy of Ballet in Encino, her family moved. She went to public school until her parents pulled her out in seventh grade, and from then on, she was homeschooled while touring the country with the Los Angeles Ballet."

Carson had mentioned that Beatriz's parents were

deceased, but I still wondered about her connection to San Ladrón "Does she have any relatives here?"

"What do I look like, Ancestry.com?"

"It was just a question."

"You already know I'm a private person. Beatriz and I have that in common."

"How well did you know her?" I asked.

"How well do sixth graders know each other? She was a kid in my class. Her family moved to Encino so she could take ballet lessons. I lived in Encino because I bounced around foster homes and ended up living with a mechanic. We didn't exactly share notes after school."

Charlie's reasons for avoiding the subject became clearer.

"What else happened when you went to see Clark?" I asked.

Charlie scowled at me.

"You're the one who set up this meeting, not me."

"I told him what I just told you. That I knew her as a kid. And I told him her fiancé—your ex—brought his car in to my shop on Friday morning, and I haven't heard from him since."

"Is it done?"

"Of course it's done. How long do you think it takes me to rotate tires?"

"That was a rhetorical question, right?"

"I finished the job on Friday and left him a message. When I found out about him and Beatriz, I assumed they were staying together. Imagine my surprise to learn he was shacked up here with you."

"There was no shacking."

"Don't you think it's suspicious that after his fiancée's partner was murdered, your ex-boyfriend spent the night with you instead of her?"

"Maybe. Or maybe he knew it would be awkward if he ran into me, so he came here to clear the air."

"With an overnight bag."

"Carson is a planner. He probably keeps a packed overnight bag in the trunk of his car for emergencies."

"Right. Or he knew his fiancée was in trouble and he followed her here without telling her. Maybe he even tried to step up and handle things and his plan went south."

The suggestion that Carson had murdered Laird Harden had sounded preposterous when Beatriz first leveled it, mostly because I didn't think Carson could be driven to murder, but also because I couldn't see his possible motivation. But this theory of Charlie's sounded plausible. A confrontation between Beatriz's past and Beatriz's future. Two men doing battle, one with something to gain and one with something to lose.

Beatriz opened the restroom door and stood there, backlit by the light, drying her hands on a paper towel. Her newly dyed auburn hair glowed under the light.

"Why'd you dye her hair that color?"

"It's your color. I had a box left from your last touch-up."

Before Beatriz made her way to us, I lowered my voice. "I found hair in the trash outside the Circle K. I took it to Clark, and he told me it wasn't her hair. How did he know?"

"That's what he called me for. Beatriz needed a way to change her appearance without attracting any attention. Clark was there when I gave her that cut."

# 17

"BUT IF YOU CUT HER HAIR AT THE SHERIFF'S OFFICE, THEN WHY was it in the trash bin outside of the gas station?" I asked Charlie.

"It wasn't."

"Then whose hair did I find?"

"Good question." She glanced at my hands. "Where is it?"

"Clark kept it."

"You just said he knew it wasn't her hair."

Right. Which meant Clark might not have believed me when I told him the hair belonged to Beatriz, but he hadn't completely discounted that the hair was relevant to his case.

"What about the rest of her things?" I asked. "The baseball hat, the sunglasses, and my sketch?"

Beatriz crossed the room and now stood a few feet from Charlie and me. "Your sketch got ruined when Charlie spilled hair dye on it. I thought I could clean it off, but between the smell and the discoloration, it wasn't salvageable. I took a picture of it after I left your store, but I tossed the original."

"Where?"

"The trash bin outside of the gas station."

I did some mental calculations. The hank of hair had been on top of the trash, with the baseball hat and sunglasses underneath. The sketch had been on the bottom. If Beatriz had thrown away the sketch, then someone could have seen her and added their disguise on top. They would have known she cut and dyed her hair. If I were right, her efforts to change her appearance had been futile.

"I'm going to call Clark and let him know you're here," I said to her.

"I'm surprised you haven't already," Charlie said.

Instead of using my cell, I used the Material Girl phone to call the sheriff's mobile unit. Clark answered immediately. I identified myself even though his caller ID would have done so already. "Beatriz Rosen came to my store when I got home tonight," I said. "She's here with me now. Charlie is here too." I didn't tell him what Charlie had told me about him calling her to assist in Beatriz's makeover. He was a cop. He could figure that part out on his own.

"Poly, this is an open investigation, and I have reason to believe Ms. Rosen's life may be in danger. If you speak to any of her mutual acquaintances, I'd appreciate you not discussing her whereabouts."

"I don't think Carson did this," I said.

"That means *any* of Ms. Rosen's friends—her wedding planner, bridesmaids, your former boss," he said. Then he waited a beat. "And Mr. Cole."

"Charlie knows," I offered. "She's a mutual acquaintance."

"You can discuss Ms. Rosen's whereabouts with Charlie."

"What about Vaughn and Adelaide? They're mutual acquai—"

He interrupted me. "Poly, this is not up for negotiation. I'm conducting a homicide investigation that may or may not involve members of our community. The more you interfere, the more difficult my job becomes. Businesses in San Ladrón have already suffered because of this tragedy, and they will continue to suffer until this is resolved. Do you understand?"

I understood more than I cared to admit. If the murder had taken place in Material Girl, my store would have been closed indefinitely. That meant a loss of income, which meant late loan payments, suspended vendor accounts, and lack of liquidity for future business moves. My shop was small potatoes compared to the Waverly House. It was the crown jewel of San Ladrón, a certified landmark that boasted a restaurant, a monthly murder mystery party, the most exquisite gardens in the town, and now, a full calendar of wedding parties, all of which were on hold, or canceled, or scrambling to find another place to tie the knot.

"Yes," I said. "I understand."

"Thank you for your cooperation," Clark said before hanging up.

The phone call had accomplished one good thing: it had removed any doubt I had about Beatriz's trustworthiness. Maybe she alleviated stress by stretching, but I was tired, achy, and in need of some feline companionship.

"Follow me," I said. "We're moving this party upstairs."

Every once in a while, I experienced a day that felt like it contained more than twenty-four hours. Today was like that. This time last night, I'd sat in my living room, drinking scotch with Carson before he passed out on my sofa. Today, Carson was being accused of murder by his wayward-ballerina fiancée.

I gestured toward my living room. Something about the interior troubled me, but I couldn't figure out what. The stack of pillows, sheets, and blankets that Carson had left behind had been knocked off the arm of the sofa by Pins, who was now dozing in their place. A furry orange tail with a white tip jutted out from underneath the pile of bed coverings. I bent down and poked the pile, and the tail flinched. It disappeared under the pile, and the lump moved, and Needles's head poked out. He meowed at me.

"Back atcha," I said. "Who wants something to drink?" I asked my human companions. "I have wine, scotch, beer, and water."

Charlie requested beer, and Beatriz requested water. I had a glass of wine. Carson's scotch sat on the kitchen counter where I'd left it last night. I put each of the beverages on a lacquered tray along with some grapes, cheese, and crackers. Aside from Carson's smoothie, so far today, I'd eaten only doughnuts, cake, and half of a deviled egg, and I needed something more than that.

I set the tray on the coffee table, and we each took our drink. Charlie sat in a rocking chair. I sat in the club chair, and Beatriz was curled up next to the arm of the sofa. She'd kicked off her sneakers, and her feet, in socks, were tucked underneath her.

I pulled a branch of grapes off the vine and popped one into my mouth. Maybe it was because the scene felt familiar, but I asked the same question I'd asked Carson.

"How did you and Carson meet?"

Beatriz stared into her water glass. "It was a coffee shop in Los Angeles. I was in line ahead of him, and I'd left my wallet in my car. He offered to pay for my drink. I waited for him in the parking lot to pay him back, and he said I could buy him a drink in return. We went to the hotel bar next door and had a room within the hour."

The only detail their two accounts shared was the coffee shop, and I wondered which of the two of them was lying. Carson's version made him out to be rich, successful, willing to go for what he wanted. Beatriz's version cast her as confident, capable, and forward.

"Do you remember what you were wearing?"

I felt Charlie's stare, but I held my wineglass and popped another grape into my mouth, acting as if I were just making conversation.

Beatriz shrugged. "Nothing special. I'd just come from practice, so it was probably a pair of jeans over my leotard and a wraparound sweater. That's practically my uniform."

"And Carson?"

"A custom suit. I remember telling him he looked like a corporate attorney." She smiled to herself. Whatever the truth was about their first meeting, it seemed to be a pleasant memory. I wondered how she'd gotten from that memory to the accusations she'd leveled when she first arrived.

"Tell me about Laird," I said.

"Poly," Charlie said.

I held up my hand to silence Charlie and pointed at Beatriz. "You're here because you're scared. And Sheriff Clark asked me to keep your whereabouts secret, which puts me in a difficult spot. All of this has to do with your former partner's murder, yet I know nothing about him. One of the suspects central to the case spent the night on that very sofa. I think I'm well within my rights to ask for some information."

Beatriz held up her water glass. "Can I get something a little stronger first? You said you had scotch?"

I stood up and carried Beatriz's glass to the kitchen and set it on the counter. I pulled a tumbler out of my cupboard and added two ice cubes then poured her an inch of Carson's scotch, which seemed like the appropriate amount if Mae West movies were accurate. I carried the glass into the living room and handed it to her then reclaimed my seat and grabbed a few more crackers.

Beatriz tasted the scotch and, after it appeared to meet with her satisfaction, dumped the contents of the glass down her throat. She stared into the empty glass for a second then held it out to me. I set my handful of crackers on a napkin and stood then went to the kitchen and refilled her glass. This time, I carried the bottle with me to the living room and set it on the coffee table. She sipped the contents and wrapped both of her hands around the glass.

"I met Laird when I was sixteen. He'd been dancing since he was ten, and his family moved him to Los Angeles much like my family had moved me. He was the new kid. I expected him to observe the ballet company and figure out where he fit in, but he showed up and announced that he was better than the rest of us and challenged each of us to take him on. We held a dance-off after warm-ups. By the end of the day, he'd secured the lead in the next production."

"Were you the female lead?"

"Not at the time. Not long after Laird showed up, the principal ballerina injured her ankle in a difficult jump, and I took over the role as her understudy."

"What happened to the other ballerina?"

"The last I heard, she was working in the nonprofit sector."

"You don't keep in touch?"

"It's not a sorority. When someone leaves, especially due to an injury, they generally don't hang around to watch the rest of us keep dancing." Beatriz pulled at a loose thread on the quilt, first separating it from the seam then tucking it underneath a fold of fabric. She pinched the edge of the quilt between her fingers and tried to flatten it, but the texture of the batting sandwiched between layers of cotton, along with decades of washing and drying cycles and more recent attacks from small kitty claws, had left the coverlet puffy in patches, and her unconscious efforts were futile.

"But wouldn't there be other jobs for a retired dancer? Coach or choreographer or something?"

"There are notoriously few career paths available for ballerinas, and the more successful you are, the fewer opportunities exist."

"Why is that?"

"The ballet company treats you like their commodity. They leverage your artistic and physical abilities to sell tickets, and in order to fulfill the promise made to their audience, you spend ten hours a day training. You spend every night hand sewing ribbons onto your pointe shoes, and you exist on a diet of high protein to keep your body strong and lean. The more successful you are, the more ballet becomes your life, and the fewer options you have when you retire."

"Would that apply to Laird too?"

"It's different for men. First off, ballet isn't as abusive to their bodies. There's also a gender problem in ballet. Outside of the dance company, the field is disproportionately white and male. A few years ago, the New York City Ballet featured twenty-first century choreographers, and when they published the poster featuring five white men, there was a backlash. But even after that, not much has changed."

"How did Laird fit into this boys' club?" I asked.

"Laird had a dark side. He was suspended more than once for scalping tickets to sold-out performances. He failed a mandatory drug test, and when the producers looked the other way, he did it again. There have been accusations of him manipulating some of the younger dancers into unwelcome situations, but the accusations were all settled out of court, so nothing was ever proven."

"And yet, you didn't leave him," I said.

"Until recently, Laird was nothing more than my dance partner. It's a job, and he's one of the best. When you're a performer and your career depends on not just yourself but the person cast opposite you, you appreciate the best more than you care about the other stuff."

I narrowed my eyes. "Why did you say 'until recently'? What happened to change things?"

She shrugged. "I got engaged, and my press agent leaked my engagement to the media. It came at a good time." She untucked her feet and reached down to her toes, which she covered with her fingers. "What Ursula didn't leak was that my doctors discovered a fracture in my fifth metatarsal. It's a death sentence for a ballerina. My career is over whether I want it to be or not."

"Don't tell me you're getting married as a backup plan," I said with an unexpected surge of defensiveness on Carson's behalf.

"I didn't expect Carson to propose, but when he did, I said yes. Not because I needed a backup plan but because I saw a future with him. My whole life has been about dancing, and when I got the diagnosis, I couldn't see beyond the bad press and the inevitable stories that I was an old maid and that it was time to make room for the next up-and-comer to take my place."

"How come I never read those articles?" Charlie asked. She'd been so quiet from her side of the room that until she spoke, I didn't know if she'd even been paying attention.

"I gave the press a new story: 'Prima Ballerina becomes private dancer to self-made millionaire banker.' Nobody knows the truth," Beatriz said. She cupped her hand over her toes and said, "Correction. Very few people know the truth."

"Did Laird know?"

Beatriz shook her head. "I told him I was going to retire after I got married. His life had been like mine— ballet, ballet, ballet to the point where you start to think you don't get to have a life other than the one you give your audience. I thought he would understand."

"But he didn't, did he?" I asked gently. "That's why he followed you to San Ladrón."

Beatriz stared into what was left in her glass of scotch. She nodded, but that was her only response.

"That's what you two were arguing about when I saw you on the street, wasn't it?" I prodded. "He wanted something from you. He told me you only cared about yourself. He knew if you left the Los Angeles Ballet, he'd have to dance with someone else, someone who might not be as forgiving as you with his extracurricular activities."

She looked up. "Laird Harden was a jerk. He hurt a lot of people. And I let him, all because it was good for me. Now he's dead, and I don't know who killed him or why. I don't know if his murder had something to do with me, with something I know, or with something I pretended never happened."

"If that's all true, then why did you tell me you think Carson did this?"

"Because the last time I spoke to Carson, we fought. Carson said he wanted to tell Laird about my injury, and I blew up at him. I said he had no right to talk about my personal problems to anyone, and I told him Laird would use that information to destroy any chance I had of retiring with grace. I'd go from being a highly respected ballerina who left the dance for love to being a desperate has-been who was getting married for security. And I refused to be that person. I told Carson we were through."

"But you're not through. You came here to select a wedding dress for your ceremony on Saturday."

"Because Carson said he'd fix it. He said he'd take care of things so Laird couldn't ever hurt me again."

# 18

It was hard to hear those words and not think they were tantamount to a threat.

I could say a lot of things about Carson, but they were informed by the time we dated, not the time since then. The main reason for our breakup wasn't that I wanted to move to San Ladrón and reopen the fabric store; it was that I'd wanted to chase the unknown. I wanted to wake up every day and know that the next twenty-four hours had the possibility of being different than the previous twenty-four. I wanted to experience the struggles of trying to make ends meet, because that gave me purpose, and I wanted to celebrate both the highs and the lows of trying something that was not insured against failure.

Carson wanted security. He wanted to know what came next.

The trajectory of my future took a hard left when I moved to San Ladrón. Carson and I stayed in touch, mostly because, aside from the hurt at accepting our long-term relationship hadn't panned out the way we'd both expected, we were friends. We knew each other in a way a lot of people never got to know from living together and sharing the struggle of our post-college days. The last time we'd talked had been after I asked his advice on a financial matter, and he went behind my back to leverage the opportunity for his gain. Not only had I been infuriated by his actions, but my personal life had been dinged too; Vaughn could have given me the very same advice and been hurt that I hadn't turned to him.

Vaughn. He planned to go to the elementary school with me tomorrow when I talked to Beatriz's teacher. How was I supposed to tell him I no longer needed to investigate Beatriz Rosen's connection to San Ladrón when I wasn't allowed to tell him about tonight?

I sliced a piece of cheese and stacked it on a cracker then bit down and made a noisy crunch. Beatriz now rested her head on the arm of the sofa. Her eyes were closed, and she didn't respond to the sound of me eating. I swallowed and crunched into the second half of my cracker and cheese.

"Geez, woman," Charlie said. "Make a little more noise, would you?"

I glanced at Beatriz. "I think she's asleep."

"She drank two glasses of Clark's scotch when I cut her hair and two glasses here in the past ten minutes. I don't think she's asleep. I think she's passed out."

"I guess that means she's spending the night on my sofa."

"Is that a problem?"

"I'm supposed to spend tomorrow with Vaughn."

"And?"

"And Clark told me not to say anything."

"You're kidding me, right? Do you not hear me, or do you actively choose not to listen to me?"

"What are you talking about?"

"What did I tell you the other day when you accused me of being a capitalist?"

"You said you do what's right for you."

"Right."

"You think I should tell Vaughn."

"What *I* think shouldn't matter. It's what *you* think that counts."

"But Clark said—"

"That's the other thing you never seem to hear. Leave Clark to me."

Charlie stood up and stretched. She crossed the room, and I followed her down the stairs.

"I'm going to be busy at the auto shop all day tomorrow. I'll call after I close."

Since Monday was the day off for the rest of us, it was the day we handled things like car repairs and doctors' appointments. Charlie was one of the few businesses open on Bonita Avenue, and she said it was consistently her best day of the week.

She reached for the dead bolt, and I stopped her. "You did a good thing for her," I said, pointing at the ceiling. "And I don't think it had anything to do with your personal agenda."

"Sure, it did," she said. "Now Clark knows our standoff is over."

"That's why you helped her?"

"My motivations are nobody's business but my own." She grinned and left.

I waited by the back door while she got into her Camaro and drove away then closed the door and relocked it. I'd gotten a lot of information tonight, and I was too tired to make sense of it all. I went back upstairs and took a cat inventory—they were curled up in the bottom of my closet, next to my shoes— before locking the door at the top of the steps. It was quarter after nine. Beatriz had stretched out on the sofa, her rhythmically rising and falling chest the only sign that she was sleeping. I picked up the quilt I'd covered Carson with last night, draped it over Beatriz, then washed my face and went to bed.

I slept fitfully. I wasn't accustomed to having overnight company, and now, for two nights in a row, my quiet time had been infiltrated. Until this case was solved, I saw no way of getting my space back.

My difficulty sleeping wasn't entirely due to my occupied sofa. Beatriz's accusation of Carson troubled me more than I wanted to admit. Something about him had changed since we were dating, and it was more than just his buzzed haircut and upgraded suits. Even the story Beatriz had shared, if it was true, painted him in a more confident light than the one I knew. Carson had achieved what he'd set out to achieve in college, and the taste of success had been enough positive reinforcement to keep him steady on his path. I never would have thought he'd be capable of murdering someone when we were dating, but did I know this version of him? What if it had been an accident, a simple confrontation that had gone off the rails and resulted in Laird's death? Could I draw a line from his behavior then, mild though it was, to now?

I tossed and turned, drifting in and out of sleep for the next few hours, while my thoughts tortured me. Carson had been here, *right here*, last night. What did that say about my ability to read people? Nothing I would want to brag about.

The worst part was his actions were starting to seem suspicious. Just this morning, when I extended the offer to stay here if he wanted, he'd been grateful. But after we closed the store, he'd disposed of the doughnut box and left, and I hadn't heard from him since. It was like he'd seized the opportunity to disappear, and that behavior reeked of guilt. Beatriz had gone to Clark and told him what she knew, but Carson was in the wind.

Hold up.

That was it—*that* was what didn't feel right when I'd brought Beatriz and Charlie upstairs. Carson's copy of *The Art of War*, which he'd left on my coffee table, had been gone. And only one person aside from me had access to my keys. The same person who'd used my keys to unlock the stockroom when I asked him to take the doughnuts out to the trash and who never came back.

I had a hunch I knew what it meant, but I didn't like it. If I was right, then this was bad. This was more than bad. I would never fall asleep now.

I threw the covers off and woke up the cats, who had joined me sometime during the night. I smoothed each of their heads and gave them both kisses then slipped my feet into slippers and pulled on a black sweatshirt. I crept out to the kitchen and got a flashlight out of my junk drawer. I peeked into the living room, where Beatriz was sleeping. The grandfather clock indicated it was a little after one. I quietly opened the door and tiptoed down the stairs to the fabric shop.

In the dark, with only a narrow beam of flashlight to illuminate the interior, the shop reminded me of those first impressions when I hadn't yet landed on the decision to reopen the place. With everything that had happened, I'd pushed off the task of straightening the store after Sunday's busy day of sales, and now, bolts of fabric sat cattywampus on the cutting station and next to the wrap stand. Fabrics had been extended from their bolts and now hung too long, covering the bolts underneath them. A few of the tilted bins had empty spaces where a roll of fabric needed to be returned or replenished.

I cast the light to my left and right, half expecting someone to jump out of the shadows. I crept forward and reached the wrap stand then slid open the drawer under the register to confirm my suspicions.

My master set of keys was missing.

I pulled the drawer all the way open and felt around the interior. I pricked my fingers on some loose pins in the back of the drawer and retracted my arm quickly. I set the flashlight down and squeezed my fingertip, and a dot of blood appeared. I quickly sucked the blood away like a vampire, tore the corner off a sheet of tissue paper, and wrapped it around my finger to stanch any additional bleeding.

Once I was convinced my keys weren't in the drawer, I checked the various nooks and crannies of the wrap stand and went to the stockroom. The knob turned under my hand. Using the flashlight had been more about not shocking my nervous system, but I was kidding myself if I wanted to believe I wasn't already wide awake, so I flipped on the light and immediately squeezed my eyes closed to block them from the assault of brightness. I blinked a few times to adjust to the light then looked around the room.

The last time I'd seen Carson was after I sent him in here to collect the doughnut box and dispose of it outside. I'd seen the pink box in the dumpster, so it was easy to draw a line between my instructions and his actions. But he hadn't acted suspicious at the time. Nothing about his behavior indicated that he planned to take off. And the Carson I knew didn't take spontaneous actions. I would have known if leaving with my keys had been his endgame all along, wouldn't I? Or had he changed more than I wanted to admit?

Now that my eyes had adjusted to the light, I was able to see the stockroom more clearly. Where the store showed signs of a busy day of business, the stockroom looked mostly intact. The card table where I'd set the doughnuts was empty and had been wiped clean of crumbs. The small trash bin that I kept under the table had been emptied, too, and now sat just inside the stockroom door. For someone who had split with my keys a few minutes later, Carson had acted very responsibly. *This* was the Carson I knew. So, what had happened after he cleaned my stockroom and took out my trash? Maybe he hadn't planned to take off. Maybe someone had, what? Thrown him into their trunk? Strong-armed him into a suspicious white van? Beamed him aboard the Starship Enterprise?

I needed sleep.

After one last glance around the stockroom, I pulled the door toward me and started to leave. And stopped. Something—

I turned back around and looked inside. There was a lot to see: bins of buttons, bolts of fabric, boxes of scissors and rotary cutting tools in their flat plastic packaging. Spools of thread. All shades of colors from bright to muted, patterned and solid, enough to keep anybody from seeing something that didn't belong.

But I wasn't anybody. I lived and breathed fabric, and this stockroom had been set up for maximum productivity for one person: me.

Once I realized something was out of place, it took me only a few seconds to find it. A thick book, wedged on the end of a shelf next to a clipboard, where I documented out-of-stock items that I needed to reorder. A black Sharpie hung from a thin ribbon next to the clipboard so I never had to worry about finding a pen.

I knew what the book was before I pulled it off the shelf: Carson's copy of *The Art of War.* I opened it and stared at the words written on the flyleaf.

*I'm sorry, Poly. None of this was supposed to happen.*

Well, now, crap. If his words to Beatriz sounded like a threat to Laird, then these sounded like a proclamation of guilt.

# 19

I FLIPPED THROUGH THE REST OF THE BOOK, BUT THERE WERE NO other notes or markings. I closed it and wedged it back onto the shelf. If I needed to tell Clark about it, I wanted it to be as close as possible to how I'd found it. The decision to tell Clark would wait until tomorrow when I was thinking more clearly.

At least I was able to discount the *Star Trek* possibility —for now.

I left the stockroom and went back upstairs. My efforts to be quiet while reentering my apartment were lost on Beatriz, who was sitting up on the sofa and texting. The living room was dark save for the glow that emanated from her cell phone screen. My eyesight was compromised thanks to the darkness downstairs and the subsequent brightness in the stockroom, so taking a page from Charlie's playbook, I switched on the floor lamp. Beatriz looked up and squinted against the light, dim though it was. She set her phone on the sofa next to her. She'd picked up the pillow and sheets from where Pins had knocked them over and made a temporary bed. She had no way of knowing that when I left this morning, Carson's overnight bag had been underneath that pile or that he could return at any minute.

"I couldn't sleep," I said.

"Neither can I."

I sat down on the other end of the sofa and pointed at her phone. "Carson?"

She nodded. "I couldn't help it. I wanted to see if he was okay."

"Is he?"

"I don't know. He hasn't responded."

I toyed with the idea of telling her what I'd found, but something kept me from sharing that information. It wasn't that I didn't trust her—she was in my apartment, on my sofa, under my favorite quilt, after all—but Carson's note had been addressed to me specifically, and there had to be a reason for that.

Beatriz picked up her phone and glanced at the screen then leaned forward and set it on the coffee table. "I'm scared, Poly."

"For him?"

"For him. For me. If this case goes unsolved, it'll hang between us. I'll always wonder who—or what—or why." She paused for a moment then continued. "Anything that happened to Laird might as well have happened to me."

"From what you've told me, Laird wasn't worried about alienating people. Isn't it possible he made enemies that had nothing to do with you?"

"Anything is possible," she said.

I chewed on a piece of information Carson had shared with me when he was here and made the decision to go directly to the source with it.

"When we spoke earlier about Laird, you alluded to knowing something you pretended never happened. What did you mean?"

"There were rumors about our dance company. That younger dancers were being groomed, and I don't mean getting help with their performances. One of the members of the troupe came forward and leveled accusations, and Laird's name was mentioned. He was heavily involved in the recruiting process, and I heard he used abusive text messages and emotional manipulation to control the new recruits when they first arrived. It was a game to him."

"Did anybody try to stop him?"

"I don't know. I don't even know how true the rumors are. He didn't pull those stunts with me, but I couldn't deny that the newcomers were under his spell."

We lapsed into silence. From the first time Laird had shown up at Material Girl, I'd taken an instant dislike to him. Brash and bullying, he'd walked into a closed appointment as if the rules that applied to the rest of the world didn't apply to him. It was easy to see that if this was how he'd lived his life, he would leave a path of enemies scattered in his wake.

But this was an ugly side to entitlement, that Laird preyed upon younger dancers hungry to advance in a cutthroat world. The thought turned my stomach.

"Did you tell this to Clark?"

"Of course." She sat back and played with the frayed edge of the vintage quilt that covered her legs. "The media likes to say I have a history of aligning myself with domineering men. My dad, then my ballet coach, then Laird. Carson was supposed to be the opposite of all that, but maybe I'm not built for a different life."

I glanced at the grandfather clock along the wall. It was the middle of the night or the middle of the morning, depending on whether you were a night owl or an early riser. I was neither. I regularly got seven hours of sleep regardless of whether I went to bed at ten or at one. It was my favorite thing about owning my business: that the most important part of my job was getting up in time to unlock the doors.

Tomorrow—or today—being Monday, I could have slept in.

"Wait here," I said. I stood up and stubbed my toe on the foot of the sofa. "Ow!" I exclaimed.

Beatriz tossed the quilt off and stood. She put her hands on my arms just below my shoulders and guided me to the sofa. "Sit," she said.

I sat.

She picked up my ankle and rested my foot on the sofa. "I'll get you some ice."

"It's fine. I'm fine. I've stubbed my toe a hundred times before in my life."

"Wait here," she said, ignoring me. She went to my kitchen, and I heard the sound of drawers opening and closing, then my freezer, and then the rattle of ice. I closed my eyes and focused on identifying the sounds to distract me from the pulsing pain in my big toe, and when I felt the cold ice pressed against my foot, I flinched and kicked it out of her hand.

"Sorry," I said automatically.

She picked up the plastic bag and pressed it against my toe again. "Hold that there," she instructed.

I leaned forward and held the bag, and she picked up two sofa cushions, lifted my ankle, and laid the cushions underneath it. "Rest. Ice. Compression. Elevation."

"It's a stubbed toe," I said. "I'm klutzy."

"You're not klutzy," she said. "You were in a hurry, and you didn't look where you were going."

"Trust me. I can trip when there's no obstruction in my path. Ask anybody who knows me. I'm uncoordinated."

She positioned herself by my foot and held the ice bag in place. "I can teach you exercises to improve your balance. They're part of my—of every dancer's—warm-up routine. But a stubbed toe can ruin a ballerina's career. You say it's nothing because it hasn't affected your life. You think you're fine because you can still run your fabric store. But imagine if you couldn't. If that one freak accident changed your life and kept you from doing the one thing you knew how to do. Imagine having a career and losing it in a split second."

"Is that what you're facing with your injury?"

"No," she said. "My injury is a direct result of dancing en pointe. Metatarsal fractures are the most common reason ballerinas stop dancing, even if that's not the reason they say they retire."

"If it's so common, then why hide it?"

"The world of ballet is highly competitive and not just among the dancers. If a coach or a producer or a sponsor gets wind of a possible injury, they won't touch you with a ten-foot pole. Nobody wants that kind of press. And the assumption is that a dancer with the first signs of an injury might try to dance through it to prove she's the exception. If she becomes reckless, then she puts her partner in jeopardy too."

"Have you danced since getting your diagnosis?"

"Yes."

"Was that wise?"

"I went against doctor's orders, if that's what you're asking. I was just like everybody else. I thought it wasn't as serious as the medical team said, and I thought I'd be the exception if it turned out that it was. When I saw the X-rays, I knew I was done."

"Was this before or after you met Carson at the coffee shop?" I asked gently.

"It was that same day. I didn't have my wallet because I left it in my car on purpose. I'm not proud of this, but I spent a portion of my life getting validation from men. I went into that coffee shop with a fake story because I wanted to pick up a stranger, and a forgotten wallet was a convenient cover story. I wanted to be treated like I was the most desirable woman in the world without it having anything to do with ballet."

"And Carson fit the bill."

"He was perfect."

"Did you ever love him?"

She looked surprised by my question. "What makes you think I don't love him?"

"You caught him with a honey trap," I said.

"And after I got to know him, I wanted more," she said. "Maybe we were meant to meet. Or maybe everything in my whole life led up to that day."

I watched Beatriz rationalize her actions on that fateful day, and my heart went out to her. From the age of ten, she'd known what it was she was going to do with her life, and a medical prognosis had had the power to change all of that. On the same day that her career received a death sentence, she'd met the man to whom she was now engaged, and she was rationalizing the way those two things fit together to make one of them more palatable and the other less crass.

It was interesting to think of Carson's life in the terms in which Beatriz had imagined it. If they'd been destined to meet, then our break-up had been destined too. One door closed, and another one opened—that was the way life happened.

The longer we sat on the sofa with the bag of ice resting against my toe, the less the stub hurt. When the pain had all but subsided, I set the bag of melting ice on the floor and said, "Wait here." I slowly raised my foot from the sofa cushions and went to the kitchen, favoring my foot and stepping carefully over the thin metal strip that divided the rooms. I prepared two mugs of hot cocoa. Before leaving for France, Genevieve had been tinkering around with a recipe of powdered chocolates and hot red pepper, brewed with a mild lavender tea as the base instead of water, and I'd been her test-kitchen audience. In the interest of saving time, I heated the water in the microwave and stirred in the premeasured ingredients until they dissolved then carried them to the sofa.

I handed one mug to Beatriz and sat down on the sofa, careful not to spill my own. She sipped the contents and groaned with delight.

"This is amazing," she said. "Chocolate and something spicy, and... what is that other taste?"

"Lavender," I said. "My friend Genevieve runs a tea shop a few blocks away. This is her invention."

"I have to get some of this to take back to Los Angeles when I leave."

I didn't tell her that Genevieve's shop was closed or that Genevieve was in Paris for her dream vacation. "Genevieve was born to run a tea shop," I said. "She's had a few hiccups along the way, but I can't imagine her doing anything else with her life."

"Like you and fabric?"

I nodded. "And from what I've heard, like you and ballet." I studied her face. In the amber glow of my floor lamp, her complexion looked sallow. Beatriz didn't have the coloring to carry off the auburn shade Charlie had used to dye her hair, and the shadows and sleeplessness only made it worse.

"Tell me how you knew you wanted to be a dancer."

"People always think it was like a lightning bolt, but it wasn't. My parents were like every other set of parents. They exposed me to a lot of different things when I was a kid to see if any of them stuck. Somewhere out there is the guitar they bought me when I was six. And the karate outfit, the tap dance shoes, the ski suit, and the chemistry set." She shook her head at this last one, and a faint smile tugged at her mouth at the memory. "Nothing stuck until dancing. I loved it. I loved going to class and learning the steps with the other girls. I didn't know at the time that I was better than them or that I had some innate talent. I just thought we were kids and we got to play together in leotards and tights. I kept getting picked to play the lead, and the kids who I thought were my friends started to treat me differently. They didn't ask me to warm up with them, and they didn't ask me to spend time with them after practice."

"Were you bullied?"

"Not in the way you think. It was the silent treatment. It was as if I didn't exist."

"That couldn't have been easy for a kid. I'm surprised you didn't quit."

"I've wanted to quit a thousand times since then, but by that point, the train had left the station, and too many people were on board. My parents, my teacher, my nutritionist. My dance coach and my weight coach. My parents found local businesses to sponsor me so they could afford it all."

"How old were you?"

"Eight." She picked at a loose thread on the end of the quilt. "You know those signs outside of rides at amusement parks that say if you're not this tall, you can't ride this ride?" She held her hand out even though she was sitting, which indicated a height of about two and a half feet, but I knew what she meant. "It's their way of limiting liability. Chances are nothing would happen if you did ride that ride, but by posting those signs, they're saying if something *does* happen, it's your responsibility, not theirs."

"Nobody wants a lawsuit."

"They should tell you the same thing about being in the public eye. If you're not ready to give up your privacy, to be stripped of everything that made you who you are so you can become what they need you to be, then don't get on the ride."

She sounded bitter. It was as if her brief time back in San

Ladrón had made her see her life differently and she regretted the success she'd experienced. I wondered about her life. Gossipy celebrity blogs and magazines made her life sound charmed: natural talent discovered at a young age, got her big break at fourteen, became a star before puberty. It was a version of the same story that came out of the Hollywood publicity machine over and over and over, minor details changed but the gist of it the same. Sometimes, there would be a quote from a dissenting source that said the celebrity in question would never make it, that they were destined to become a joke or a fraud or to be laughed at when the limelight eventually moved on to the next hot commodity. It was almost as if the negative press was as instrumental in the hype as the praise.

"You don't sound like someone who dances because they love to dance."

"And the public doesn't like that. Nobody wants to hear how you practice twice as hard as anyone else to keep people from thinking you don't deserve it. Nobody cares that you secretly hate the same partner you trust with your life. Nobody knows that sometimes, in the middle of the night, you hope you might land funny and break a bone that will give you an excuse to gracefully leave the only profession you've ever known or that you're terrified that if you stop doing the thing you're starting to resent, you'll shrivel up and die."

I didn't miss how Beatriz had started talking about her success in broad terms, as if she were describing the life of any performer or pro athlete who'd experienced a modicum of success, to talking about circumstances that were unique to her. Tears streamed down her face and dripped onto the quilt. I didn't offer to console her. She was lost in her thoughts, and I didn't even know if she realized I was still in the room until she looked up at me. She wiped her eyes with the back of her hand.

"Remember the vintage tulle I selected for my dress?" she asked.

"Of course."

"That tulle reminded me of my first ballet costume. I got it when I was seven. My grandmother gave it to me. It was vintage and had moth holes and was easily two sizes too big. My mom said I couldn't wear it in public, so I'd wear it in my room when I practiced my positions. Until then, dancing had been something I did because my parents enrolled me in class, and everybody else in my grade did it too. But those hours practicing in my room in that old, torn dance costume, that's what made me better than the other girls. That's when I discovered dancing was something I wanted to do more than I wanted to make friends or be popular." She screwed up her face. "Does that even make sense?"

"More than you'd think."

And now I saw something I hadn't seen before: Beatriz and I were a lot alike. The way she felt about that old torn ballerina costume was the way I'd felt about vintage dresses from the thirties. My great-aunt had taught me to buy them when they became available on the secondary market, to take them apart at the seams and use the individual pieces to draft patterns. She taught me to study the beadwork, hand stitching, and infrastructure of the garment, and by the time I enrolled in design school, I had a head start on my classmates. It was *that* education I'd relied on while designing pageant dresses at To The Nines, not the textbooks I'd purchased for classes. I could trace my love of the fabric store back to those early memories.

My conversation with Beatriz had given me an idea. The fabric store provided the perfect cover for me to operate within the boundaries that Clark had set out while also helping Beatriz—and maybe Carson too.

I stood up and held out my hand to help Beatriz up.

"There's no point in you risking exposure. Stay here today. Take my bed and sleep as long as you like."

"Where will you be?"

"I'm going to work downstairs in the fabric store. And when the rest of the world wakes up, I'm going out to find us another suspect."

# 20

Two hours later, I stood on the sidewalk outside of Lopez Donuts, waiting for Big Joe to unlock the doors and let me in. The choppy sleep I'd had had kept me going over my conversation with Beatriz, but exhaustion was settling onto my shoulders, and my body demanded caffeine.

Before leaving Beatriz to sleep in my bedroom, I'd changed from my vintage nightgown into a loosely woven black sweater, cropped pants, and motorcycle boots I'd found in a resale shop. The brisk air snaked around my exposed neck. It was chillier than I'd expected.

What made California temperatures unique was that they didn't hit their peak until around noon and started to cool off around four. Outside of that window, it was fall. I wasn't dressed for fall. I wrapped my arms around my torso and rubbed my sleeves for warmth, and when my hands got cold, I thrust them into my pockets. It was a never-ending cycle.

I hopped from foot to foot and peered into the doughnut shop. The swinging door to the kitchen moved, and Big Joe pushed through with his shoulder. He balanced a tray of doughnuts in each hand, and when he saw me staring into the store, one of the trays tipped precariously. He recovered but not without some fancy Harlem Globetrotter-like maneuvering first. He left the trays on the counter, came to the door, and let me in.

"It's Monday," he said. "I thought you shop owners slept in on Mondays?"

"A craving for a cream-filled doughnut kept me awake all night."

"Maria's out on a cleaning job with her sisters," he said. "If you're willing to work for doughnuts, I'll let you in."

"Deal."

Over the next hour, Big Joe carried trays of doughnuts out of the kitchen and left them for me to merchandise in his display case. The scent of sweet, sticky sugar clung to the air, coming out of the kitchen in bursts every time Big Joe carried a fresh tray to me. My role in the prep of the store was easier than his, and while he tended to the freshly baking doughnuts, I stocked the napkin dispenser and went in search of the sugar packets.

Other than the commands required for me to properly merchandise the doughnut displays, we didn't say much to each other while we worked side by side. When we finished, the case was bursting with strawberry-glazed, regular-glazed, chocolate, chocolate with sprinkles, and Sheriff Clark's favorite, boysenberry-jelly-filled. A row with vanilla icing and colorful sprinkles reminded me of the silly dinner with Vaughn in the kitchen of the Waverly House, and I smiled to myself.

"That smile have anything to do with one of the men in your life?" Big Joe asked after stacking the empty aluminum trays that he'd used to transport doughnuts from the kitchen.

"I don't know," I said. "There are so many men in my life

these days that it's hard to keep track. There's Sheriff Clark, Tiki Tom, my old boss Giovanni, you..."

"Funny you didn't mention the three that count."

"Three?"

"Vaughn McMichael, Carson Cole, and Laird Harden."

"How do you know those names?"

"I read the paper."

"Carson is here because he's getting married. I'm supposed to spend the day with Vaughn, and I've barely met Laird."

"Why was Sheriff Clark the first person you mentioned?"

"You just put out his favorite doughnuts."

Big Joe laughed. "You got me there." He pointed at the display. "You earned your keep. Which flavor do you want?"

"Surprise me."

He picked up a vanilla-cream-filled glazed doughnut and set it on a napkin then turned around and tapped out a disposable cup of hot, steaming coffee. He handed them both to me. I bit into the doughnut, and chunks of glazed sugar broke off and fell onto his clean counter. He picked up a bottle and sprayed the glass then wiped it down with a rag. He took what was left of my doughnut from my fingers and tossed it into the trash.

"I wasn't done with that!" I exclaimed.

"When's the last time you had a meal?"

"Thirty seconds ago."

"That's what I thought." He turned around, and I followed him. I flipped up the hinged countertop that separated the work staff from the public and went through swinging saloon-style doors. In addition to the equipment required to produce dozens of doughnuts every day, there was a flat griddle and an industrial refrigerator. A seasoned cast-iron skillet sat on the griddle. Big Joe added a chunk of butter to the skillet then turned on a burner underneath it.

"Omelet?" Big Joe asked.

"Sure."

He pulled a carton of eggs out of the fridge, removed three, and put the carton back inside. He cracked the eggs with one hand and held the shells while the contents drained into a bowl. He whisked the contents and poured them through a strainer into the skillet. While the egg bubbled up around the edges, he removed a plastic tub of Boursin cheese from the fridge, and after gently lifting the edges of the egg to check the color underneath, he squeezed the soft cheese in a line down the center of the egg. While the egg bubbled and cooked, he minced a sprig of chives. He returned to the skillet and folded one side of the omelet into the center, then the other side, and transferred the omelet to a plate. I reached out for it, and he slapped my hand away.

"I'm not done yet." He leaned back and scanned the shelves above him then grabbed a small bag of sour-cream-and-chive potato chips. He tore the bag open and crushed it between his hands. He reached in and sprinkled potato chip crumbs along the top of the omelet and garnished the whole thing with a finger pinch of the chives.

When he finished, he handed the plate to me. I took it and looked around for a place to sit and eat. He unfolded two chairs that had been leaning against the wall, and I sat in one. He handed me a knife and fork, and I was three bites into my omelet before he joined me.

"Why'd you show up on my doorstep hours before I unlocked the doors?"

My mouth was full, so I didn't answer at first. But omelets didn't require a lot of chewing, which I suspected Big Joe knew when he made it for me. I set my utensils down and swallowed.

"My ex-boyfriend's fiancée spent the night on my sofa. She seems to think he's responsible for murdering her dance partner."

Big Joe raised his eyebrows. "Do you agree with her?"

I shook my head. "I think there's something else going on. Something that has to do with her, not him. I saw Laird exactly two times, and he didn't exactly charm me. If he was holding something over Beatriz, maybe Carson confronted Laird in a moment of chivalry, but I don't think he killed him."

"Could have been an accident. Confrontations don't always follow a script."

"Yes, but I don't think Carson would have disappeared if that had happened. He's more responsible than that."

"When did you two break up?"

"Before I moved to San Ladrón."

"And that was when?"

"About a year ago."

"And you don't think he could have changed?"

"Carson is… Carson isn't…" I didn't want to admit that Big Joe had a point, but it was undeniable. Carson and Beatriz had different versions of their meet-cute, but in both of them, the Carson I'd heard about was different than the one I'd dated for years. It wasn't fair to him to think he didn't have the capacity to change. Maybe that was just what I'd told myself to feel superior in the aftermath of our breakup.

"I guess that's the problem. I think I know him, but maybe I don't. Sheriff Clark seems to think he's guilty, and now my keys are missing, and I don't know where Carson is, but if he has my keys, then he could show back up at any moment—oh no."

"What?"

"Beatriz is at my place. Carson has keys to my place. If he comes back and she's there—"

"Poly, they're supposed to get married on Saturday. Them being alone in your apartment shouldn't feel like a crisis."

I didn't tell Big Joe the details about Carson that Beatriz had shared with me, but as I entertained the thought of Carson entering my apartment while she was there, I questioned what the outcome might be.

As I ate my omelet, another recent memory came back to me. "When I was here yesterday morning, I saw a woman sitting by herself in a booth. Do you remember her?"

"Sunday's my busy day. Maria covered the counter while I baked. Why?"

Instead of answering his question, I added, "She had on a baseball hat with her hair pulled through the back, and she kept her sunglasses on while she was eating. There was a blue rabbit's-foot key chain on her table too. Are you sure you didn't see her?"

Big Joe studied my face for a few seconds. He turned around and strode to the wall that separated him from the front counter and took down a cardboard box labeled L&F. He reached in and pulled out a blue rabbit's-foot key chain. "Maria found this on one of the tables. She said the woman in that booth just disappeared. Left her coffee and doughnuts and keys. It was a busy day, but that booth looked occupied. After about an hour, Maia bussed the table and put the key chain in Lost and Found. It's got two car keys on it, so unless the owner had a spare, they're not leaving town until they get it back."

"I can take it," I said. "It might belong to someone I need to find."

I reached for the key chain, and Big Joe held it out of my reach. "That's not how Lost and Found works."

"The woman had on a pink sweater and a baseball hat. I found both items in the trash outside of the Circle K last night along with a ponytail that made it look like she gave herself a makeover in the gas station bathroom. I thought it was Beatriz, but she said it wasn't her."

Big Joe finished cleaning his skillet and dropped into the

chair across from me. He set the key chain between us. "You want to back up a bit and bring me up to speed?"

I'd turned the events of last night over in my mind enough times to have whittled them down to a concise story, and I repeated that story to Big Joe now.

"I thought everything I found belonged to Beatriz, but it turns out Beatriz got her makeover at the sheriff's mobile unit courtesy of Charlie Brooks."

"Then who ditched the stuff at the gas station?" Big Joe appeared to have gotten wrapped up in the clues and evidence and forgotten all about the doughnut shop.

"I don't know. I keep coming back to the woman I saw here. She looked like she was trying to hide her identity. I was hoping you might have remembered her."

"Sorry. I was in the back all day."

"You ran out of change, right? Maria charged my doughnuts to the card she keeps on file."

"That's right. Why?"

"Do you have a paper trail of every customer who came in here yesterday?"

Big Joe stared at me for a few seconds. He was a large, imposing man with a build that would have intimidated the opposition when he was a Marine. I'd learned that somewhere under that big, imposing frame was a teddy bear, but on the few occasions when I'd brought up his soft side in public, his response had been more intimidating than usual. I couldn't tell *what* he was thinking, only that the wheels of thought were in motion.

After an awkward stretch of silence, Big Joe stood up and went to a metal box on the shelf next to the potato chip bags. He lifted the box and set it on the table in front of my omelet plate. "You know what the worst thing is about Sunday business?"

"What?"

"The bank's closed. When we run out of ones, we can't make change." He patted the top of the metal box. "That means it's credit cards or nothing, and that means giving up three percent of our take." He flipped the latch on the box and opened the lid. The inside was full of hastily folded register tape that recorded a busy day's worth of sales.

"Is that what I think it is?"

"Sales audit copy from yesterday. Every sale was recorded. If the sales tally matches what the bank reports, it'll get shredded, but it takes a few days for the sales to post to the bank."

"What time did you run out of ones?"

"Maria forgot to go to the bank on Friday, and our second customer asked us to break a hundred. We ran out after our first three customers."

I stared at the register tape. Aside from the three customers who'd frequented the shop before it ran out of change, every person who'd eaten there had been recorded. It wouldn't look good for Lopez Donuts if it got out that he'd made that information public, but I didn't think he'd shown me the sales record on a whim.

Before I could qualify his intentions, a bell chimed from out front in the doughnut shop. Voices and laughter followed. Big Joe looked at his wrist. "Shop's open for business," he said. "Take your time finishing that omelet and rinse your plate in the sink. I probably won't make it back here for a couple of hours." He held my stare for a long moment then left me alone with the evidence.

I would have ignored my meal if I'd eaten anything of substance in the past two days, but it was so good that I couldn't help myself. I finished it off in a few bites and rinsed my plate while I was still chewing. I dried my hands and sat back down, then I pulled the register tape out of the box and started at the beginning of the day.

Yesterday, I'd arrived at Lopez Donuts before Material Girl opened, which was around eleven thirty. The shop was crowded, and the woman in the booth was there before I'd gotten there. That meant she'd arrived and bought her coffee before then. I scrolled past the first three transactions then periodically checked the date stamp on each slip until I reached ten o'clock. At that point, I went one transaction at a time. Each slip had a series of x's with the final four digits of a credit card at the end, along with a first initial and a last name. What started out as an inspired idea quickly turned into a futile task, and the only thing I confirmed in the process was that people liked sugared pastries.

And then I found a sale for two cups of coffee and two glazed doughnuts. I remembered the table in front of the woman. It held two cups of coffee, one in front of her and a full one across from her, and two doughnuts that still sat on the table after she'd left. I stared at the name on the slip, and a tingle of nerves and discovery snaked up my spine. The name was Ursula Ungaro.

Ursula wasn't a common name, so it wasn't difficult for me to remember the last time I'd heard it. Maybe it was a coincidence. Or maybe Beatriz's publicist was in town—and trying to keep anyone from knowing.

# 21

AFTER DISCOVERING URSULA'S NAME ON THE SALES AUDIT SLIP from Lopez Donuts, I had a new theory, one that involved Beatriz's publicist-slash-bridesmaid. But there'd been *two* cups of coffee on that table, not one, and while Carson had been at the store working for me, someone had been with Ursula. It was just as likely that that someone had been Beatriz.

I wasn't entirely without drawn conclusions. The ponytail, the sweater, and the baseball hat I'd found in the trash outside of the Circle K all matched the outfit the woman had worn at the doughnut shop. What had happened between yesterday morning and yesterday evening? Why sit in a booth at a public doughnut shop if you were trying to lay low? I mean, Lopez Donuts were good, but they weren't risk-arrest-after-a-murder good.

While Big Joe attended to the customers out front, I sat in his kitchen and called Giovanni in an attempt to find a back door into the wedding party. He was acting more like a brick wall than an entrance.

"No," Giovanni said wearily. "I haven't spoken to anyone from the Rosen bridal party since the last time you asked."

"The wedding is in less than a week," I said. "When are the bridesmaids coming in for their fittings? Or to pick up their dresses? What about your payment?"

Giovanni grumbled something that sounded suspiciously like "transaction declined."

I'd hit the nail on the head. The suggestion that Giovanni had his workroom making dresses for a bridal party that might never pay had pierced the publicity bubble he'd clung to since Beatriz first walked into his shop.

"When is Beatriz coming to your shop for her final fitting of her dress?" he asked. "I'll bring the bridesmaids' dresses to you, and we can finalize fittings and payment in full at that time." He probably thought he'd kept the emphasis on "payment in full" out of his voice, but I caught it all the same.

"I don't know if the wedding is still going to happen."

"Why not?" he asked. "I've got my best team working on these dresses. We could have outfitted an entire prom by now. Nobody does this to Giovanni."

"Actually, people do this to you all the time," I said, cringing at him referring to himself in the third person while also remembering how often an unclaimed custom dress ended up first in the window with a "one-of-a-kind" sign on it and later as inventory in an unadvertised warehouse sale.

"It's one thing when we make the dress out of our usual fabrics. I can control those costs. These dresses were different. Beatriz requested a design that took three times the materials we usually use on our dresses. And dancers' bodies are not like those of our usual clientele. We'll be hard-pressed to resell these without additional alterations."

"Hold up," I said. "Beatriz is a dancer, but the bridesmaids aren't. They're normal women."

"Listen to these measurements and tell me if they sound normal to you. Renee, five foot two, long neck, broad shoulders. Her bust, waist, and hip measurements are the same. Ursula, five foot one, massive thighs, and no butt to speak of. And the third girl, who I know nothing about other than the measurements on this card, is practically an ox. She's five foot nine with a flat chest and an ample bottom. I'm dressing two popsicles and a pear."

I barely heard the end of Giovanni's rant, because I'd forgotten all about something Carson had said way back when he first arrived. Those measurements of the third "girl" sounded uncomfortably familiar. They sounded like mine.

"Have you met the third bridesmaid?"

"No. Your ex dropped off a measurement card and paid her deposit."

"Did Carson tell you anything else about this mystery woman?"

"He said to give the dress healthy seam allowances, as she may have put on weight since he last saw her."

Any goodwill Carson had accumulated went out the window. I was ready to go directly to the sheriff's mobile unit and fabricate evidence to get Clark to throw him in the clink.

———

I took pictures of the register tape and re-accordioned it as I'd found it and returned it to the metal box. I put the box back on the shelf next to the potato chips and went out front. The doughnut shop was empty, and Big Joe stood by the counter, flipping through a catalog of kitchen supplies.

"That was fast," he said. "I figured you'd be eating that omelet for the next hour."

I grinned and patted my tummy. "Thanks for the sustenance," I said. "It was exactly what I needed."

I pocketed the blue rabbit's foot and left. I considered going home but ultimately decided against it. I didn't know who or what I would find there, and I wasn't ready to answer questions just yet. I pulled out my phone, reviewed the photos on it, and called Vaughn.

"Are you still up for a field trip?" I asked.

"Sure. Do you want to get a late breakfast first? I feel like I owe you a real meal."

"I just came from Lopez Donuts."

"That's not exactly the breakfast of champions."

"Big Joe made me an omelet."

"Did he use Boursin cheese?"

"Yes. Potato chips too."

"Then you've just eaten better than most of the residents of San Ladrón. I'll grab something here. Do you want me to pick you up?"

"Actually, can you meet me at the Waverly House?"

———

I HAD MORE than one reason for asking Vaughn to meet me at the historic mansion, not the least of which was that it was crime scene adjacent. Last night, Adelaide had requested that we call first to find out if the chapel was open, but I was hoping for a first view after the crime scene tape came down. I was also hoping to chat with her about the wedding party.

Powered by Big Joe's gourmet omelet and two cups of coffee, I made it to the Waverly House in record time. It was close to ten, and caffeine had taken over where adrenaline had left off. I wondered how far I would get into Monday before I crashed from lack of sleep, but I pushed those questions out of my mind. Nothing I could do about that now except go home and nap, and Goldilocks was currently sleeping in my bed.

It was almost as if I'd sabotaged common sense on purpose.

Mondays in San Ladrón were quiet. During the school year, things were quiet from eight to three. The Waverly House amended their hours by closing the museum floor but opening the restaurant had been a necessity ever since the historic mansion started renting out guest rooms.

The parking lot was mostly empty save for cars parked in the employee area. Vaughn's silver BMW wasn't there yet. I imagined Adelaide in her office, having her morning café Americano with a fresh blueberry scone while she calmly assessed the day's schedule, making notes on who to reschedule, what to prioritize, and where to begin. Or maybe she reviewed the week's menu first so Chef could make the appropriate food purchases. In my mind, the running of the Waverly House was very civilized, not the crazy haphazard method I'd adopted for Material Girl.

"This is unacceptable," a female voice exclaimed from inside the chapel. "How do you expect me to handle this?"

The voice had an edge that was neither calm nor civilized. But I recognized it nonetheless; it was Adelaide. I went directly to the chapel doors and pulled one open to find her standing on the discolored runner between two rows of clear ghost chairs that faced the pulpit. She was dressed in a blush-pink twinset and narrow gray pleated trousers. She stood with her hands on her hips. She appeared to be talking to one of the ghost chairs, which concerned me not just a little bit. She spotted me and held her finger up to her lips, pointed at the chair, and waved me inside. It wasn't until I was nearly by her side that I saw her phone on the chair.

Sheriff Clark's voice came out. "Don't you have a maintenance fund?"

"What I have is a nasty stain on the carpet of the wedding chapel and a fully booked weekend thanks to your request that we postpone the ceremonies that were scheduled over the past few days."

"As of this morning, you can reopen the chapel."

"That's easier said than done."

"I'm sorry, Ms. Brooks. You have your job, and I have mine."

Adelaide bent toward the chair and tapped the phone screen. She straightened up and shook her head. "That man doesn't have a romantic bone in his body."

"Considering his victim met his fate in a wedding chapel, it's not that hard to believe."

"I don't need any more reminders of what happened in here." She stepped back, and I saw the problem.

When I'd found Laird Harden's body in the chapel, it hadn't been difficult to see that he was dead. His head wound, and the blood surrounding it, had provided ample evidence. And now that his body had been taken to the morgue, only one part of the scene I'd happened upon remained.

"You get one end, and I'll get the other." Adelaide strode to the end of the carpet nearest the pulpit and bent down to grab the carpet.

"Mom, put that down," Vaughn said. He cast a *shame-on-you* look in my direction. "I'll get it."

I shrugged in a *What? She's only seventy* response and held the corners of the carpet. Adelaide stepped back, and Vaughn took her place, and together, we rolled the carpet ends toward each other until we met in the middle. I glanced around to try to figure out what to do with it next.

Adelaide said, "Take it to the dumpster outside. The garbage men are due to empty the trash any minute now, and I'd rather it be gone from the property so no one accidentally happens upon it."

I had to admit, the rolled carpet was heavier than I'd anticipated. Adelaide had brought in a plastic tarp, and we wrapped
the tarp around the carpet, which eliminated the ick factor but
added some difficulties in getting a good grip.

I backed out of the chapel with Vaughn holding the other
end and looked for the dumpster.

"In the corner of the lot," he said.

I conserved my breath and stayed quiet while we trudged
across the lawn. I should have known the inevitable would
happen, but I didn't, and I tripped over a tree root and sprawled
out on the ground. I dropped my end of the carpet, which
threw Vaughn off balance, and he landed next to me. The
carpet tumbled to the ground, and the plastic tarp fell aside.

The ground was cold underneath me, and I suspected my
awkward landing was going to leave a bruise. Normally when I
face-planted, I was quick to hop back up and pretend nothing
had happened. Today, I sat on the ground, rubbing my hip and
staring into Vaughn's face.

"I'm not used to having company on the ground," I said.

"Where you go, I go, Poly."

I raised my eyebrows and tipped my head toward the
carpet. It had unrolled upon landing, and the stained portion
was on display. Vaughn followed my line of vision and paled
when he saw the discoloration. "My mom wasn't replacing the
carpet to match a wedding party's color scheme, was she?"

"Not exactly." I stood up and held my hand out to Vaughn
then leaned back as a counterweight while he stood. "Let's get
this thing into the trash before one of us realizes we don't want
to touch it."

"Deal."

I grabbed one end of the carpet and waited for Vaughn to
grab the other, preparing to reroll it or fold it in the middle or
just lug the darn thing across the lawn to where the trash

waited for collection. But something on the bottom of the carpet caught my attention. I turned it over and peered closer at the plastic backing. Vaughn was unprepared for the motion, and he dropped his end.

"What now?"

"There's something here," I said. I used my fingernail to scratch the backing and free something that had gotten trapped under the carpet. At first, I thought it was a random piece of trash, but as I flattened it across my palm, I recognized it as something I'd seen days ago.

"What is that?" Vaughn asked.

"It's a clipping of vintage tulle," I said. I looked up at Vaughn. "I gave it to Beatriz the day she came to Material Girl to discuss her wedding dress."

"This chapel has been sealed since you found Laird Harden's body."

"Right," I said. "Which means either Sheriff Clark did a poor job processing the crime scene, or someone snuck in and planted evidence."

# 22

I STARED AT THE TULLE AS IF IT COULD SPEAK TO ME. WHICH WAS it? Did someone drop this during a confrontation with Laird? Or did someone plant this in here, like they could have planted the sweater and shorn hair in the trash outside of a public restroom?

Various pieces of information weren't lining up. The hair in the trash didn't fit with the haircut Charlie had given Beatriz at Clark's request. The apology from Carson in his book didn't fit with Carson's suspicious departure from my apartment.

Last night, Beatriz had been wearing a blue hoodie. She had a fresh haircut and color. She showed up scared, and with Charlie as her backup, I believed everything she'd said. I still did—otherwise, I wouldn't have let her stay in my home. But now, my suspicions were raised. Somebody wasn't telling me the truth.

Before I could formulate a plan or a conclusion, the trash truck rounded the corner. The driver slowed and pulled into the parking lot then drove up to the dumpster and engaged the hydraulic arm to lift the bin and dump it into the back. I had an urge to race forward and tell him to stop, but it was too late. If other clues were in the trash, they were destined for the local landfill.

Adelaide exited the chapel. She spied Vaughn and me on the lawn by the carpet. She spotted the carpet in our hands and turned toward the trash truck. "Do I want to know why that carpet didn't make it to the dumpster for trash pickup?"

"No, Mom, you don't," Vaughn said. "But you might want to call Sheriff Clark and ask him to come over for an unofficial chat."

———

SHERIFF CLARK, Vaughn, and I sat facing each other in the chapel. Adelaide, though clearly curious about what we'd found, had been called inside the Waverly House to deal with a demanding guest. There would be time to clue her in later.

Clark sat with his elbows resting on his thighs, the piece of tulle in his hands. Finally, he looked up at us. "There's a forensics course at the local community college. It's a new class, and there are only a handful of students. I agreed to use them on active cases so they could get field experience."

"Did you use them on this case?" I asked.

"Yes."

"And now you're wondering if one of them missed this," Vaughn asked.

"No."

"No?"

"Part of my agreement with the school is that ultimately, I'm responsible for their work. That's why I didn't release the crime scene yesterday. I went over that place with a fine-tooth comb to make sure the students didn't miss anything. I've never seen so thorough of a job. I've already contacted the school with a glowing endorsement."

"I don't want to jump to any conclusions, but it sounds like you're saying there's no way they—or you—missed that piece of fabric," I said.

Clark studied me, glanced at Vaughn, then looked back at me. "Vaughn, can you give Poly and me a moment?"

Vaughn looked bemused by the request. He stood. "I'll go see if my mom needs any free labor." He left. I was surprised that Clark was willing to trust me with details of his case after constantly telling me that doing so would compromise his investigation. Then he spoke, and I discovered how wrong I was.

"Here's how I see this," he said. "Your ex-boyfriend has a clear motive for murder. The victim had a relationship with Mr. Cole's future bride, which could have inspired jealousy. I have a witness who can place Mr. Cole in San Ladrón at the time of the murder and another witness who can speak to Mr. Cole's animosity with the victim. I get that you don't want to believe he could do this, but your statement puts him in close proximity to the chapel on the night of the crime."

"I said Carson came to my *shop,* not the Waverly House."

"Your shop is less than a block from the Waverly House. Less if you take the alley and cut across the lawn. He could have learned of the shortcut from you. Don't pretend you don't know how easy it would be to get from one to the other."

I couldn't deny that Clark was right, but I didn't have to like it. "If someone came forward to implicate Carson, then maybe that person has a motive for pointing the finger. Did you ever consider that?" I asked.

"It won't help to throw suspicion on Beatriz Rosen," Clark said. "I've confirmed every detail of her statement. She's no longer a person of interest."

"I know," I said defiantly. "She spent last night on my sofa, and right now, she's asleep in my bed."

Clark's eyes widened.

"She was waiting for me when I got back to the fabric shop. Charlie showed up and told me about her late-night pop-up salon. If you're going to start giving suspects makeovers, then maybe you want to make arrangements with the local beauty school too."

Clark tucked the piece of tulle into one of the breast pockets of his uniform. "I need a female present if I question a female suspect. My mobile sheriff's unit is provided to San Ladrón by contract from the Los Angeles Sheriff's Department, and until they approve my request for a female sheriff, it's me full-time."

"You questioned me before, and you didn't have a female present."

"If I recall that night correctly, you came to me. There was no way for me to know you planned to show up."

"Seems like a convenient excuse," I mumbled. He wasn't wrong, but this might not be the time to get into it with him.

"Someone has been going around town impersonating Beatriz Rosen," Clark said. "Similar build, same clothes, same hairstyle. Calling Charlie in helped accomplish two things. Without notifying anyone else, we changed Beatriz's appearance."

"What was the second thing?"

"I got access to Beatriz's DNA." Clark looked overly pleased with himself.

"You can't get DNA results that fast. Life isn't like CSI."

"Usually, I'd say you're right. But that's the other thing about the forensics course at the community college. They have a lab, and they need to learn how to use it."

"How, exactly, did a town like San Ladrón get a fully functioning forensics lab?"

"You might want to ask Mr. McMichael."

"Vaughn funded it?"

"His dad did. Not sure he wants it to be common knowledge. That's why I asked his son to leave."

My impulse to contact Clark and share my clue with him had dissolved into a warm puddle of resentment and annoyance. He'd listened to me chirp on about the tulle under the carpet, but now that I'd shown my hand, instead of putting his cards on the table, he folded. I was no smarter about the evidence of the case than I'd been when he first arrived, and now, my one solid clue was literally in his pocket.

Clark also knew how much I hated learning about the influence Vaughn's wealthy dad had in the development of San Ladrón. I'd gotten to know the man a little bit since moving here, and I no longer saw his role as venture capitalist as pure evil, but I couldn't help questioning why one man felt the need to control the future of a small California town. I kept those questions to myself because of my feelings for Vaughn, but I also couldn't help wondering how much of his father's plans Vaughn knew—and agreed with.

I was annoyed enough with Clark's little bombshell to end my half of the Laird Harden case recap. "Speaking of Vaughn," I said, "he's probably getting curious." I stood and put the ghost chair back into its row. "If you're not leaving yet, I'm sure Adelaide would appreciate you putting your chair back too."

Truth was, I wanted Clark to leave with me. He didn't. And I couldn't come up with any plausible excuses to stay behind, especially now that I knew about his crack team of forensic trainees. I had a deficit of clues on my balance sheet and was right back where I'd started.

I walked out of the chapel and plunged my hands into my

pockets. I'd forgotten all about the blue rabbit's-foot key chain that I'd found this morning at Lopez Donuts. I rubbed my thumb against it while I sought an excuse that would get me out of sharing my other piece of evidence with Clark, then I spotted Evan Grant in the parking lot. Today, the dandy wedding planner wore a dove-gray suit with a powder-blue dress shirt and a lilac pocket square. He was bent over, peering into the windows of a black sports car that had been parked in the lot for a few days.

I shoved the key chain into my pocket and crossed the lot. "Hi," I called out. He looked up at me, but it was difficult to read his expression behind his mirrored sunglasses. "You're Evan, right? Evan Grant?"

The older man straightened and faced me, but since he had his Ray-Bans on, I couldn't see his eyes. "Yes," he said after appearing to assess me. "You have me at a disadvantage."

"I'm Poly Monroe. I'm making Beatriz Rosen's gown."

"Ah. Is it almost done?"

"It's—" I stopped speaking suddenly. I hadn't done a thing about Beatriz's wedding dress since she'd picked out the tulle. From the cheap seats, it didn't look as if there would even be a ceremony. Surely, her wedding planner would know that. Wouldn't he? "It's still in the conceptual stages," I finished. "Have you spoken to Beatriz about the ceremony lately?"

"We spoke this morning," he said. "She's supposed to meet me here for final approval on the menu, but she's late." He glanced at his Cartier tank watch and scowled.

"When did you make plans to meet her?"

"Last night. She'd just returned to her hotel."

"That's the San Ladrón Hotel, right?" I asked.

He nodded.

"I need to get in touch with her about the dress. I left her a couple of messages, but she hasn't returned them. We're getting down to the wire, and if I don't get her in for a fitting, she might end up with a dress that came off the rack."

"No!" he exclaimed. He glanced to his left and right. "No," he said again. He pulled his phone out of his pocket and tapped the screen with his thumbs. He looked at me over his glasses. "Did you try to reach Renee or Ursula?"

"That's a good idea. Do you have either of their numbers?"

"Don't you?"

"Why would I? A shop in Los Angeles is making their dresses."

"Right. I can't believe Beatriz let her groom convince her to use that tacky sweatshop. Who ever heard of black bridesmaids' dresses?"

I felt a wave of defensiveness on Giovanni's behalf, followed immediately by a nauseating contrast of regret and gratitude. Maybe Giovanni did usually use cheap fabrics he bought in bulk and marked up for a generous profit, but this time, he'd used an expensive fabric at the bride's request. He'd complained about the possibility that there wouldn't be a wedding because he'd gone out on a limb to accommodate the bride by paying up front for the materials. And now I'd discovered the dresses were black. Evan might have been wrong to assume the dresses would be of poor quality, but he was right about Carson's involvement in more than one of these choices; Carson knew the only way I would agree to be in his fiancée's bridal party was to wear what had become my signature color.

Instead of getting distracted by Carson's ill-conceived ideas, I stayed on task. "Can you give me Ursula's number? To coordinate the bachelorette party," I added hastily.

He tapped the screen and looked up. "Tell me when you're ready."

I reached into my pocket and pulled out my phone. The

blue rabbit's foot came out and landed by my foot. I bent down to pick it up but not before Evan saw it.

"I thought you said you didn't know Ursula," he said.

"I don't."

"Then what are you doing with her key chain?"

# 23

"This is *Ursula's* key chain?" I repeated.

Evan bent down and picked it up. "Yes," he said. "It's her good luck charm. Beatriz gave it to her when she signed on as a client."

I reached out for the key chain, but Evan pulled it away from me. "You didn't know," he said. "That's suspicious."

"No, it's not. Ursula must have left it behind at the local doughnut shop. I planned to give it to Beatriz when she saw her."

It was not only plausible; it was true. But Evan wasn't ready to trust me just yet. "Ursula eats a macrobiotic diet. She wouldn't be caught dead in a doughnut shop." He slipped the rabbit's foot into his suit jacket pocket. "I'll tell Beatriz to call you when I see her."

It was my turn to call his bluff. "Considering I spent a portion of last night with Beatriz, and it wasn't at the San Ladrón Hotel, maybe you're the one who's not telling the truth." I pointed at his pocket. "The next time *I* talk to Beatriz, I'll ask her to tell Ursula that *you* have her lucky key chain."

I turned around and left the eccentric wedding planner in the parking lot. Something about Evan Grant rubbed me the wrong way, but I couldn't put my finger on it. I doubted Beatriz would show up to finalize the menu, but I wasn't in love with the idea that Evan planned to spend the morning alone with Adelaide.

Vaughn came out of the Waverly House, and I spun my hand in a circle to gesture for him to turn around and go back inside. He stood in the doorway, half in, half out, while I crossed the yard. He backed away from the door, and I scaled the steps and went inside.

"Do you know if your mother has an appointment today?" I asked.

"Yes. She's meeting with a wedding planner. Why? Is she here?"

"She's a he. His name is Evan Grant. Have you met him?"

"Evan Grant is a wedding planner?"

"Yes. Why? Who did you think he was?"

"He's the reason she canceled on me for dinner on Friday. He was her last-minute date to the ballet."

Vaughn and I stared at each other. It didn't seem possible that we'd somehow not connected two halves of the same story, but here we were: him having been stood up by his mom for a gentleman caller who'd invited her out for an evening of culture, me having interacted with the suave wedding planner who seemed to resent my involvement in the wedding he'd been hired to oversee.

I grabbed Vaughn's arm and pulled him down the hall, around the corner, and out the exit. We were on the opposite side of the parking lot where I'd left Evan.

"Are you serious about your mother and Evan?" I asked.

"I wish I weren't."

"Then that's why he keeps coming around."

Vaughn's face paled. "I thought that wedding was off."

"Carson said the wedding was off, and Beatriz said the wedding was off, but I don't know if Carson and Beatriz have told *each other* the wedding is off. I know neither one of them told Giovanni the wedding is off."

Vaughn held up his index finger and pressed a number on his phone. "Hey, Mom," he said, keeping his finger by his lips so I would remain silent. "Is the Rosen-Cole wedding still on?" He paused then nodded. "Have they finalized their menu?" He paused again. "I know you're under the gun because of the—" Two couples who'd been strolling the lawn came within earshot, and Vaughn lowered his voice. "The thing that happened on Friday, so if you need me to pick up anything while Poly and I are out, let me know. Love you too." He hung up.

"What did she say?"

"Carson and Beatriz have not told my mother the wedding is off."

"I can't help thinking there's one obvious conclusion to draw from what we've just learned."

"That the wedding isn't off?"

"Yes. Both the bride and the groom have suggested that the other might have killed Laird, but neither one of them has turned on the other. If one of them calls off the wedding, it becomes public, and the accused's reputation won't bounce back." I thought about what that meant. "They're covering for each other," I said, light dawning on me.

"It's romantic," Vaughn said.

"Yes, but it's also dumb. They're putting themselves—and a whole town—at risk, and if they're not careful, someone else is going to get away with murder."

I CONVINCED Vaughn to leave his BMW in the Waverly House parking lot. We walked back to my place. I didn't know if Beatriz was still inside, and at the moment, I didn't care. I unlocked my Bug and drove to the San Ladrón Elementary School. I had too many disparate pieces of information swirling around in my mind to make sense of them, so I took advantage of Vaughn's relative captivity in my car to broach another topic.

"Did you know your dad invested in a forensics lab in San Ladrón?"

"Where'd you hear that?"

"Does it matter?"

"I always like to know who's spreading rumors about my family."

"So, it's not true?"

"My dad is a venture capitalist. He built his career on managing portfolios of other people's money. Why would he care about forensics?"

"Maybe because there have been three murders in San Ladrón in the past year? Maybe he recognizes that we might need more than a sheriff's mobile unit that's funded by a contract with the Los Angeles Sheriff's Department?"

Vaughn turned away from me and looked out his window. He rolled it down, and cool air circled through the car. I fought against a shiver. He didn't say anything for the duration of the drive except for "Take the next two lefts" and "Turn right at the light."

I entered the lot. A few cars were in faculty spaces, but otherwise, it was empty. I parked by the tennis courts. Vaughn unclipped his seat belt and got out. I followed. We were halfway to the school when he stopped and put his hand on my arm.

"I'm not angry," he said. "It might seem like I am, but I'm not. I just don't want to spend any more time talking with you about my dad."

"Fair enough," I said. "As far as I'm concerned, we're here to talk to a fourth-grade teacher." I flashed him a grin.

He smiled back and took my hand. We walked side by side like that until we reached the doors. He held the door open and said, "I should warn you. I had a *major* crush on Ms. D."

"When's the last time you saw her?"

"Sixth-grade graduation." He stared off into the clouds and sighed. "The day I became a man."

I slapped his arm playfully. "Thanks for the heads-up. A woman likes to size up her competition." I took the door from Vaughn and led the way.

The San Ladrón Elementary School was a typical brick building built during California's population expansion in the 1950s. The exterior was red brick topped with clay tile to minimize the effects of the hot sun on the classrooms inside. Bright-blue lockers lined the hallway, each locked with varying versions of the same padlock. A banner cheering on the football team hung overhead, and a small directory indicated the path toward the principal's office. I turned to the right to follow the indicated path, and Vaughn caught me by my elbow and pulled me to the left.

"Trust me." He continued to lead the way, turning through the hallways like he'd been here yesterday and not decades ago. We arrived at a room with the door propped open.

A pretty older woman with ash-blond hair sat at a desk by the window. She looked up. "May I help you?" she asked. She addressed both of us, but after a moment, her expression softened, and she stood. "Vaughn McMichael," she said. "You haven't changed one bit."

"Ms. Demeulemeister," Vaughn said. He approached her, and they hugged. He turned to me and introduced us. "This is Poly Monroe."

"Of the fabric store?"

"Yes. How did you know?"

"You look just like Millie."

"Millie was my great-aunt."

"She was a lovely woman."

It wasn't often that I encountered people who'd known my great-aunt and -uncle, but it also wasn't an entirely rare occurrence. Their version of the fabric store had been a destination spot in the small town, and Millie and Marius had been valued members of the community.

"She was," I said.

"I've read about you in the papers. It's wonderful that you reopened your family's shop."

It would take a long time for me to get used to the way news spread through San Ladrón. Coming from Los Angeles, where half of the residents actively pursued fame, it never ceased to amaze me how fame had found me through minimal effort of my own. After taking over the shop, I'd planned a grand reopening, printed up coupons, and took out ad space in the local paper, but I could have saved the money and gotten the same results. People loved the fabric store. They loved that a piece of the town's history had been saved by a relative and not snatched up by a greedy tenant. They overlooked the fact that I'd changed the store's name—apparently, that happened all the time—but to the longtime residents, it was as if the store had never been closed after my great-aunt was murdered. My willingness to become one of them after that seemed to indicate a level of acceptance on my part, an ending to an unfortunate chapter in the town's mostly peaceful history.

I found myself reaching for small talk. "Did you always teach fourth grade?" I asked.

"Yes. The school system wants you to think sixth grade is the pivotal year for most students, but I always preferred fourth. Ten years old—that's when you see a child blossom before your eyes. Their ability to reason, to apply logic and critical thinking skills... It's when they first come into their own."

"You taught Beatriz Rosen, didn't you? You were the one to recognize her talent and suggest her parents find her an appropriate school to nurture it."

Janet seemed surprised by my knowledge of this little-known fact. "You've been talking to Adelaide," she surmised.

"Yes, but that's not where I heard about your influence on Beatriz's life."

She smiled, and her face lit up. "She has mentioned me in interviews, which is more kindness than one would expect."

"I heard about it from her fiancé," I said. "He said that's why she wanted to get married here in San Ladrón. That you're the closest thing she has to family. It must be very fulfilling to you to have watched her blossom from an average ten-year-old into a world-famous ballerina."

Sadness colored Janet's face. "Nothing about Beatriz was average. She was a troubled child who needed boundaries and structure. I encouraged her parents to become more involved in her life, not to pull her out of school. I've often regretted that parent-teacher conference."

"But surely Beatriz's success indicates they did the right thing," I pointed out. "If she hasn't told you that by now, she will."

"I'm not sure I agree. Beatriz may have found success on the stage, but she never learned to play well with others. As far as I know, only one person has said no to her in her life, and he's not here to talk about it."

"Who was that?" I asked, afraid to hear the answer.

"Her partner, Laird Harden. They danced together from the age of fourteen till recently. It haunts me to think if that girl had gotten the guidance she so desperately needed, that man might still be alive today."

# 24

THIS SOUNDED LIKE SOMETHING. YOU DIDN'T SPEND TEN YEARS working and training closely with a member of the opposite sex without developing feelings for them. Nobody ever said those feelings had to be love.

In the version Beatriz told me, Laird had been a barely tolerable bad boy who tested his boundaries and tried to make her a coconspirator in his actions. And Carson's version was similar: Beatriz danced with Laird, but otherwise, there was nothing between them.

Yet Carson's and Beatriz's versions of their meeting varied wildly, providing evidence that neither was opposed to a little creative license when it came to their memories. And I couldn't help seeing that in both versions of their story, Laird was the one who needed Beatriz, not the other way around. Laird's interests were being rewritten, too, and that could only mean one thing: Laird was in San Ladrón because he wanted something, and whatever that was had led to his murder. Which fit into the interaction I'd had with him when he told me, with not just a little hostility, that Beatriz only cared about herself.

"Did you ever meet Laird?" I asked the teacher.

"Once," she said. "It was after a performance. Beatriz was kind enough to arrange for me to see her debut performance as lead ballerina, and she asked me to visit with her backstage when it was done. That's not the kind of opportunity a fourth-grade teacher gets every day." She smiled at the memory. "It was after a performance of *The Nutcracker* in Los Angeles. I can still picture her face when she came here to invite me. She was excited and nervous, filled with anticipation and doubt and enthusiasm and nerves. Everything she'd worked for came down to this one performance."

"That can't be true, though, can it? If she'd been an understudy, then it's not like this was her first break."

"It was the first time the spotlight was solely on her because of her, not because she had to step in to cover for someone else. This time, she'd been cast in the role of Clara from the onset, and it was important to her to perform exceedingly well. Under the circumstances, I understood. She did everything I'd always believed she could do, and the reviews were glowing. The next day, she was named the lead dancer in her touring company, and she's danced the lead role ever since." Janet opened a drawer in her desk and pulled out a scrapbook. She flipped through several pages and stopped at one a few pages from the back. A waxy paper envelope had been secured to the page with little white corners and adhered to brittle black paper. "I keep a scrapbook of my students' accomplishments," she said. "It's a small indulgence to make me feel like I've had an impact on a much bigger world." She slid a program out of the envelope and handed it to me. On the cover was a picture of a ballerina midleap. The dancer's face was heavily made up, and her hair was slicked against her head, but still I was able to recognize Beatriz. A signature had been scrawled across the program's cover in a blue marker.

"She signed this?"

Janet nodded. "I didn't ask her to. She volunteered. She said it was her first performance and she wanted there to be a record of it somewhere. I remember that because her partner made a disparaging remark about her talent. Rather, about her interest in fame because of her talent. It was as if he resented his gift and wanted her to resent hers as well."

"How did she respond to that?"

"Poly," Vaughn said. "Maybe Ms. D. doesn't want to talk about this."

"Vaughn McMichael, I seem to recall a young boy in my class who resented his parents' money enough to pick fights with other students and get tipsy on wine at his fourth-grade birthday party."

Vaughn turned beet red. I'd never seen him get embarrassed like this. I was ready to pull out my checkbook and make a sizeable donation to the teacher's fund on the spot.

Mrs. Demeulemeister reached across her desk and placed her hand on top of Vaughn's. "I also recall that same boy showing a natural inclination for math, data analysis, organization, and public speaking, all of which were on display when he turned in a business plan as his creative writing assignment and argued that it was as imaginative as an essay about what he'd done over Christmas break."

"You remember that?" he asked.

"Of course I remember that. I had to ask the math teacher to help me grade it. And I remember how proud I was, years later, when you moved back to San Ladrón to help your father with his business. Sometimes life comes full circle, and we embrace the very thing we used to resent."

"Is that what you saw in Beatriz?" I asked.

"Beatriz had been told that she had a gift, and I do think she resented it on some level. The other students weren't nice to her, and until her family moved her to Encino, she had to learn how to navigate jealousy at a very young age. But she didn't understand Laird's attitude toward dancing. From what she told me, performing as Clara was the happiest time of her life."

I opened the program and flipped through it until I reached the bios. The story printed in here lined up with what I'd learned about Beatriz. She'd been a member of the Los Angeles Ballet for years, but this was her first lead performance.

After scanning her bio, I read Laird's. Unlike Beatriz's, Laird's bio simply stated when he joined the conservatory, where he'd studied prior, and how many seasons he'd been with them. There were no personal details, no quotes from his coach or his fellow dancers, nothing to humanize him.

"How did Beatriz respond to Laird when he said that stuff?"

"Poly, this has to be fifteen years ago," Vaughn said. "Mrs. D. probably doesn't remember."

"She responded with adoration," the teacher said after casting a *give-me-some-credit* glance at Vaughn.

I stifled a smile.

"That's the only way I can describe the way she looked at him: adoration. She tried to joke about how he was jaded but it was her first time and how he should try to remember how his first time as lead felt. He said—" She stopped speaking abruptly.

I glanced at Vaughn. His attention was focused on his teacher. Mrs. Demeulemeister straightened her posture and finished her sentence. "He said if he'd wanted to dance with a mediocre dancer, he wouldn't have gotten her the lead."

"*Gotten* it for her?" I asked. "That's awfully pompous of him. She had to have earned it through hard work and talent."

"Yes," Mrs. Demeulemeister said. "Absolutely." She seemed conflicted by something. "I don't know if I would have believed that story if I hadn't heard him say it myself."

I flipped through a few more pages of the program. A newspaper clipping fell out from the back pages and landed by my foot. Vaughn bent down and picked it up then nudged my foot and handed it to me without Mrs. Demeulemeister seeing. I felt my face contort with confusion, and he pointed at it and made an expressive face that had a note of urgency to it. He sat up and asked his teacher if she'd seen any other ballet performances, and they conversed idly while I glanced at the clipping, immediately seeing exactly what it was Vaughn thought was so important.

It was a review of the *Nutcracker* performance Mrs. Demeulemeister had attended, but this review included details that both the teacher and the program had failed to mention. Yes, it had been Beatriz's first lead, and yes, she'd been awarded the role on her merits. But what hadn't been said until now was the reason the company had held those auditions in the first place: The prior lead had shattered her ankle when Laird failed to assist with her landing during a rehearsal. It was the same story Beatriz had told me last night.

Two photos were included in the article: one of Laird and Beatriz dancing and one of the dancers whom Beatriz had replaced. Her hair was slicked back, and her makeup was severe, but her eyes were familiar. The caption confirmed my suspicions that I'd already met this dancer but not as anyone connected to Beatriz or her wedding.

The dancer was credited as Katya Petrova. It was Katie, the shy blond bride who'd shown up at my store the morning of Beatriz's first appointment.

# 25

THE TIMING OF KATIE'S VISIT TO MY STORE HAD FELT unfortunate. She'd walked in on the same morning I'd agreed to remain closed for Beatriz, and I'd had to ask her to leave when Beatriz finally arrived. And she came back on Sunday, the same day that Carson had tried to get her to leave by telling her we were closing, right before he disappeared out the back door.

Suspicions that I'd never once considered assaulted me. Had Carson recognized Katie? Was that why he tried to get her to leave? Did he harbor latent hostility toward her based on something Beatriz had said, or did her accusations implicate Beatriz in the ballet company's rumored impropriety?

There were other questions that needed answering, but if I didn't want to raise suspicions, I needed to sit back up and pretend everything was fine.

On instinct, I folded the newspaper clipping and shoved it into my motorcycle boot next to my ankle. I sat up and smiled at Mrs. Demeulemeister, hoping I looked as calm and innocent as I'd been when we arrived at her classroom.

"You said something about the circumstances of Beatriz getting the lead," I said. "What did you mean?"

"Nothing, I believe," she said dismissively. "And I also don't believe in repeating gossip, no matter how old it may be."

Mrs. Demeulemeister took the program from Vaughn and slipped it into its waxy envelope. She secured the envelope to the brittle scrapbook page, slipped the book into her desk drawer, then pulled out a different book. I couldn't think of a reason for Vaughn and me to stay, but I also couldn't come up with a plausible excuse to have to leave suddenly, considering our surprise drop-in. I looked at Vaughn for help, but Mrs. Demeulemeister had the final say.

"If you two aren't in a hurry, I do have incriminating photos from that notorious birthday party." She set another scrapbook on her desk and folded her hands on top of it then looked back and forth between our expressions eagerly.

And so, despite the clue burning a hole in my boot, we shot the rest of the afternoon.

———

I WAS ITCHING to get to the car. The first thing I did was to pull off my boot. The newspaper clipping was already yellowed with age, and I was afraid I'd ruined it. I tossed my boot into Vaughn's lap and unfolded the small piece of paper.

"You took the newspaper clipping?" Vaughn asked.

"Didn't you want me to?"

"I didn't want you to steal from my favorite teacher."

"Then what was that face you made?"

"What face?"

I tried my best to imitate the expression I'd seen on Vaughn's face after he looked at the clipping. He laughed.

I set the clipping on the dashboard, took my boot from him,

then bent over while I pulled it on. "You wanted me to look at the clipping, and when I saw what it said, there was no way I wasn't taking it with me."

"Why?"

I started my car but left it in park. "How did you know the clipping was important?"

"The headline says, 'Ballerina Scandal Threatens to Overshadow *Nutcracker* Performance.'"

"You didn't read it?"

"Poly, I saw it about two seconds before you did." He studied me for a moment then looked out the windshield. "Besides, I didn't have my reading glasses on, and the rest of the article was too small to read."

"You wear reading glasses?"

He looked embarrassed. "When I read the newspaper over breakfast. And at night when I read in bed."

"How come you've never worn them around me?"

"You're not in my apartment when I read in bed. Or when I'm reading the paper over breakfast either."

I raised my eyebrows involuntarily. I'd seen Vaughn flush red a few times over the past day, but this time, he smiled his lopsided smile. Sunlight highlighted the gold flecks of his eyes, and I leaned across the center console and planted a kiss on his lips. When I pulled away, it was Vaughn who was left with the raised-eyebrow expression. He recovered quickly and looked over each shoulder. "Careful," he said. "You'll make Mrs. D. jealous."

I couldn't help laughing but sobered quickly when I realized I'd just stolen a precious piece of memorabilia from Vaughn's fourth-grade crush. I slid the clipping toward me and smoothed it out against my thigh.

"It says here the reason the ballet held auditions for *The Nutcracker* was because the lead ballerina sustained an injury after a bad catch during a practice session. It also says Laird and Beatriz were rumored to be romantically involved and that the management team cleared the way for unscheduled auditions that led to Beatriz being cast in the role of Clara." I held the clipping toward him. "There's a magnifying glass in the glove box if you need it to read."

Vaughn swatted my hand away. "It sounds like the article implicates Beatriz, but you said Clark has undeniable proof that Beatriz didn't commit the murder."

"It's not the first time Clark had 'proof' that turned out to be false," I said, using air quotes around the word "proof." "That's not what troubles me about this article." I tapped the picture. "This is one of my customers. She came to the store the morning of Beatriz's appointment, and she recognized Beatriz. I thought it was bad timing, but now, I'm not so sure."

"You think she was there on purpose?"

"It feels pretty coincidental, doesn't it? The lead dancer who was forced to step aside and give Beatriz her big break was in San Ladrón on Friday morning."

"That's the same time Laird was at your store, wasn't it?"

"Yes," I said, pleased that Vaughn had been paying attention. "I thought she was a random customer, but now her presence seems a little too convenient."

"Did you tell Sheriff Clark about her?"

"There didn't seem to be a reason to." I scanned the rest of the article. "The thing is, Beatriz told me she was scared for her life. She thinks whoever killed Laird might come after her too. Beatriz and I spent a lot of time talking last night, and she told me how few career opportunities exist for a ballerina, especially if she's forced to retire suddenly. What if Katie thought Laird and Beatriz conspired to cause her injury?"

"I know you're starting to trust Beatriz, but don't you think her story lets her off the hook? And that maybe her getting the lead *was* a backroom deal? If you were the dancer in the lead, wouldn't you be suspicious?"

I drew the paper close and found the line I was looking for. "It says here that Beatriz's performance in *The Nutcracker* answered any doubts about her qualifications as prima ballerina."

Vaughn considered this. "Still, you can't deny that Katie's presence at your store was suspicious. What did Beatriz do when she saw her?"

"Nothing." I thought back to Beatriz's reaction to Katie. She'd had her oversized black sunglasses on at the time, and one could argue that she didn't recognize her. But Katie...

"I didn't think much about it at the time, but Katie started to say something that she didn't finish. 'I can't believe she didn't...'"

"She said *didn't*?"

"I'm pretty sure she did. 'I can't believe she' could have meant a hundred different things, but 'didn't'? Maybe she meant she couldn't believe Beatriz didn't recognize her."

"It's a stretch."

"It's not that much of a stretch, though."

"You were there. Maybe Beatriz did recognize her, and maybe she snubbed her."

"It's possible. But Beatriz had dark sunglasses on, and Katie"—I tapped the newspaper—"didn't look like this. She didn't have on any makeup, and this article was from fifteen years ago."

Vaughn considered this. He opened my glove box and pulled out the magnifying glass, shot me a *don't-judge* glance, then scanned the article. I couldn't suppress my laughter.

"What about Laird? You said he showed up that morning, right? Did Katya see him too?"

"Maybe. I don't know. He didn't arrive with Beatriz, at least not in her car, so I don't know if Katie saw him too."

"What happened with her?" He pointed at the newspaper clipping.

"I had to ask her to leave." I thought back to that morning. I remembered the look on Katie's face when Beatriz arrived, and at the time, I thought it was because she was starstruck, but maybe it was something else. Maybe Katie—Katya—hurried out of there because she didn't want a confrontation. But she came back on Sunday. I didn't know if that was significant.

I held up my finger and pulled out my phone then scrolled through my recent calls until I found the one I wanted. I tapped the number and put the call on speaker so Vaughn could hear. I waited for Katie to answer. If she didn't recognize my number, then she would probably let it go to voicemail. It was what I would do.

It became clear she wasn't going to answer. I left a brief message. "Katie, this is Poly Monroe from Material Girl. I'd like to talk to you about"—I glanced at Vaughn, who nodded his encouragement—"Beatriz Rosen. I know the two of you used to dance together. Please call me back, either at the store or on my cell." I left my number and disconnected.

# 26

THE RESULT OF THE PHONE CALL, AFTER THE BUILD-UP OF discovering Katie as the dancer Beatriz had replaced, was anticlimactic. I kept the phone in my hand and stared at the screen, willing it to ring with a return call. Seconds ticked by and stretched into a minute. If Katie was screening her calls, she would have had time to listen to my message by now. Maybe leaving details hadn't been the right move.

I put my phone back into my small cross-body pouch and reached for my seat belt. There seemed to be nothing left to do at the school. A muffled ring came out of my bag, and it took me a moment of fumbling with the seat belt to release it so I could access the pouch underneath and pull out my phone. The caller wasn't Katie. It was Charlie.

I flashed the screen at Vaughn then answered. "Hey," I said. "I'm waiting for a call."

"From the ballerina?"

"No, from a..." There was too much new information to pack into a brief description. "Customer," I finished.

"Then I'll keep this brief. I'm at the Broadside, and I'm pretty sure one of Swan Lake's sidekicks is here."

"How do you know?"

"She came in and asked for a takeout order for Beatriz Rosen."

"What does she look like?"

"White. Ponytail. Pandas. Basic."

"Sounds like Renee."

Charlie's voice dropped to a whisper. "If you want to talk to this Renee, you've got a short window of time. Sam screwed up her order, so now she has to wait while they fix it."

"Sam never screws up a take-out order."

"Work with me. I told Sam to do something to keep her here. Do you want to talk to her or not?"

"I'm on my way." I reclipped my seat belt and peeled out of the high school lot.

"What did my sister want?" Vaughn asked.

"She said Renee's at the Broadside, waiting for a take-out order. I left her a message on Friday, and she hasn't called me back, which seems suspicious, right?" I hit the gas to blow through a yellow light, and Vaughn checked his seat belt to make sure it was secure.

I made it to the Broadside in record time and parked around the back. Trucks from construction companies filled most of the spaces. A pack of Harleys was parked by the door. The Broadside had a mixed clientele, and even with Duke's efforts to change that, my anxiety rose as I approached the entrance. I was happy to have Vaughn by my side if only because two were better than one when it came to a fight.

Charlie was seated at the bar. She raised her eyebrow at my arrival with Vaughn then spun halfway around on her stool and glanced across the interior. A woman with long brown hair under a knit San Ladrón hat from the visitors' center stood next to the front entrance, reading something on her phone. She wore a pink wraparound sweater and jeans, just like Beatriz had.

For someone who wanted to lie low, she didn't seem to be particularly aware of her surroundings.

I nodded and turned to Vaughn. "Wait here with Charlie for a moment. I don't want Renee to feel cornered."

I made my way across the bar as if I'd arrived alone.

"Renee?" I asked.

She looked up as if expecting someone else. Recognition played across her features, at first showing fear then suspicion. "Poly," she said. She jammed her phone into her back jeans pocket. "What are you doing here?"

"I live across the street," I said. "You could call me a regular." I smiled in what I hoped was a nonthreatening way to gain Renee's trust. "What about you?"

"Takeout," she said. "This place gets high reviews on Yelp, but they screwed up my order twice."

I stifled a smile. "Twice?"

"Yeah. I've never heard of such a thing."

I turned around and glanced at the bar. Sam wiped down the counters. He looked up at us. "Your Impossible Burger will be out shortly. The cook had to clean the grill to remove the taste of beef."

She shook her head. "Whatever."

It was after five, and we were squarely in the middle of happy hour. Sounds of billiards clinking interrupted Jerry Lee Lewis singing from Duke's internet jukebox. Conversations blended together and blurred into indecipherable white noise. I didn't doubt for a second that Charlie was behind the delays and order screwups, but sooner or later, Renee's order would be ready, and she would leave. If I was going to get anything out of her, it was now or never.

"How's Beatriz holding up?" I asked.

"Haven't you spoken to her?"

It was an odd choice to answer my question with a question, and I sensed Renee was fishing to see what I knew. Instead of giving her a yes or no, I said, "I tried to reach her at the San Ladrón Hotel, but she must have registered under an assumed name. The number she gave me was yours, and you haven't called me back."

"Our reservations are under Ursula's name. Beatriz is staying with an old friend. Honestly, I don't know if she's still planning to go through with the wedding."

"If she's going to cancel her plans, she should notify the businesses that she engaged."

"Like yours?" she asked. "Beatriz's dance partner was murdered. Her relationship with him was a lot longer than the one she has with this new flavor of the month. She's in mourning, and all you care about is getting paid."

I was going about this all wrong. Renee had been defensive on Beatriz's behalf from that very first appointment at Material Girl, and my questions were doing little more than triggering her loyalty. She was the kind of friend I would like to have in my corner if someone came after me, but in this case, I sensed an undercurrent to her loyalty. It took me a moment to realize that Renee's criticism of me was a case of the pot calling the kettle black.

"You're not just one of her bridesmaids, though. You're her assistant too."

"What are you getting at?"

"You stand to profit from Beatriz's life whether she gets married or not. Probably more if she doesn't. Are you the one who suggested she cancel her wedding plans?"

I could tell from the look on Renee's face that I was right. Her fair complexion colored an unfortunate shade of dark pink, and her lower lip trembled as if she were about to cry. I was close enough to see her eyes well up with tears, confirming that she was on the brink of an emotional display. I put my hand on her upper arm and steered her toward a private booth. While she sat, I glanced back at Charlie and Vaughn, who were deep in conversation and appeared not to be paying attention to us.

"I'm right, aren't I?" I asked gently. "You're afraid that if Beatriz gets married, you're going to be out of a job."

Renee pulled a napkin from the dispenser and blotted her eyes. The coarse paper left faint scratches on her skin. She crumbled the napkin in her palm and left the ball on the table.

"Beatriz hired me because I didn't come from her world. She wanted someone who would be more loyal to her than to the ballet company. She treats me like a friend, not an employee. And she's been so generous with me, more than most people would. She knows I don't have the same income as her, and she pays my way when we travel so she has a companion. But getting married—that's going to change everything. She won't need a companion anymore because she'll have *him*."

"Has she told you any of this?"

"No."

"Then aren't you making yourself crazy by worrying about it?"

"You don't understand," she said. She leaned back in the booth, and her shoulders slumped. "I've got massive debt. I need this job. I can't sleep at night when I think about her letting me go."

"You need to talk to her, let her know your concerns. You said she's your friend as well as your employer. Trust her to see things that way too."

Sam arrived at our table with a brown take-out bag. "Here

you go," he said. "Sorry about the inconvenience." He set the bag on the edge of the table.

Renee wiped the tears from her face with the backs of her hands. She slid out of the booth, and I followed. I felt a window closing, my chance to ask her questions before she had second thoughts about telling me anything slipping away.

"Renee, there's one other thing I wanted to ask you about."

"What's that?"

"When Beatriz was at my shop on Friday, I gave her a clipping of tulle. Do you know what happened to it?"

"Sure," she said. "She gave it to Evan, her wedding planner."

# 27

"EVAN GRANT?"

"Yes. He wanted to know what her dress would look like, so she gave him your sketch and the clipping of tulle." On seeing what could only have been an expression of alarm on my face, she added, "It's standard practice to coordinate the wedding theme to the bride's style of dress. Didn't you know that?"

"Like I said on Friday, I'm in the fabric business, not the wedding dress business."

She shrugged. "It probably doesn't matter now."

As I watched Renee make her way toward the exit, my thoughts raced. I'd already learned that Evan was Beatriz's wedding planner. I'd also learned that Adelaide had been spending a lot of time with him. And now, I'd discovered the snippet of tulle that I'd given Beatriz, which she'd given to Evan, had ended up under the carpet in the wedding chapel where Laird had been murdered. I felt like I was following breadcrumbs, but I was afraid to eat the loaf.

Charlie and Vaughn watched me. I waved them over to my booth.

As was often the case when I got preoccupied with something else, my dietary needs had been ignored. The last thing I'd eaten was Big Joe's hearty omelet. A growing sense of unease had been creeping up on me, and I couldn't shake it. Sam hovered nearby with a glossy laminated menu. I ordered my usual, a burger and fries, and relaxed in the booth while Charlie slid in opposite me and Vaughn sat next to her.

"So?" Charlie asked. "What's the verdict?"

"I don't know. She's worried about her future. She thinks Beatriz is going to fire her when she marries Carson. I just don't know what that has to do with Laird."

"That's the same thing you said about Beatriz."

"I know. Plus, there's another problem."

"Just one?" Charlie asked with more than a trace of sarcasm.

"Renee said Beatriz gave that clipping of tulle to Evan."

"My mom's Evan?" Vaughn asked.

"Who's Evan?" Charlie asked.

I looked back and forth between their faces, trying to decide which question to answer first. Finally, I held my finger up to silence Charlie and addressed Vaughn. "I think you should check on your mother."

Vaughn was out of the booth with his phone to his head before I finished my sentence. As he walked toward the exit, I heard him say, "It's important. Can you find her for me?" He pushed the door open and left.

"Should I worry about that?" Charlie asked.

"Wedding planner. Adelaide has been spending time— socially—with him. Do with that what you will."

Charlie leaned back against the booth and stared at the door through which Vaughn had left. For one of the rare moments in her life, she didn't have a clever retort. I gave her space to decide whether she wanted to follow Vaughn. After a few moments, she turned her attention back to me. "What did you say to make the assistant cry? You usually have a softer touch."

"I said if Beatriz was going to call off her wedding, she should notify the businesses around town, and she accused me of only caring about myself. I turned the tables on her and pointed out that she was on Beatriz's payroll, too, and that if Beatriz got married, Renee would probably be out of a job."

"Judging from the waterworks, I'd say she's already thought of that."

"She said she's not just an assistant, she's Beatriz's regular companion. She's afraid that when Beatriz marries Carson, she'll be done."

"Seems like Beatriz would have told her that if that's the case," Charlie said.

"Right," I said. "I can understand that she doesn't want Beatriz to get married, but I can't figure out what that has to do with the murder of Laird."

Vaughn returned to the booth. "Mom's fine," he said, quickly casting a glance at Charlie, "but annoyed. Aside from disrupting the schedule at the Waverly House, Clark still won't let the weddings take place. She's already had to reimburse deposits for two weddings and reschedule a third."

There was no denying the monetary impact of the upcoming nuptials, but I couldn't figure out what they had to do with Laird. On one hand, we had the bride's former dance partner—a bad boy who had a rough past of his own. On the other, he'd been here, in San Ladrón, for no other reason than to confront Beatriz. And he'd been murdered in the wedding chapel where she and Carson had planned to exchange their vows. Those two pieces of information seemed to validate that his murder had to do with their wedding.

Charlie and Vaughn had ordered at the bar, and their food

came first. I ate a few of each of their fries to stave off my hunger until my food arrived too. We tore into our burgers, and by the time we finished, there was nothing left in any of our red plastic baskets. Sam came by to drop our check on the table, and I pulled out my wallet.

"Put it away," Charlie said. "My brother's buying."

Vaughn dropped a couple of bills on the table. "Fine, but you owe me an oil change."

"Sure," she countered. "Bring your Beemer in tomorrow. You're probably due for a new timing chain or an alignment. Bring your checkbook with you too."

"I've got work tomorrow."

"Your dad owns the company. Tell him you're working in the field."

We left together. I dropped off Charlie and took Vaughn to his car at the Waverly House. Orange cones sat around the entrance to the chapel, one of them lying on its side. The parking lot was empty save for Vaughn's silver BMW.

"I had fun today," Vaughn said. "And not just because we saw Mrs. D."

"I had fun too. We make a good team. Too bad work will get in the way tomorrow."

"Pesky people expecting us to grow their investment portfolios and sell them fabric."

I laughed at the contrast of our wildly different jobs. "Good night, Vaughn."

He leaned across the seat and kissed me unexpectedly. "Good night, Poly."

I drove home. This morning, I'd left Beatriz sleeping in my bed while I headed out to talk to her teacher. I'd gotten more details from Clark about what was going on, but I'd also met with his trademark resistance. I knew I had no right to be angry about him not discussing the case with me, but still, it stung. I wasn't just a fabric store owner. I was the ex-girlfriend of the fiancé of the dance partner of the victim. That should count for something.

Before I got into my car, I glanced up at the windows to my apartment over Material Girl. They were dark. I had one of my living room lights on a timer, but it didn't switch on until five. At the moment, my apartment looked empty, and I felt relief. After the past few days, I just wanted to be alone with my cats.

I drove around the back of the store and parked. It had been a long, productive day, but in terms of rest and recharge for a six-day week of work, it had hurt more than helped. I was wise enough to the aches and pains of my body to know I was facing a losing proposition, so I called in the original unpaid staff of the fabric store: my parents.

"Hi, Mom," I said. "I have a favor to ask."

"Does it involve rubber gloves or a month's worth of carpet fibers?" She sneezed.

"Excuse me?"

My mother's voice dropped. "I accidentally vacuumed up one of the diamond stud earrings your father gave me for our anniversary. I'm sorting through the"—*Achoo!* —"contents of the vacuum to find it, but"—*Achoo!*—"the dust keeps making me sneeze, and if I"—*Achoo!*—"can't keep quiet, he's going to find me in the garage."

"How long have you been out there sneezing?"

"Not long. I mopped the hallway and told him he couldn't walk on the floors until they're dry. That bought me about an hour."

I was used to the shenanigans of my parents. They maintained a playful relationship of negotiations that seemed more like entertainment to each of them than an actual attempt to get what they wanted.

"Eureka!" she exclaimed then followed it with another sneeze. "Okay. Crisis averted. Now, what was it you needed?"

"Help at the store this week. Are you free?"

"Free? I have more commitments now that I'm retired than I did when I worked."

"Come on, Mom. You told me once you loved working in the fabric store. It'll be like old times."

She sighed. "Fine, Poly. But I'm not lying to your father, so you better come up with a job for him too."

---

I WAS A SEVEN-HOURS-A-NIGHT SLEEPER, and when I chiseled away at my seven hours, in time, my body retaliated by sleeping through my alarm. Tuesday morning was that retaliation. I woke at ten fifteen, only forty-five minutes from when I was due to open the fabric store. There were a number of missed-call notifications on my phone along with a series of messages of escalating concern. Each message included some version of this: "Poly? This is your mother. We're in your parking lot. Where are you?"

I threw on underwear, a coarse black V-neck sweater, baggy black trousers, and white leather sneakers, told the cats I would be right back, and raced downstairs. I unlocked the back door and opened it to two people who looked as though their confidence that I could successfully run the family fabric store had diminished greatly.

My mom eyed me up and down. "You're due for a haircut." She entered the shop.

My dad followed. He gave me a hug and handed me a shopping bag filled with groceries. "Your mother figured your fridge is empty."

She wasn't wrong. I ran the groceries upstairs, fed the cats, and used some gel to smooth my hair into place and make my haircut needs less in-your-face. I swiped on cranberry lipstick and went back downstairs. My dad was behind the register. My mom stood in front of the bridal display.

"What's this?" she asked.

"Bridal dress designs. The Waverly House gets a lot of weddings, and I thought I could take advantage of that with a dedicated display of suitable fabrics."

"How's it working?"

"It's been a good week," I said, referring to business and not murder investigations. "Just last week, a bride picked out one of my designs and bought a hundred and one yards of vintage tulle from the original store stash."

"That's great," my dad called out from across the shop. "I knew you could do this."

"How will that work?" my mom asked. She was a savvy one, my mother, not prone to handing out compliments until she got the full story. "It's your design, but who will make it for her?"

"Me. She asked if I would, and I said yes."

"Correct me if I'm wrong, Poly, but this is a wedding dress, and you don't make wedding dresses. You barely sew."

"It's no big deal," I said. "The wedding might not even take place."

"And why is that?"

"The groom is suspected of murder."

My father had joined my mother, and I sensed the tides of support turning against me. "Before you say anything else, there's something you should know. Carson is the groom."

"Your Carson?"

"He's not my Carson, Mom."

"Thank heaven for small favors," my dad muttered under his breath.

"You two don't like Carson?"

My mother tucked my hair behind my ear. "He was never good enough for you." She dropped her hand and cocked her head. "Is this why you needed our help? So you can help the police find out what happened?"

I nodded.

She turned to my dad. "You take the registers. I'll handle the cutting table. Poly, you've got us for the day. Go do whatever it is you need to do."

I kissed my parents goodbye and left. I didn't know exactly where I was headed, so I called Vaughn from the car.

"Remember how Charlie wanted you to take a day in the field so she could work on your car?" I asked.

"Good morning to you too."

I chuckled. "Sorry. Top of the morning to ya, mate."

"Ah, so I'm your mate now? That's progress."

"You can be my coconspirator if you take the day off like Charlie asked. I brought in the A-team to run my store for the day."

"Your parents?"

"Yes. Are you in?"

"I'm one step ahead of you. Charlie's been working on my car since seven. If you don't want her to talk you into auto work, too, you can pick me up on the corner."

"Deal." I left the alley and circled around back roads until I came out at the stop sign by the Waverly House then drove to the cross street and pulled up next to Vaughn. He had on a gray William & Mary sweatshirt and jeans. The breeze had ruffled his dark-blond hair, leaving it tousled.

He hopped into the car. "Where to, mate?"

I didn't have a where to, but it turned out I didn't need one. My phone rang with an incoming call. I recognized the exchange as Katie's, and I answered and put the call on speaker.

"Hello?"

"Is this Poly?" a soft, sweet voice asked. "Poly Monroe?"

"Yes," I said. I turned a hard right into the parking lot of a grocery store. Vaughn looked at me like I was nuts.

"This is Katie."

Vaughn's expression changed to one of understanding.

"I tried calling you back earlier today, but your mailbox was full. My boyfriend and I decided on a small civil ceremony back home. I won't be coming back to San Ladrón."

"Does that decision have anything to do with the murder of Laird Harden?"

Vaughn looked shocked at my direct approach, but I was emboldened by the silence on the other end of the phone, so I pressed forward. "Katie," I said, "or should I call you Katya? I know who you are, and I know the real reason you were at my store on Friday morning."

There was an awkward stretch of silence on her end of the phone, almost enough to confirm my suspicions of guilt. But when she spoke, she said, "It's not what you think."

"You don't know what I think."

"Can we meet somewhere to talk? In private?"

"We can meet but not in private." I widened my eyes and stared at Vaughn, hoping he would help me come up with a suitable suggestion. I mouthed, "Waverly House?" and he shook his head. He mouthed, "Material Girl?" and I shook my head. I mouthed, "Clark?" and he shook his head.

"What about the doughnut shop on the corner?" Katie asked.

Vaughn and I stared at each other. It wasn't the worst suggestion. He nodded.

"Meet me there in ten minutes," I said.

"I'll be there as soon as I can." She ended the call.

I left the phone balanced on my thigh. "She didn't sound guilty," I said.

"She didn't," Vaughn agreed. "She sounded scared."

"So, what do we do next?"

"I don't know," he said. "We're in your wheelhouse now."

# 28

BEING GIVEN THE POWER TO DETERMINE HOW TO HANDLE OUR meeting with Katie was equal parts exciting and nerve-wracking. This was a complete turnaround from how it felt to make decisions with Carson, who'd always thought he knew better than I did, and Vaughn's confidence in me didn't go unnoticed.

"Lopez Donuts is a public space with a former marine on site," I said. "I don't think we need to call Sheriff Clark just yet."

I drove to Lopez Donuts. It took longer than I'd expected thanks to a couple of red lights, and by the time we got a parking space out front, more than ten minutes had passed.

"If she's not already here, then let's take two booths," I said. "I'll sit in one, and you sit in the next one and listen in. I don't want her to think we're ganging up on her."

"You don't know this woman," Vaughn said. "Based on what you've told me, she might be dangerous."

"That's why I want you in the next booth. She's never seen us together. I'll go in first, and you come in about a minute after."

My plan was for naught, because Katie was already seated

at a booth inside the doughnut shop. She had a cup in front of her and a doughnut on a napkin.

I waved at Big Joe and slipped into the opposite side of the booth. The second thing I noticed, after her body language, was the pale-pink wraparound sweater she wore over a plain white T-shirt. It was almost identical to the one Beatriz had worn when she came to the store, the same one I'd found in the trash outside the gas station and that the employee was going to take home for his cat.

"Where did you get that sweater?" I asked accusatorily.

She looked down at herself as if needing a reminder of what she wore. "I don't remember," she stammered. "I've had it forever. Why?"

"Beatriz Rosen had the same sweater on when she came to my shop on Friday."

The last thing I expected Katie to do was laugh, but she surprised me by doing exactly that. "It's standard ballet attire," she said. "I have over a dozen of them. Beatriz probably does too. We wear them over our leotards."

"Then you admit you know Beatriz."

"Of course I know Trix," she said, using a version of the nickname Carson used for Beatriz. "We were both members of the Los Angeles Ballet before I quit."

"Right." I'd come to the doughnut shop prepared to confront Katie with what I'd learned and to press her for details about her past in the ballet company. I wanted to grill her with my theory that her residual animosity toward Laird had led her to murder him in the chapel. So far, she hadn't required pressing. In fact, she seemed almost eager to tell me about that time in her life.

"You didn't say anything about the ballet company when you were at my fabric shop," I said.

"When you first meet someone, do you lead with the details

of your life before moving to San Ladrón?" At my silence, she added, "I didn't think so."

"How do you know I had a life before moving to San Ladrón?"

"I looked you up," she said. "After I found out Trix had an appointment at your shop. It seemed too random that she would select a fabric store in a small town. She could have contacted any number of Los Angeles-based designers to create her wedding gown, and I wanted to know why she picked you."

I held up my hand. "How did you know about our appointment?"

"Her press secretary told me. Trix wanted three brides-maids, and Ursula thought I was the third. She called me with your address in the event I wanted to come along to help pick out the fabric for her dress." She shook her head. "But Trix never asked me. I guess she had second thoughts."

"You being at my store on Friday wasn't an accident," I said.

"No, it wasn't. I knew she was coming to see you. Trix and I used to be friends once, and when Ursula told me about the wedding, I thought maybe Trix was going to leave the past in the past."

"What came between you?"

"Laird came between us," she said. She tore her doughnut in half and offered a piece to me.

I waved it away even though I wanted it. "He was your partner when you had your injury," I said.

She looked up from the doughnut and I added, "I know things about you too."

Katie nodded. She continued to decimate the doughnut with her fingers, leaving behind chunks of fluffy dough and a small mess of broken glaze on a napkin. It was a waste of a perfectly good doughnut.

"Then you know about my injury?" she asked after she'd reduced the doughnut to a pile of crumbs.

"I know it happened, but I don't know much more than that."

"It was a freak accident at practice. It could have happened to any of us, but it happened to me."

"Do you blame Laird?"

"No. Maybe I should, but I don't."

"Why should you?"

"We'd been out drinking the night before, and I was hung over. Maybe he was too. Maybe I miscalculated my jump. Maybe if I'd had my regular shoes that day, I would have landed properly."

"Whose shoes were you wearing?"

"They were mine—they were new. I thought I'd broken them in properly, but maybe it wasn't the right day to test them out. Look, Poly, I went through a pretty dark time after that accident. I've finally accepted that it happened and that it was the end of my dance career. I can't undo the damage, and if I continued to dance with my injury, I would have only made it worse."

"Was that an option?"

"Not for me," she said. "But that's what Trix and I fought about."

"She wanted you to keep dancing? But then she wouldn't have become the prima ballerina."

"She overheard Laird pressuring me to stay," she said. "He said we could use my injury for publicity. To sell out my final performance."

"Was this before or after auditions?"

"It was the day of. And before you get the idea that Trix got the lead by default, you should know it was no contest. She was ready. She blew the judges away."

"So why would Laird want you to stay? Wouldn't he have seen the same thing, that it was her time?"

"He didn't have any doubts about her ability. Trix was always going to become the prima ballerina after me, and maybe I'm lucky that it happened after an injury and not because she outdanced me and made me look like a has-been. But Laird liked to control people, and he couldn't control her. That was their biggest problem."

The conversation flowed freely, more so than I would have predicted. "Could Laird control you?"

She chewed her lipstick, leaving behind a bare patch in the middle of her otherwise plum-colored lower lip. "Laird had dirt on me that he held over my head, and he used it to keep me on his side."

This conversation was starting to feel like something Sheriff Clark should hear, but unless he was due for a boysenberry doughnut, my choice of venue precluded him from listening in.

"Look, Katie, I don't know how else to say this. Laird is dead, and you were in town at the time of the murder. When the sheriff hears that you had opportunity, he's going to need to know if that dirt Laird has on you was enough to kill him."

"You're going to tell him, aren't you?"

I nodded.

"Why?"

"I thought you said you looked into me."

"I did. I discovered that you inherited a closed fabric store about a year ago and reopened it under a new name not long after. I thought maybe you and Beatriz were friends from childhood, but when I saw you with her at your store, I knew that wasn't the case. You were so apologetic about having closed the store for her appointment that it was clear you didn't have a clue who she was. And if this had to do with Laird, I'd know that too."

"How?"

"You first."

Katie was closing up, and if I wanted to keep her talking and have a chance at convincing her to go talk to Clark, I needed her to understand my motivations. I didn't know where Vaughn was sitting, and I didn't know if he thought me confiding in our latest suspect was a good decision. He'd trusted me thus far, so I followed my instincts.

"Beatriz Rosen is engaged to my ex-boyfriend," I said. "He and I broke up when I moved here to reopen the fabric store. He recommended she come to my store for her dress because he knows I took out a loan for the first year of my operating expenses, and he thought I could use the money."

"Sounds like your ex still cares about you."

"My ex is a pain in the you-know-what, but I don't think he's a murderer."

"Is that what the cops think?"

"Yes."

"And you want to find them another suspect so he's off the hook for Laird's murder."

"Something like that."

"Maybe you still care about him too," she said.

I felt the back of my ears prickle with heat. My feelings toward Carson weren't easily explained. He was like an old high school friend who'd come back into my life. I didn't know how much he'd changed over our time apart, and I found it easier to assume that he hadn't changed at all.

But like it or not, Carson *had* changed. He'd achieved the success he'd always pursued, and that catapulted him to a new income level and a different way of life. He no longer worked for a boss; he *was* the boss. The Carson I knew didn't know the difference between a pas de deux and a grande jeté, didn't read books like *The Art of War*, didn't wear four-figure suits, and didn't drink green smoothies for breakfast.

"When everything about your life changes, sometimes people from your past can help you feel anchored. Does that make sense?"

Katie nodded.

"That doesn't mean I want Carson back," I qualified.

My conversation with Katie had started out accusatory, but she'd answered every question I asked. I couldn't put my finger on it, but I sensed there was something she hadn't told me, something she didn't want me to know.

"Do you want some coffee?" I asked. "I could use a cup."

"Decaf," she said.

"Cream and sugar?"

"No and yes."

I didn't need coffee, but the trip to and from the counter gave me a view of the rest of the tables. I doctored the coffees and headed back to my seat. Vaughn had managed to get the booth behind me, which meant he'd heard everything I'd said. His back was to me, so I wasn't able to make eye contact or get a read on his response.

I slid into the booth and pushed Katie's cup toward her. She pulled the red plastic stirrer out of the cup and slid it through her lips then set it on her napkin.

"You said something about Laird," I said. "About how if Beatriz's appointment at my store had something to do with him, you'd know. Why's that?"

"I wouldn't know because of Laird. I'd know because of Ursula."

"Ursula Ungaro? Beatriz's publicity agent? Would she have leaked it to the media?"

"No. Ursula and Laird used to be married." She sipped her

coffee then set the cup back down. "You've heard of matches made in Heaven?"

I nodded.

"Their match was made in a much hotter climate."

# 29

Now *this* was news. "You're saying Beatriz's press secretary was Laird's ex-wife? And they divorced under bad circumstances?"

"They *married* under bad circumstances. Their split was inevitable."

"And the divorce left bad blood between them?"

Katie looked confused. "What? No. Ursula was a professional. She had the marriage annulled. She wouldn't—wait a minute. You said you wanted to talk about Trix." Her face contorted from confusion to shock. "You're making her dress, and you asked me questions about my relationship with her after my injury. I thought maybe this had to do with her *wedding*. That maybe she wanted me to be a part of it after all."

I couldn't help but notice that Katie had said "maybe" more times than I could count. "Maybe you're still hiding something," I said. "You knew all along this was about Laird's murder. I said as much when I called you to meet with me."

Katie slid out of her side of the booth. "I shouldn't have agreed to this," she said. "Don't call me again." She reached across the table and grabbed her handbag, which knocked into her cup of coffee, spilling it and the cup of water next to it across the table. While I scrambled for napkins, she hoisted her bag over her shoulder and stormed out.

Vaughn and I pulled ourselves out of our respective booths at the same time. He turned to me and held up his hand, palm side out. "Not now, Poly." He followed Katie out the door, pausing to look over his shoulder. "She doesn't know not to talk to me."

I wanted to argue, but I knew he was right. My question, my implication, had chased Katie off, and running after her probably wasn't going to undo that. The thing was, after talking to her, I didn't feel as strongly about her as a suspect as I had when she first arrived. I couldn't say the same thing about Ursula.

The dumped coffee and water had seeped over the edge of the table and dripped onto my side of the booth. I glanced up to see if Big Joe had seen, but he'd left the counter unattended. I pulled a wad of napkins out of the dispenser and cleaned up the table and booth as best as I could.

Maria came to my aid with a wet rag. She bent over the table and mopped up the spill. "Your friend sure left in a hurry. Is everything okay?"

"I don't know," I said, staring at the exit.

I considered my options. Behind door number one was catching up with Vaughn. Door number two was sitting in a freshly wiped-down booth, enjoying another cup of coffee and possibly a cruller. Guilt pulled me toward door number one. Exhaustion and hunger pulled me toward door number two. But I hadn't turned over every rock just yet, and my parents were due to leave at the end of the day. When that happened, I would be back where I was before I called them for help.

I got the cruller.

During our interlude at the school, Vaughn and my energy had been easy and breezy, but that hadd changed during my talk with Katie. It was the ongoing dance of our relationship: one step forward, two steps back.

More than once, Vaughn and I had gotten our signals crossed. At first, it had to do with the circumstances of my great-aunt's murder and how they related to Vaughn's family. From there, we'd sorted through obstacles of finances and income. He had never shown any real jealousy over Carson, and I'd always assumed he recognized that my past was my past.

I checked my phone. Hours had transpired since I first picked up Vaughn outside of Charlie's auto shop, but the day was far from over. I scrolled through recently called numbers, trying to decide what to do next. It was then that I linked information that I should have put together from the start.

The San Ladrón Hotel. And Adelaide's comment: Beatriz's bridal party may be staying there, but the bride was staying with a friend in town.

I hadn't bothered with the hotel ever since learning Beatriz wasn't staying there, but I didn't need to find Beatriz anymore—I needed to find Ursula. And I had more than one reason to believe she would be there.

I scooted out of my booth with a sudden charge of enthusiasm, waved goodbye to Maria and Big Joe, and dashed out the door.

The San Ladrón Hotel was a stately building made of brick and stucco with forest-green trim. It was built in the late 1800s, around the same era as the Waverly House, and had similar Victorian details evident in the construction. Unlike the Waverly House, which had petitioned for and received national accreditation as a historic monument, the hotel had passed through a series of different owners with different ideas, each time losing a little bit of its original charm while becoming more palatable for the uninformed masses.

I parked in a visitors' space and strode to the entrance, realizing halfway there that it would have behooved me to prepare a cover story. *Too late for that.* I took my chances and marched up to the registration desk.

"I'm trying to reach one of your guests, Ursula Ungaro. Can you ring her room to see if she's here? Tell her it's about the Rosen-Cole wedding."

The woman behind the reception desk tapped something into her computer then picked up the phone. "Good afternoon, Ms. Ungaro. You have a guest waiting in the lobby," she said. She hung up her phone and said, "She'll be right down."

I sat in a plush floral chair by the windows and watched the elevators. I had a feeling that if Ursula knew who I was, she would turn around and go right back upstairs to her room. I had one element on my side: Ursula had never met me face to face. The problem with that was that I didn't know what she looked like either.

The elevator doors opened, and a woman in a black minidress, black patterned tights, and over-the-knee black boots came out. She was overdressed for an afternoon of hanging out in her hotel room. She scanned the lobby from left to right then turned to the reception desk. The hotel employee pointed at me, and I stood.

"Ursula?" I asked.

"Yes. You're here about the wedding?"

"Yes." I smiled at the hotel employee—nothing to see here, everything's cool—and lowered my voice. "I'm Poly Monroe. Beatriz asked me to make her wedding dress, but I haven't been able to reach her to schedule a fitting."

"I'll have her call you," she said. "Is that all?"

"No, that's not all," I said. Now that we were out of earshot of the employee, I played my hand. "Look. I know you're not just Beatriz's publicist, but you're also one of her bridesmaids. And I know you were married to Laird Harden. And I know you left your lucky blue rabbit's foot at the Lopez Donut shop on Sunday, where you were dressed in an outfit that you ditched outside of the Circle K."

Ursula had arrived with the confidence of a woman who was used to being in charge. But everything I said chipped away at her composure little by little until she swayed and reached out to the back of the plush floral chair to stabilize herself.

"Who are you?" she asked.

"I told you. I'm Poly Monroe. I own the fabric store where Beatriz is getting her wedding dress."

"How do you know so much about me?"

I expected Ursula to ignore me and storm out of the hotel or, worse, ask the hotel employee to escort me to my car. I didn't expect her to look like she was about to pass out. I put my hand around her, guided her to a club chair, and sat in the one opposite her. I looked up at the registration desk and saw the employee watching us. I pantomimed taking a drink, and she nodded and brought Ursula a small bottle of water.

She uncapped the water and drank some then set the cap on the table between us. "I work as Beatriz's publicist. We've been together for a long time. As my business grew, I handed clients over to my staff, but I kept her. Now, we're coming to the end of an era."

"Because she's getting married?"

"Because her married life is going to be different than her performance life. Trust me, I've seen this movie before."

"Will your business suffer from that?"

Ursula laughed. "I live in Los Angeles. I could throw a penny out a window and hit someone in need of a publicist. My business will survive."

I knew she was right. In Los Angeles, being a publicist was as recession-proof as being a personal trainer.

"Why did you go to the doughnut shop on Sunday?" I asked her.

"I didn't."

"Yes, you did. I saw you sitting in the booth. Some kids were behind you, and one tugged on your ponytail. You were with someone, weren't you? There were two cups of coffee. You left your key chain on the table. I checked the sales audit slip and saw your name on the receipt." There were enough details to pin Ursula down to a place and time, and I didn't know how she could possibly deny it.

She sat back and crossed one leg over the other. Her knit sweater dress rode up her thigh, and she made no move to tug it down. "You're right. That was me at the doughnut shop. Your small-town sheriff is looking at all of us for Laird's murder, and sooner or later, he's going to learn about my past with him."

"You don't appear to dress like Beatriz. Why were you dressed like her that day?"

"After we heard the news about Laird, Beatriz got scared. She said whoever wanted him dead would come after her next. But she had appointments set up all over town, and we thought it would look worse if she suddenly canceled everything. Like she had something to hide."

Ursula was laying the groundwork for an explanation, but I still wasn't following. "But she hasn't kept her appointments," I said.

"She hasn't, but I have." She finished her bottle of water. "It's not the first time I impersonated her to give her a cover story. Sometimes, it's the best way to give her some privacy. We're the same height and build when I'm not in a push-up bra and heels. The wig is a close match for her hair, and it's less obvious when I put on a baseball hat and sunglasses. I look like a celebrity who doesn't want to be noticed. Here, nobody knows Beatriz, so it seemed like an easy fix." She shook her head. "But then she got that haircut. That's not like her to do something so spontaneous without talking to me first. It's her image, and we usually consult on those decisions. She called me after it was done, and I did my best to cut and dye the wig, but I didn't have the best scissors. After I butchered it, I got frustrated and tossed it all."

"In the bathroom at the Circle K?"

"Yes." Her eyes showed confusion, but her forehead remained smooth. The clear conclusion must have presented itself to her without me needing to explain. "You found it."

I nodded. "I found it, and I took it to the sheriff."

"And Beatriz didn't tell them it was mine."

I shook my head. A cloud passed over Ursula's features, and I wondered if that was significant. If Beatriz *not* telling Clark that Ursula occasionally impersonated her meant Beatriz saw the benefit of having Ursula as a scapegoat.

"You need to talk to the sheriff," I said. "You need to tell him what you've just told me."

The color drained from her face. I couldn't place her reaction, but it didn't seem like that of a person caught in a lie. Ursula Ungaro wasn't a fool. She'd quickly pieced together bits of information that came from me, from Beatriz, from Clark, and from some sources I probably didn't even know yet and filled in the narrative herself. I respected her for her quick thinking and ability to parse what was going on, but it wasn't lost on me that much of what she'd told me conveniently filled in holes in what I knew and cast her in a just-doing-my-job light.

"You don't know who you're dealing with," she said. She stood and glared down at me. "Leave it alone, Poly. Nothing good is going to come from you pulling at threads."

# 30

URSULA SHOWED NO SIGNS OF HER EARLIER SHAKINESS AS SHE strode toward the elevator banks. She jabbed the button and got on, whisked away to her room upstairs while I dealt with her bombshell.

She was scared. Her sudden departure was rooted in fear, not guilt. Someone, or something, had gotten to her, but I was no closer to learning who or what.

My day had been filled with conversations—Katie, Renee, and Ursula—and I was no closer to knowing what had transpired at the chapel on Friday night. I hadn't heard from Vaughn since he'd followed Katie out of the doughnut shop, and I didn't know if I would. I'd wanted time to figure things out, and now I was confused by more than just the investigation.

Sometime during my conversation with Ursula, the sun had dropped. It was after six, and if I'd followed my normal routine, I would be counting the day's sales tally right about now instead of contemplating motives for murder.

I drove back to my store and parked by the back door. I went inside, taking care to lock the door behind me.

A note in my mother's handwriting was taped to the register. *Hope your day was productive. We're headed back to Burbank. xo, M&D.* A second note, in my father's handwriting, followed: *I lost one of your cats in the fabric store.*

While I read the note, Pins ran up to me and meowed loudly. He turned away and went a few steps then turned back toward me and meowed again.

"What's wrong?" I asked. I bent down to scratch his head, and he turned and trotted toward the stairs. My heartbeat increased, and I followed him but not before scanning the interior of the fabric store. Everything appeared to be as I'd left it: general disarray after a busy day of business. I checked the sales logs. Not too shabby. I should call my parents for help more often, but then I would have to start getting regular haircuts, thus eating up all of my profit.

I followed Pins up the stairs. I turned the knob and found Needles on the other side of the door. This morning, I'd left Beatriz sleeping in my bed, and I didn't know if she would be there when I entered. She wasn't. The bed was made, and the glasses we'd used last night while indulging in Carson's scotch were all rinsed and loaded in my dishwasher. The only sign that Beatriz had been in my apartment was a sheet of paper on my dining room table that listed daily exercises to improve my balance. I couldn't help smiling at that. The two cats circled each other, shared some nose butting and butt sniffing, and left me behind in favor of the kitchen. Needles swatted his food bowl and howled so loudly I expected animal control to arrive within the hour.

I scooped Pins up and held him. "How'd you get downstairs?" I set him on the kitchen counter and pulled out a can of food then picked up Needles and gave him an equal amount of affection before doling out their dinner. I mixed the canned food with some dry food and set it back down on the floor then refilled their bowl with fresh water. They noisily slurped their food while I sorted through the groceries my parents had brought and fished out a loaf of bread and a pack of turkey. I slathered mayo on the bread and added lettuce and a slice of tomato then sat at my kitchen table and chowed down too.

Today's mail brought another postcard from Genevieve. This one featured the Tuileries Garden. On the back of the riotously colorful picture of flowers was Gen's note: *Paris! C'est tres jolie, non? xo, G.*

Duolingo had served her well.

I'd wanted to be alone with my cats, but now that I was, thoughts I'd been keeping at bay crept in. Thoughts about Carson. About Vaughn. About Beatriz and Katie and Laird. I was three bites into my sandwich when I accepted that the thing bothering me had nothing to do with the murder. It had to do with the big lie I'd been telling myself.

Ever since moving to San Ladrón, I'd prided myself on my ability to change. To move away from Los Angeles and reopen the fabric store. I'd made a new set of friends and felt almost superior to Carson and Giovanni and anyone else I'd left behind. I'd used Carson as a benchmark to judge how far I'd come. While he stayed behind in his routine of a life, I was moving on to my next chapter. And the further I found myself from that shared life, the more secure I felt in my decision. I was the risk taker, the one who got away. And while I never wanted Carson to chase me, it felt good to know I'd surprised him with my choice to expand my world in a direction nobody could have predicted.

But when you got right down to it, what had I accomplished? Sure, I'd moved to San Ladrón, but I simply reopened a store that had already been established. I gave up life in a big city for life in a small town, and my experiences shrank accordingly. And while I'd been struggling to make loan payments and feel good about working six days a week in a business that still felt like it belonged to my great-aunt and -uncle and not me, Carson had moved on. He'd become a millionaire. He'd started his investment firm. He'd met someone and gotten engaged. If he was my benchmark, then I was moving backward.

It wasn't just Carson, either. From the article I'd read, Katie had sustained an unexpected injury during a routine practice, and the only life she knew had vanished. A similar fate befell Beatriz, though she'd kept the injury secret and attributed her retirement to her upcoming marriage.

I'd spent yesterday talking to Vaughn's fourth-grade teacher, a woman who was still teaching fourth grade. Adelaide had managed the Waverly House for decades. Everybody here had been here forever, and they accepted life as the way it was, and I'd fallen for their routine as easily as I'd fallen for Carson's Meatballs on Monday.

And then there was Vaughn. I couldn't think of Carson's impending wedding without comparing it to my lack of forward motion in my personal life. Vaughn and I had dated a few times, and I knew we had a connection, but I'd kept him at arm's length, and why? Because our bank accounts had varying balances? Even I could see that was little more than a convenient excuse. Vaughn had never once thrown his money in my face, and I wasn't exactly starving. For all I knew, in five years' time, he could lose everything on a poor investment, and I could have the most profitable fabric store in the country.

Stranger things had happened.

I finished half of my sandwich and wrapped up the other half for later. I didn't have much of an appetite, and it had nothing to do with my eating schedule. I added Genevieve's postcard to the stack of mail. Vaughn's job application was on the bottom, and I pulled it out and read over it again. This wasn't the first time he'd made a gesture to show me how he felt. Maybe it was my turn.

In the time that I had sat at my kitchen table while wallowing over my life, Pins and Needles finished their food. They ran into the bedroom, and a few seconds later, I smelled something not particularly fresh. I followed the smell and found a mess in the litter box. There was nothing like cat poop to take your mind off your own crap.

I scooped the clumps into a plastic bag, knotted the top, then added fresh litter to the box. Needles stood by my side supervising while Pins charged around my bedroom like the wild child that he was.

I knotted the bag inside another bag and carried it downstairs, leaving the apartment door closed behind me so both Pins and Needles could have a post-dinner run around the store.

I searched through my inventory of novelty cotton prints. These were vital for the quilting community, and with each passing season, there was a theme.

At the end of September, I'd moved the back-to-school prints to a sale rack to make room for the Halloween prints. Among the bolts was a yellow-and-black print that featured pencils, a green-and-white one that looked like a chalkboard, and a black one with words like "science" and "genius" and "knowledge is power," along with images of pencils, school buses, chalkboards, and composition books. I pulled out this last, colorful bolt and carried it to the cutting table. I had an idea. I pulled a sixteen-ounce denim from my shelf and set to work making a book bag.

Sometimes, when an issue was weighing on my mind, the best thing I could do was sew. There was a rhythm to the process: measuring pieces, serging edges, pinning components, sewing it all together.

It felt good to push details of Carson, Beatriz, and Laird Harden out of my mind while I sewed. The project was easy enough: rectangles for the body of the bag, a cross-body strap with a buckle for adjusting the length. I used a heavy, durable denim for the exterior and strap of the bag and lined it with the silly back-to-school print. It was called a one-hour project by the pattern company, and I'd made it enough times to shave off a few minutes.

I laid the book bag flat in a gift box, tied a ribbon around it, then tucked a note under the ribbon. The note said, *I can't speak for Mrs. D., but you get an A+ from me. xo, Poly.* I'd deliver it tomorrow.

It was as good a time as any to get the store back into shape for tomorrow's business. I scanned the shop to figure out where to start. I was close enough to my back door to hear the sound of a key entering into the lock, and before I could do anything, the door swung open, and Carson strode in.

# 31

"Hey, Poly," Carson said. "What's up?"

"What's up?" I repeated. "You just let yourself into my locked store and all you have to say is 'Hey, Poly, what's up?'"

"No, actually, I have a lot more to say than that, but I thought I'd start with a greeting instead of jumping in with 'Does your small-town sheriff still think I killed my fiancée's former partner?'"

"How did you get in here?"

He held up a single black key. It wasn't on a key chain. He pulled my spare keys out of his pocket and dangled them in the other hand. I snatched them from his fist.

"You stole my keys," I accused.

"Borrowed," he said. "To make a copy."

"That's illegal," I said.

"You have a copy of *my* keys," he said. "You gave a set back to me, but I know you had more than one."

"You don't still live in that apartment."

"Yes, I do. Trixie and I are looking for a place to move. And you know you're always welcome to drop by unannounced. That's what friends do, Poly."

I narrowed my eyes and looked at the key in his hand. "Why is your spare key black?"

"You always wear black, so I got a black key for your place so I would remember who it was for."

I wanted to smack him, but I also wanted to hug him. Carson getting a black key so he remembered it was for me was just like him.

"You could have called me first," I said.

"I did call. Check your phone."

I looked down at myself and patted my pockets then realized where I'd left the phone. "It's in my car," I said.

He shook his head. "You haven't changed one bit."

It was the wrong thing to say.

I picked up the bag of cat poop and carried it outside. I flung it into the empty dumpster then unlocked my car and sat in the driver's seat. My phone was where I'd left it, resting in the cup holder. I closed the door and checked it. There was a missed-call notification from Carson's new number.

Carson had been back in my life for a sum total of five days, and in those five days, I'd entered a downward spiral of doubt. About who he was, who I was, and what we'd been to each other. I'd questioned my choice to move on while leaving him behind, and I questioned whether I'd moved on all that much in the first place. And now he was here, in my house.

I had two choices: suck it up and deal with it, or call Sheriff Clark and turn Carson in. And as attractive as the second option sounded, it was a temporary fix. Getting Carson out of my life wasn't the problem. The way I viewed my life was.

I went back inside Material Girl and locked the door behind me even though it seemed a futile act. Carson leaned against the fixture of cashmere fabric, dangling a piece of ribbon over Pins's head.

"I'm sorry," I said.

Carson looked at me, and Pins took that moment to jump, grazing Carson's fingers with his sharp cat claws.

"Ow!" he said. He dropped the piece of ribbon and checked his fingertips. "Nice cats you got here."

"Funny, they've never attacked anybody else."

"Ha ha."

He stuck his fingertip in his mouth and sucked the teensy tiny drop of blood away, and the most unexpected, profound thought occurred to me.

"You haven't changed," I said.

Carson didn't seem to realize this was a life-altering revelation. "Change is overrated," he said.

I left him standing by the cashmere display and got a small flexible bandage for his "wound." Without saying anything, I removed the bandage from the wrapper and stuck it on his finger. He winced, I rolled my eyes, and he grinned. Then his grin slid off his face as concern took over.

"Trixie doesn't do things like this," he said.

"She probably thinks you're old enough to put on your own Band-Aids."

"That's not what I meant. She's not a take-charge person like you. She's more of a, well, she likes me to handle things and take care of her."

"Is that what happened with Laird?"

"I'm not going to lie to you," he said. "Trixie knew something bad was going to happen because of him. She told me she was worried. That's the reason I came to San Ladrón."

Carson's hand was still in mine. I closed my fingers around his and stepped backward, pulling him with me. "We need to talk, Carson. And this time, we're drinking wine."

I rallied the cats to follow us, and somewhere between the fabric store and the door at the top of the stairs, they took the lead in our parade. I let us in, and they charged into the bedroom. I went left and led Carson through the kitchen. His bottle of scotch sat empty on the counter. He picked it up and raised his eyebrows.

"I had company on Sunday night," I offered as an explanation, though the bottle had been half full when I last saw it.

"Anybody I know?"

I was tired of keeping secrets, of trying to figure out whom to trust and who was lying. Deep down, I didn't believe Carson was capable of murder, and he was closer to this case than anybody else.

"Your fiancée." I stared at him, waiting for a reaction that never came. "We stayed up talking for most of the night."

"About what?"

"Her. You. Laird. Ballet."

Carson scratched the top of his head. The timer on my floor lamp switched on and cast a glow around the room. Carson's face, initially in shadows, turned a sallow shade of ochre, which made the purple bags under his eyes stand out in contrast.

I left Carson on the sofa and opened a bottle of Petite Sirah. It was a deep-purple color with a peppery bouquet and a plummy taste. As much as I liked it, it was too heavy for the hot, humid days of summer, but the break in the temperatures had made tonight the perfect night to uncork it. I poured the whole bottle into a decanter, grabbed two glasses, and set it all on my living room table. I expected Carson to give the decanted wine time to breathe, but he leaned forward and filled a glass then swallowed two gulps in an uncivilized manner.

"Don't judge me," he said when he caught me staring at him. "I've seen you get drunk on blueberry wine coolers."

I crossed my arms over my chest and averted my eyes.

After the requisite amount of time to pout, I poured a glass of wine for myself. I couldn't remember the last time Carson and I had talked for hours, but tonight, in my living room, under the light from the vintage Tiffany floor lamp that had sat in the corner for fifty years, talking came easily.

"Beatriz told me about her metatarsal injury," I said. "She said it means the end of her ballet career."

"Did she tell you the day she got her diagnosis was the day we met?" he asked.

I nodded.

He swirled his wine. "It didn't happen like I told you," he said. "The real story is that she was at her lowest point, and she was looking for validation of herself, not as a dancer but as a woman. I showed up at the coffee shop at the right time. I might as well have been following a script."

"Whose idea was it to go to the hotel bar next to the coffee shop?"

"Hers."

"Whose idea was it to get a room?"

"What room?"

"She said she offered to buy you a drink, you went to the hotel bar next to the coffee shop, and you booked a room within the hour."

"There was no room. We had a drink, and I took her to dinner. The next day, I sent two-dozen roses to her attention at the ballet conservatory. I didn't know if she would be there, but I knew by then that her choosing to spend time with me wasn't all about chemistry. She'd let me know enough for me to figure out that if it wasn't me, it would have been someone else, so I had to make a move to change the outcome of the game."

"The game?" I asked. "Since when is dating a competitive sport?"

"Why don't you ask Vaughn McMichael?"

"Vaughn doesn't play games."

"Right. And you're legitimately accepting job applications for the position of companion."

I flushed. "You weren't supposed to see that."

He laughed. "If you didn't want me to see it, you wouldn't have left it sitting out in the center of your table when you left to go to the doughnut shop. Games, Poly. Offense, defense, strategy. It's all in *The Art of War*."

"I don't think relationships are supposed to feel like a battlefield."

"Pat Benatar would disagree."

I stifled a smile and silently conceded a point to Carson. "Why did you send Beatriz's flowers to the conservatory?"

"I knew if Beatriz wasn't there when the flowers arrived, the other dancers would talk about it and that attention would make her feel special. I figured at the least, she'd call me to say thanks, and I'd have a second chance to ask her out."

"Did she?"

"She called my office and asked if I would accompany her to an industry event. I said yes without asking what it was." He smiled to himself at the memory. "It was a recital at a local dance studio. The kids were between six and twelve."

"You had no idea?"

"None," he said. "When we first got there, I thought it was a publicity stunt. But then I saw how she treated those kids, and I knew when she watched them dance, she saw herself. I think that's the night I realized I was falling in love with her."

"Did you ever tell anybody about that night?"

"No." He hesitated for a moment. "At first, it was because I didn't want to share the details with anybody else. After we started dating exclusively, she warned me that the press would want to know those details, and she asked me if I would tell an alternate story. She was afraid the media attention would blow back onto the kids, that people would start going to the recital as a novelty to see her and not them. She didn't want their big event to become a sideshow act."

This story felt like the truth. It wasn't the version Carson had first told me, and it wasn't the one Beatriz had shared either. But this one had details you couldn't fake. This one, I believed.

"I'm happy for you," I said gently. "You found what you were looking for."

"And I owe it all to you."

"For what?"

He laughed. "For changing your whole life and inspiring me to do the same."

"Your life changed when that predictive algorithm went public. That had nothing to do with me."

"I didn't write the algorithm. I just invested in it." Carson finished his first glass of wine and poured another. He glanced across the table at my glass, still untouched, then set the decanter back down. "When you asked me if I'd approached the doughnut shop owners about franchising, I lied. I did. I can spot an opportunity a mile away, but that's my lane. You were able to take this place over and turn it into something new. My role is to write checks."

"That's not true," I said.

He continued as if I hadn't protested. "If you hadn't left, I'd never be where I am. You inspired me when you gave up your job at To The Nines and moved here to reopen this store. That choice shook me to my core. I knew we weren't right together. I saw it too. I wasn't ready to admit it, but deep down, I knew you were right to leave. And if I wanted the kind of passion you showed with this store, then I had to take risks too."

The last thing I'd expected when Carson let himself into my shop with stolen keys was this acknowledgment that my actions had inspired him to reassess his life. The old Carson, the one who made me roll my eyes and fight his days-of-the-week routine had been replaced by the man in front of me.

"I was wrong," I said softly. "You've changed a lot."

He set his glass of wine down on the table and leaned back against the cushions. "Call your sheriff, Poly. You never needed me to protect you, but there's a murderer in your town. Maybe if I cooperate with the investigation, I can protect you anyway."

# 32

I MADE TWO PHONE CALLS. THE FIRST WAS TO SHERIFF CLARK. The second was to Charlie. I invited each of them to my place and they arrived at the same time, offering no explanation as to whether that was coincidence or if they'd been together when I called. Even though Clark was out of uniform, he was all business. Charlie waggled her eyebrows behind him and pretended to goose his rear. He turned around and caught her gesture. "Charlie."

"Ryan," she said.

"Sheriff Clark," he corrected.

"Whatever," she said.

"When you two are done figuring out what you're going to call each other, let me know."

Clark tried to look over my shoulder. "Where is Mr. Cole?"

"Carson is upstairs in my apartment."

Charlie waggled her eyebrows and made another butt-squeezing gesture.

"I think Sheriff Clark will back me up if I change my mind about you sitting in on the conversation," I said to her.

"You two are no fun," she said.

I led the way up my stairs. Carson had moved from my living room sofa to my small dining room table. He'd brought the decanter and our wineglasses with him. Three empty chairs sat around the table. Charlie grabbed the one across from Carson, and Clark shook his head. He pointed at the one next to him. Charlie relinquished her original seating choice and turned my dining room chair around, straddling it and resting her arms on top. I shook my head, and she stood up, turned her chair around, and sat like a normal person.

"This is practically a dinner party," she said. She glanced around. "Where are the hors d'oeuvres?"

I was starting to think inviting Charlie had been a bad idea.

"I'd like to talk to Mr. Cole alone," Clark said.

"Absolutely not," I said. "You're here because I called you and invited you to my home." I glanced at his black shirt and jeans. "You're not even in uniform."

I pulled two fresh wineglasses down from a cupboard and set them in front of Charlie and Clark. Charlie picked up the decanter and filled one of the glasses to the brim as if it were grape juice and not wine. She filled the second one to just shy of half, approximately the same amount that Carson and I had in our glasses. She picked up the full glass and set it in front of Clark. He tried to pretend he wasn't fighting a smile, but he didn't do a particularly good job of it.

I sat next to Carson and tried to think of something to say. What had started out as a good idea was now awkward. I didn't know how to get these two men talking to each other, and I knew the dialogue had to happen between them and not me.

I stood up abruptly and said, "Charlie, can you come with me? I want to show you that thing we talked about."

"If that isn't the vaguest excuse for leaving a table, I don't know what is." She stood. "Play nice in the sandbox, boys." She followed me out of the dining area and down the stairs to the fabric shop.

"You sure about leaving them alone?" she asked.

"No, but I don't know what else to do. Carson needs to tell Clark what he told me—about Laird, Beatriz, everything. It won't do any good for me to act as an intermediary."

"And how do you plan to find out what they talk about?"

"I'll ask Carson when Clark leaves, and you can ask Clark. We'll share intel over doughnuts."

"You just assume I'd be down for breaking Clark's confidence?"

"If you don't, then I'll know there's more between you and Clark than you let on."

"Checkmate." She looked around the store's interior. "You don't have something to show me, do you?"

"Nope, but I could use your help cleaning up the store."

I gave Charlie the task of tidying up the fabric rolls around the room while I put a Booker T. & the M.G.'s CD into my boom box. A room filled with fabric absorbed sound like a sea sponge with a spill, so I cranked the volume to compensate. The music was loud enough to make conversation difficult, so we both focused on our respective tasks. While Charlie moved from display to display, rerolling the fabric to a uniform length, I spent the next half hour taking bolts of fabric from the cutting station and returning them to their original displays.

The CD ended. I pulled out my box of CDs and flipped through them to choose another. Charlie walked to my bridal display and stared at the sketches. She pointed at the space where Beatriz's requested sketch had been pinned.

"Did someone buy one?"

"Sort of. That's the dress Beatriz wants."

"Where is it?"

"It isn't. I haven't started it."

"You said it was a big job. You said you didn't know if you could get it done on time."

"Right and right." I set the CDs down and joined Charlie by the display. I unpinned one of the sketches by the bottom of the display and moved it to the empty space. It didn't completely solve the problem. "Considering both the bride and the groom are under suspicion of murder, there probably isn't going to be a wedding."

"And if you believed either one of them was guilty, you wouldn't have invited one to spend the night and the other to sit around your living room drinking wine."

"I don't know what to believe anymore."

My attention was half on what Charlie said and half on the display. It was the tail end of the wedding season. Adelaide didn't like to book wedding parties in November or December because of the holidays, so after October, the Waverly House would go back to business as usual. With no referrals, there would be no point in keeping this display together.

When I'd first set it up, I'd seen it as a talking point for potential customers. I didn't want to get into the wedding dress business, but I didn't mind giving away ideas for possible dresses, not if it inspired someone or helped them make a big decision. Moving my white fabrics into one display had been out of necessity; my initial display needed more than just a few drawings to sell my point. But once I moved my white and near-white fabrics into place, the display became more than an afterthought. It had become a destination.

I adjusted a bolt of white duchess satin and picked some threads off of my sweater. "Scratch that, it's not true. I believe *someone* wanted Laird dead. And I believe that someone knew Carson and Beatriz were the likeliest scapegoats. Laird knew they were coming to San Ladrón. Someone else must have known it too."

"Walk me through the list of people you've met since this all started."

I pulled one of the chairs away from the table and sat down. Charlie remained standing.

"There's a lot of them. Evan, Beatriz's wedding planner. I've found him at the Waverly House discussing the wedding needs more than once. There's Beatriz's assistant, Renee, who is also a bridesmaid. She came with Beatriz to her appointment on Friday."

Charlie nodded. "Who else?"

"Ursula, her press agent. She's another bridesmaid."

"Does this woman have any bridesmaids who aren't on her payroll?"

"One," I said, then clarified, "me."

Charlie stared at me as if I'd just told her I'd had an alien love child. "You didn't tell me that."

"Technically, I don't know if it's true. But when Giovanni gave me the measurements of the three bridesmaids, two of them matched up with Ursula and Renee. The third set was mine."

"What color are the dresses?"

"Black."

Charlie tipped her head back and stared at my ceiling. "He asked her to include you."

"Yep."

"Could be to buy your loyalty. Make you feel like part of the family so you don't go accusing either one of them of a felony."

"I know. Giovanni knew about Beatriz's appointment with me, which means he could have told any number of people that she would be here."

"Did he?"

"I don't know. He wants her to endorse his store publicly. It's not in his character to acknowledge the wedding dress is being made here if he wants her to give him credit for the work being done there."

Charlie turned around and leaned against the wall. "Is there anybody else on your radar?"

"Katya Petrova was the prima ballerina at Beatriz's conservatory before Katya had an injury that made her retire. She was here on Friday."

"Whoa," Charlie said. She sat down and propped her elbows on the table. "Does Clark know about her?"

"I don't know what Clark knows. I thought she was just a random customer who had the unfortunate timing of showing up during a private appointment, and I felt bad about turning her away. I didn't think I'd ever see her again, but after I found out who she was, I pressed her to meet with me at Lopez Donuts. She wasn't exactly forthcoming. She ran out of the shop, and Vaughn followed her. I'm hoping he got her to talk to Clark."

"I wondered if you included Vaughn in this whole thing."

"Why wouldn't I?" I asked.

Charlie tipped her head back again and looked at the ceiling. "Your ex-boyfriend spent the night in your apartment two days ago, and now he's back. This whole thing has to do with you looking out for him. It doesn't take a venture capitalist to see you still care about him."

"I'm not pining after him. He's a putz."

"I know he's a putz. I've known he's a putz since five minutes after meeting him. But I'm not the one who dated him for ten years."

"Well, I don't still care about him," I said, possibly doth protesting too much.

"Of course you do. You lived with him for a decade. And if he moves on to happily-ever-after with the Black Swan, then you're off the hook for any guilt you may be carrying around about having dumped him when you moved here."

"I don't have any guilt about moving here." It was one denial after another, and each time, the denials felt less true.

Charlie scooted her chair closer to the table. "How many investigations have you been involved with since moving to San Ladrón?"

"Four if you count this one."

"Right. And how many times, aside from tonight, have you invited Clark to your apartment?"

"None."

"Some people might find that curious."

"I have a history with Carson. And I thought I moved on and left him behind, but it turns out he moved on too. He moved on so much that I'm the one who looks stuck. He met someone, wooed her, got engaged, and set a wedding date. Vaughn and I have been on a couple of dates, but that's it."

"Maybe that's all it's ever going to be."

"You don't think he likes me?"

"Of course he likes you. He shows up at my auto shop with Van Halen bootleg CDs the day after your dates to ask if you said anything about him."

"No way," I said.

"Yes, way. Vaughn isn't the one keeping your relationship in park, Poly. You are. Maybe there's a reason for that, and maybe that reason is sitting upstairs at your kitchen table."

Everything Charlie had said made sense, but if there was one undeniable fact to this whole thing, it was what I told Charlie next. "I'm not still in love with Carson. I've just had a lot going on with reopening the store and managing my loan payments, and there hasn't been a lot of time to commit to a new relationship."

"Sure," she said. "I get that. And Vaughn probably gets that too. But it wouldn't hurt for you to make a grand gesture to eliminate any doubts."

A grand gesture. It was the same thing Carson said he'd done when he met Beatriz—sending flowers to the conservatory instead of contacting her agent for an address. He'd swayed the tide of public opinion in his favor so she would be receptive to an offer. It was Business 101, and Carson might not have been an expert in romance or ballet, but he knew business. He'd used his language to speak hers. That one gesture had kicked off a string of events that had led to their impending nuptials.

I picked up my "gesture," which was not exactly grand but significant in a way I hoped would be noticed: the box containing the book bag I'd made for Vaughn. I couldn't deny that an innocence had clung to my time with him from the start, almost as if we'd both wanted to come at a relationship without the baggage of past liaisons and emotional scars.

I flipped the card and wrote Vaughn's name on the back then tucked it under the ribbon and handed the box to Charlie. "Will you give this to your brother when he picks up his car?"

She took the box and shook it next to her ear. "Nothing in here that's going to get me in trouble with the cop, right?'

"What exactly do you think it is?"

"It's probably something cute and romantic, and if Clark gets wind of it, he might expect that behavior to rub off on me."

"You? Allow yourself to change?" I asked in mock surprise.

"Change is inevitable." She winked. "You can pilot the change, or you can let it steamroller over you. Your choice."

I turned away from Charlie and studied the wall of bridal sketches. "You know," I said slowly, looking up at the wall of sketches from my chair, "if someone is trying to frame Carson or Beatriz, the last thing they'd expect is for the wedding to go forward."

"True."

I stood, held out my hand, and pulled Charlie to her feet. "Which means we have to go full steam ahead. We have to make the real killer think Carson and Beatriz aren't suspects anymore so whoever killed Laird gets nervous and does something drastic."

"You have a plan."

"You bet I have a plan. This wedding is going to happen just like Beatriz said. I'll get Adelaide and Clark on board."

"What about you?"

"Go into my stockroom and grab a bolt of vintage tulle. Beatriz needs an impossible wedding dress, and it's going to take more than just me to do it."

# 33

I DIDN'T WASTE TIME FLESHING OUT MY PLAN DOWNSTAIRS. Charlie followed me back upstairs, where we found Clark and Carson playing poker. A pile of cash sat in the middle of the table.

"You're *gambling?*" I asked.

"My idea," Clark said. "I thought it would be a good way to pad the department's budget."

"Who's winning?" Charlie asked.

"Who do you think?" Carson said. He set down his hand and pulled the pot of cash toward him.

I knew a few things about the men at my table. One: Carson liked money. Two: Clark played in a regular poker game. Three: A friendly game of poker between adversaries was a perfectly good way to discover what one of said parties looked like when he was bluffing.

Point: Clark.

Clark, who confirmed my suspicion by getting up from the table, nodded at me. "Thanks for the invitation, Poly. Charlie? Are you ready to leave?"

"Just because we arrived together doesn't mean we're leaving together."

"Hey, Charlie, remember that thing you told me downstairs?" I asked. "About keeping your car in park?"

"This isn't that," she said.

"If you say so."

She turned to Clark. "Come on, Ryan. You can buy me a beer."

I followed the two of them to the front gate and let them out. Clark thanked me for the invitation. I didn't ask if he still suspected Carson, because the answer to that was obvious.

When I went upstairs, I found Carson pacing back and forth in my kitchen. "Geez, Poly. You left me alone with the cop investigating Laird Harden's murder case. He could have arrested me."

"Relax, Carson. Clark knows you're not guilty."

"That's not what his last four messages implied."

"Do you think the town sheriff would leave me alone with you if he thought you'd committed murder?"

Carson stood still. He looked at the pile of cash on the table, at the window that faced Bonita Avenue and then at me. "Did he let me win?"

"Probably." I pulled the pile of cash toward me and made a pile that I tapped on the table until it was in a neat stack. I held the wad of bills toward him. "Clark has a regular poker game. He probably wanted to see if you had any tells when you're bluffing."

Carson took the cash and fanned his face with it. "Too bad for him I don't have any tells."

"Carson," I said. "When you bluff, you scratch the tip of your nose. You pretend it's not a big itch, but the itch doesn't go away until you tell the truth. By then, your nose is red from all the scratching." I walked toward my bathroom and gestured for him to follow me. Once inside, I pointed at the mirror. Carson's face was still pale from the lack of sleep and the abundance of stress, but his nose was scarlet. He rubbed at it as if he could make the redness go away, then he pinched it between his thumb and forefinger and held. When he spoke, his voice came out nasally.

"He tricked me," he said.

"Yes, but he also let you win."

Carson folded the cash in half and shoved it deep into his jeans pocket. "He might not suspect me, but that doesn't mean he doesn't suspect Trixie."

"That might not matter."

I outlined my plan for Carson: a wedding—his wedding— just like he and Beatriz had planned but on Friday night, not Saturday. A candlelight ceremony at the Waverly House chapel. A manageable crowd for Clark and a near-impossible deadline for me.

I didn't tell Carson that last part.

A lot more of the planning fell onto my shoulders than Carson's, but if he didn't track down Beatriz and make peace, it wouldn't matter if I used every yard of fabric in my store to make her dress. He sat across from me with a blank look on his face, nodding occasionally but otherwise remaining silent.

When I finished outlining my plan, I said, "Somebody doesn't want your wedding to take place, so we're going to flush them out. It's what you both wanted in the first place, but you haven't said anything since I started talking, and I can't tell if you're on board or not."

Carson's face broke out in a wide smile. "I was practicing my new poker face. Gotcha!"

———

WHERE LAST NIGHT, I had a plan, today, I had problems. How, exactly, was I going to make a one-hundred-and-one-yard wedding dress in two days plus run the fabric store all by myself?

Simple answer: I wasn't. I called the one person whom I needed.

"Yes," Giovanni said. "I'll help you."

"Thank you," I gushed. "I have the fabric at my store. If you bring two—or maybe three—of the women from your workroom, they'll be able to get this done in time."

"Not so fast," Giovanni said. "I said I'd help you, but you have to help me first."

"What do you want?"

"Payment in full for these bridesmaids' dresses," he said.

"I thought you were going to charge the credit card you had on file."

"I tried. The sale declined. That gives me even less confidence that I'm going to be compensated for my work."

"Fine," I said. I reached for the credit card Carson had left with me to handle such demands and gave Giovanni the number. "Is that it?"

"No. I want design credit for the gown."

"No way! I designed the gown."

"And unless you plan to revise your business plan to include wedding dress production, which will drastically crimp your ability to staff the fabric store, then credit for the design won't do you one bit of good. To The Nines, on the other hand, will benefit greatly."

I didn't have a lot of options, and of all of Giovanni's skills, recognizing when someone was out of options was at the top of the list.

"Fine," I said. "Bring three seamstresses. And every single note you've ever taken on the Beatriz Rosen party. I want the measurement cards, the muslins, the client file, and whatever you scribbled on the paper cube you keep next to your phone."

"You must need this wedding to take place."

"There's more riding on it than you might think."

Giovanni and I wrapped up our negotiations, and I hung up.

My next call, which should probably have been the first, was to Adelaide.

"Poly," she said. "I spoke to Sheriff Clark about the Rosen-Cole wedding. Chef is working on a menu as we speak. Evan is coming to the Waverly House this morning to work through the rest of the details, including the flowers for the chapel. I can call Rosie's Posies now if you happen to know the color of the bridesmaids' dresses."

"Black."

"Excuse me?"

"The bridesmaids' dresses are black, which might not sound particularly wedding-like, but—"

"Black dresses! How edgy. I know you're going to have your hands full with business today, but Chef is sending over a platter for your team for lunch. Batten down the hatches, Poly. It's full steam ahead."

"Adelaide, how many café Americanos have you had today?"

"Poly, dear, we're planning an emergency wedding to flush out a murderer. I've gone straight to espresso."

Call number three was to Sheriff Clark. "The wedding is happening," I told him. "I just need one thing."

"Poly, I'm running an investigation with limited resources. I'm not in a position to grant requests to local businesses."

"I've asked several people to come to my store to help with Beatriz's wedding dress. Until this case is solved, there's a murderer out there, and I'm not comfortable putting people I know at risk."

"This case has nothing to do with you and your fabric shop," Clark said.

It was true, but it didn't particularly assuage my feelings of anxiety. He added, "I'll tell the Senior Patrol to keep an eye on your store. That's the best I can do."

It wasn't the same as having a class of rookies from the local community college patrolling my store, but it would have to do.

We had two days to get the details locked down for a Friday candlelight vigil, and that included spreading the word. My final call of the morning, which took place just under the wire before I opened for business, was to Ursula.

"This is Poly Monroe," I said. "I don't know if you've heard, but Beatriz's wedding is back on. It will be at the Waverly House on Friday night. The whole town of San Ladrón is getting involved. I can give you details on the wedding gown if you want to leak them to the media, but if you prefer, you can see it in person when you come for your fitting."

"Is this a joke?" Ursula asked.

"It's no joke. I know there have been issues regarding the ceremony, but it's full steam ahead," I said, borrowing Adelaide's phrase.

"You don't listen, do you? I thought I made myself clear when I told you to leave it alone."

"Carson and Beatriz shouldn't be punished because of what happened to Laird Harden. We have the full cooperation of the sheriff's department, and both the bride and the groom want this to happen."

"And this event will pour a sizeable amount of cash into your local economy, won't it?" she asked. "I'm sure the bride and the groom aren't the only people who want this to happen."

"Anything more than a civil ceremony at the courthouse would put money into an economy," I said. "That's why weddings are such big business."

"Then you tell Beatriz that the business of her wedding is going to happen without me. I hope to never see your small town again. Anyone who attends that ceremony is a fool, and I want no part of it."

# 34

FROM THE MOMENT CLARK GREENLIT THE IDEA OF MOVING forward with the wedding as if the case were closed, we'd known that somewhere along the way, we would meet with resistance. I hadn't expected that resistance to come from Beatriz's press agent. I'd been counting on Ursula to leak the event to the media and help draw out the killer.

"What happened to Laird is horrible. And the local sheriff's department is close to an arrest. But even though our town is small, Beatriz has a connection here, and this is where she chose to have her ceremony. As her press agent, and one of her bridesmaids, surely you can do this for her."

"My job as her press agent ended the day she chose to retire. This shotgun wedding may be a celebration for the rest of you, but to me, it marks the end of her career. Like I told you, Poly, I want nothing to do with this ceremony. Beatriz is no longer a client, and as soon as I get my deposit back from that tacky dress shop, I'll no longer be a part of her wedding party."

I didn't know what to say, which was just as well since she disconnected the call.

THE NEXT DAY and a half passed in a blur of fabric, fittings, and Motown.

Aside from the business of Carson and Beatriz's wedding, business was slow. Giovanni arrived at Material Girl on Wednesday afternoon along with two of his best seamstresses and three bulging garment bags. He pulled out a box of Frownies and handed them to me. "Those are for the groom, but you might keep a pair for yourself. This town is giving you premature forehead creases."

We had a brief meeting where he showed me the bridesmaids' dresses, and I created a new wedding dress design on the fly: a strapless gown with a fitted bodice and lace overlay and a skirt with so many fluffy layers of tulle that it would fill most guest bedrooms. It was close enough to the original sketch to please Beatriz, I hoped, but the slight changes I made would make it easier for us to construct on our impossible timetable. While Giovanni and company commandeered my sewing machine display, I loaded a cart in my stockroom with vintage tulle, marquisette, boning, lace, and ribbon.

Every single person who'd been contacted with a task for the wedding had agreed to participate, and the town was abuzz with excitement. One fairly huge problem remained: No one knew the whereabouts of Beatriz. If I didn't know better, I would say she was a runaway bride.

But I did know better, and that was thanks to Carson. He swore Beatriz would be at the chapel come Friday night, and I believed him. And not only because I wanted my sofa back. I also believed he understood there was more riding on this than his vows—that if unsolved, this murder would cast a cloud over their entire marriage.

———

By Friday afternoon, the activity inside Material Girl was slowing to a halt. My hand was calloused and cramped from cutting out panels of tulle. After a healthy dinner catered by Adelaide, we fueled ourselves on a steady diet of doughnuts, and the sugar boost and crash had a cumulative effect. By the time Giovanni announced that the dresses were done, all I wanted was a nap.

If everything went as planned, I could nap my way through the weekend.

At three o'clock, I carried my black gown upstairs then showered off the past two days and got ready. While the rest of the bridal party had taken the day to get ready at Tina's Salon, I didn't have that luxury. I put a little extra effort into my hair and makeup and stepped into the black ball gown that had been made to my measurements. As an act of rebellion, I slipped on my white leather sneakers under my gown and left my bedroom.

Carson stood in my living room, facing a mirror. "I never could get the hang of tying a bow tie," he said. He turned to me, holding the ends of his white-satin tie in each hand. "Can you help me out, Poly? For old times' sake?"

I didn't say yes or no. I stepped into his personal space and took the fabric then knotted it into a neat bow. I tugged on the loops with equal effort and squared it off.

"Thank you," he said quietly.

I looked up at his face.

"I know how much you've done for me this week, and I know you didn't have to. I used to think you'd eventually come back to me, but maybe that's not how this story ends."

"Does Beatriz make you happy?" I asked.

"More than I ever could have imagined."

"Then she's perfect for you."

"What about you? What's going on with McMichael?"

"My personal life is none of your business."

"Don't wait too long, Poly. You don't want to get stuck in first gear."

I gathered a sewing kit for last looks, and we left. Adelaide had set the ceremony for seven thirty, and it was quarter to seven now. It was twilight, and the waning sun cast a golden glow over the property.

In the time that I'd been holed up at Material Girl making dresses, Adelaide and Evan had been busy too. Pink rose petals had been scattered on the grounds outside of the chapel, and pink-blooming plants had been placed outside of the chapel doors, rooted in glossy black planters. Softly twinkling lights were draped along the eaves of the chapel, and battery-powered tea lights, nestled among the path of rose petals, directed people toward the doors. Using black as a wedding color outside of a chapel where a friend of the bride had been murdered had to have been a challenge, but the addition of the rosy-pink hue elevated the somber palette to one of elegance. I left Carson with the justice of the peace and followed Adelaide's directions to the back room, where Beatriz was getting dressed.

Renee was waiting for me. Her long hair had been styled in a neat French twist, and two curled tendrils hung down on either side of her face.

She handed me a shoebox. "We're going with pink shoes," she said. "I didn't know your size, so I guessed... eight?"

"Seven," I said. "Tall person, small feet. That's why I'm so klutzy. But don't worry. Nobody's going to see my sneakers."

"You can't wear sneakers!" she said. "But I can fix the size with toe pads." She rooted around in her bag and pulled out toe pads, gauze, and a pair of scissors. She snipped the cotton into small wads and went to work on the pink-satin pumps despite my protests. Twice, she handed me the shoes to try on until finally they fit well enough for me to walk in them.

Beatriz came out from behind the privacy screen. "How do I look?"

The dress was a marvel. The fitted satin bodice hugged her torso. Cups had been sewn into the dress, creating a bustline even though Beatriz's dancer body lacked womanly curves. Satin met with a burst of tulle at the waist and exploded in layer upon layer that cascaded to the floor. There were so many layers of tulle that the seamstresses had forgone the use of the marquisette to give the dress structure. It would have served only to weigh the dress down.

The seamstresses had been forced to make decisions to streamline the production of the gown in the short amount of time we had available to us, so instead of attaching a pattern of seed pearls like my sketch had indicated, a wide faille ribbon with beads already attached had been placed at Beatriz's waist, cinching the dress and furthering the illusion of an hourglass figure. Beatriz looked, simply put, stunning.

But there was something else about Beatriz's appearance: Thanks to her quickie haircut and color, her appearance matched mine: chin-length bobbed auburn hair in my very shade, no less. It seemed wrong on so many levels that Carson's bride had become my lookalike instead of looking like herself.

"We have to cover your hair," I said. I pointed at her head. "You can't marry Carson looking like—not like you."

Beatriz stared at me. I was barefoot, and she was in five-inch heels, and we were close to the same height.

"We never thought about a veil," she said. "Can you make one out of"—she glanced at my sewing kit—"something here?"

"I brought a needle, thread, and scissors," I said. "We used everything. There's not enough tulle left for a veil. But..." I had an idea. "I have a vintage headpiece back at my place. How much time do we have?"

Renee checked her watch. "The ceremony's supposed to start in twenty-three minutes."

"I can get there and back if I hurry," I said. "Where are my sneakers?"

Renee held one up and looked at me apologetically. She'd removed the shoelaces. "I thought you could use these to tie the pink pumps onto your feet."

I didn't want to admit it, but this felt like my fault.

Beatriz broke the silence. "It's fine," she said, though anybody who saw the expression on her face would know that it was anything but.

"I'll be fine in these," I said and left.

I grabbed my keys and took off. On the way, I called Charlie.

"'Sup?" she answered.

"There's a problem. Your makeover left Beatriz looking like me."

"That makeover was for her benefit."

"I know. But she's about to marry my ex-boyfriend, and don't you think her wedding memories—their wedding memories—should be of them and not of him and a Poly impersonator?"

"Was she worried about that?"

"Not until I mentioned it. I'm on my way to my place to get a vintage headpiece. I should be back before the ceremony is supposed to start, but just in case I cause a delay, can you let Clark know what's going on?"

Charlie's voice dropped. "Are you sure this isn't just an excuse to keep your ex from moving on?"

"I'm not trying to keep Carson from getting married," I huffed as I hurried down the alley. "I'm trying to be considerate and give them the closest thing I can to the wedding they deserve."

"You sure about that?"

"Just give Clark the message." I hung up.

I resented Charlie's implication, but the only way to prove she was wrong was to get the vintage headpiece and get back before the ceremony started. I hoisted my black dress up and cursed the too-big shoes on my feet. Halfway to my shop, I kicked the satin pumps off and left them under a tree then ran the rest of the way on cold, bare feet.

I let myself into my shop and scrambled up the stairs. My apartment was as I'd left it: Carson's copy of *The Art of War* on my coffee table and the box of Frownies that Giovanni had given Carson next to it with two empty wrappers.

I went to my closet and pushed my clothes aside. In the back, stored in their garment bags, were the clothes my great-aunt Millie had collected during her life. She'd been the one to teach me that I could learn garment construction from deconstruction, and she'd started me on my lifelong journey of collecting damaged vintage items to use as inspiration for new designs. And among the gowns—hers and mine—I found the velvet pouch that stored the vintage headpiece Carson had given me. It would perfectly coordinate with Beatriz's dress. I removed the cap from the pouch and stared at it. Was it perfect? Or was this the worst possible item I could lend Beatriz for her wedding to Carson? Was Charlie right? On some deeper level, did it bother me that Carson was moving on?

There wasn't time to worry about that—not now. I slipped the cap back into the velvet pouch and dangled it over my wrist. I turned toward my bedroom door and realized I wasn't alone.

# 35

RENEE STOOD IN THE DOORWAY TO MY BEDROOM, WATCHING ME. Her eyes moved from my face to the velvet pouch and back to my face.

"You were gone longer than we expected," she said. "I thought something might have happened to you." She held up my pink satin pumps that I'd kicked off on the way.

"I was going to get them on my way back." I held up my wrist. "We can go. I've got the headpiece."

Renee backed out of the doorway and turned to leave, but she stopped when she reached the landing. "Why is that book here?" she asked. She pointed into the living room, and I followed the extension of her arm.

"It belongs to the groom," I said. "He has funny ideas about marriage."

But Renee didn't seem to find any humor in the joke I'd made at Carson's expense. She stared at me as if I'd slapped her in the face.

"Seriously, he probably owns multiple copies, but I'll make sure he gets it after the wedding is over."

"He was here? When?"

"Last night. He and I—we're—friends."

It felt odd to refer to Carson as my friend, but after everything that had transpired this week, I knew it was the truth. I could see it so clearly now. Carson's news hadn't meant anything about where I was in my life. My journey would happen on its own time.

"Carson needed a place to crash, so I offered up my sofa. Don't worry. He's in love with Beatriz. He'd do anything for her. And nobody wants them to get married more than I do. Trust me."

What I'd intended to be words of encouragement about the strength of Carson and Beatriz's bond turned out to be the wrong thing to say. Renee's face turned red, and her fists balled up.

Something had affected Beatriz's PA in a way I couldn't have anticipated, and I didn't know what it was. But the longer we stood there, the surer I was that Renee had something to hide —something that Beatriz's wedding would expose. I'd gotten lost in my memories, distracted by personal issues that could wait until tomorrow, but Renee's response sucked me back into the present.

My brain sought details to piece together, facts that would combine to tell a story other than the ones I'd fabricated over the past week, but I felt like I was trying to bake a cake with ingredients for beef stew. I'd been focused on Laird and Beatriz's ballet pairing, but Renee had been by Beatriz's side all along. What did Laird have in common with Carson? And why would Carson marrying Beatriz threaten Renee?

"She's not going to leave you," I said. "You told me yourself that Beatriz has been generous with you. She trusts you to handle things for her. Her marriage to Carson isn't going to put you out of a job. Carson cares about money. Finances. He's not going to want to organize her social calendar."

Renee turned on me. "He's going to find out what I did. He's going to ruin everything."

For the first time since I'd discovered her in my apartment, I felt fear. Sure, I was bigger. Taller. But I was also barefoot in a ball gown and with a tendency to trip over my own two feet, and suddenly, those two feet became the most unreliable appendages of my body.

I leveled my voice. "We should get back," I said. "If we don't, someone will come looking for us." I hoped I was right, but more than that, I hoped the threat of someone arriving would keep Renee from doing anything drastic.

An hour ago, Renee had been in the bridesmaids' dressing room alongside the Waverly House wedding chapel. A hairstylist and makeup team from Tina's Salon had made her picture-perfect for the ceremony. But now, tendrils of hair had escaped her French twist, and her eye makeup had smudged, leaving behind a frazzled, frantic-looking woman. The heavy-handed makeup that had been applied kept her face porcelain-like, but her neck and chest were flushed, making her look like she'd gotten a sunburn while wearing a bag on her head.

Renee stepped toward me, and I moved around the opposite side of the coffee table. I bent slightly forward to shore up my balance and held my hands out in front of me in a *calm down* gesture.

"Listen to me, Renee. Carson isn't going to care if you continue to work for Beatriz! He'll probably want to keep you on their payroll. He'll probably give you a raise."

Renee bent down and flipped the book open, and Carson's inscription stared up at her. *I'm sorry, Poly. None of this was supposed to happen.*

Whatever it was that Renee feared from Carson, the inscription temporarily confused her.

"What did he mean by that?"

"It's—it's Carson being Carson. His heart is in the right place, but his actions don't always take direction from his heart. He thought having my shop involved in his wedding was going to be a good thing for me, but it turned into a nightmare because of—" I didn't say Laird's name.

The clock ticked while we stood on opposite sides of my coffee table, and any chance I might have had at getting back to the chapel on time was slipping by. But the wedding didn't matter anymore, not to me. Because the whole point of us mounting this ceremony was to draw out Laird Harden's killer, and as those seconds ticked by, I became more and more certain that she was here with me.

"Why did you do it, Renee? What did Laird do to you?"

She sank down onto the sofa. "Before I became Beatriz's personal assistant, I worked on costumes for the ballet company. I repaired tutus and leotards and pointe shoes. I saw a lot of things from backstage, including how Laird manipulated the dancers for his entertainment. He dated Beatriz, but he cheated on her with other girls, and he blackmailed them into keeping quiet. He knew I knew, and he made my life miserable. But one day, he apologized. Almost as if he'd seen the error of his ways."

"Laird didn't impress me as the self-reflective type."

She glanced up as if she'd forgotten I was in the room. "He handed me a pair of pointe shoes and asked me to reinforce the ribbons. They were for the lead ballerina at the time. That was the day she misjudged her landing and injured her ankle. She never danced again."

"You felt responsible."

"I *was* responsible. And Laird knew it. And after Beatriz got the lead, he used what he knew to blackmail me." Her eyes were bloodshot and wide, and the frantic energy I'd seen earlier when we faced off across the table returned. "He said he'd spin it as the greatest scandal in the world of ballet. That Beatriz used me to sabotage Katya's shoes for her personal gain. After everything she'd done for me, I couldn't let that happen."

"You paid him off."

She nodded. "But he kept asking for more until I didn't have anything left. I thought he'd go away when he realized I was broke, but he didn't. He told me if I didn't have the money, I knew where to get it."

"You stole from Beatriz?"

"Yes. I was going to pay her back in time. But when she got engaged, there was no more time."

The cloud around the details I'd sought through this investigation started to clear. Carson's love for Beatriz wasn't the problem here. It was his love of money. Not in an Ebenezer Scrooge way but in an I'm-going-to-go-over-my-new-wife's-books way.

"Why did you meet Laird on Friday night?"

"I needed it to be over. I told him I was going to come clean and tell Beatriz everything—about the ribbons on Katya's shoes, about his blackmail, about me stealing from her to pay him off. I knew it was going to be the end of our relationship, but it was the only way."

"Laird didn't accept that, did he?"

"I didn't care if he accepted it or not. I'd already made up my mind. But then he told me—" Her breath hitched, and she stood. "He told me he was the one who sabotaged Katya's shoes. He was behind her fall the whole time. He manipulated the situation to make me believe, all this time, that *I* did it. That I ruined a promising career. I've been paying for something I never even did. I snapped. I charged him. He tried to pivot out of my way, but when I shoved him, he lost his balance. He fell back and hit his head on the ground. He just lay there, still. And I got scared."

"You left?"

"No. I crept over to him to see if he—to see how he was—and he grabbed me. He reached up and grabbed my shirt and held me in place. And I didn't know what else to do. I pulled off my shirt and started to run, but I knew there was nowhere I could run. There was nowhere I could go to get away from him. I grabbed a candleholder, and I turned back around, and I swung. He was right there, and he—"

"And this time, he didn't get back up."

"No," she said. "He didn't."

"You killed him," I said. "You have to turn yourself in. You were ready to put an end to it all at once. If you want it all to be over, you have to tell Sheriff Clark what happened."

"No." Her eyes widened, and she stood. She glanced from side to side as if confirming that it was just her and me, that we were alone in my living room while the rest of the town congregated at the chapel for Carson and Beatriz's wedding. "No," she said again. "I almost got away with it. You're the only one who knows the truth."

As soon as she said it, I knew she was right. And I knew how bad that was for me.

All this time, I'd been worried that the world was moving on without me. I'd questioned whether my move from Los Angeles had been about changing my life or about hiding from it, and I'd kept myself busy with the investigation into Laird Harden's murder instead of examining my feelings—about Carson, yes, but about Vaughn too. I'd put boundaries in place to keep me from moving on too fast, but the only person who could know how fast was too fast was me.

The next thirty seconds happened in slow motion.

Renee planted her foot on the table and lunged toward me. I ducked from her grasp. She grabbed a table lamp and swung it from the base, and I grabbed the only thing within reach to defend myself: Carson's copy of *The Art of War*. I swung against the lamp like it was the bottom of the ninth in the World Series and I needed a home run. The book bounced against the lampshade, but the momentum was enough to knock Renee off her balance. She tilted backward and released the lamp. Her arms flailed wildly through the air as she fell. I reached out to catch her, but she swatted my hand away. Her head glanced off the chair behind her, and when she hit the floor, she lay still. Her eyes fluttered, not opening fully but not closed either. She tried to stand, but pain flashed across her face.

"I'll call 911," I said. "But you're going to have to tell them everything."

Renee nodded as if the fight had left her.

"She just did," said Clark.

I was surprised to find the sheriff standing in my doorway. "I'll take it from here," he said.

"You don't want me to stay?"

"No," Clark said. "You're needed at a wedding."

# 36

Contrary to everything I'd imagined over the past week, the wedding ceremony went off without a hitch. I even stepped into the recently vacated role as maid of honor. Katie was the other bridesmaid, and Mrs. D. walked Beatriz down the aisle. Between the three of us, we represented Beatriz's distant past, her recent past, and her present day. Carson represented her future, and I couldn't have been happier to watch her marry him.

And I meant that.

A lot had transpired over the past week, not the least of which was an examination of my life. I'd tricked myself into believing that I'd changed, but had I? Not really. I was the same Poly I'd always been, just in a new setting.

When a town came together to handle a last-minute wedding, a town deserved a celebration, and that was exactly what we got. The mayor closed the block of Bonita Avenue, and we held the reception outside. It was a perfect October day, probably one of the last warm days before the temperature dropped. It wasn't cold by the rest of the country's standards but chilly enough for us to don jackets, scarves, and sweaters and collectively pretend it was winter.

I hoisted the fabric from my ball gown into each fist and walked toward Bonita Avenue.

"Hey, Poly! Wait up." I turned around and saw Carson waving at me. I waited for him to catch up.

"Shouldn't you be with your bride?"

"I've got my whole life to be with her," he said. "You? Not so much."

"We don't have to be strangers, Carson."

"Yes, but let's be honest. You have your life here, and I have my life there." He reached into his tux jacket and pulled out a white envelope. "Even if we don't talk regularly, I'll always know you have my back. Thank you, Poly. For today. For this week. For everything."

I took the envelope. "What's this? Beatriz already paid for her dress."

"Open it."

I reached into the envelope and pulled out a check. It was made out to Material Girl, not to me, and it was for the balance of my loan to Mr. McMichael, down to the penny.

I slipped the check into the envelope and handed it back. "I appreciate the gesture, but I don't want to owe you."

He didn't take the envelope. "Officially, you undercharged Beatriz for her dress," he said. "Unofficially, the way I see it is that I might never have found this whole life if not for you and that fabric store. And you might not find the life you want if you let that loan hang over your head." He put his hands into his pockets. "Keep it, Poly. I can't think of anybody I'd rather give a check to than you."

Now that the murderer was behind bars and the wedding was over, my mind was clear for new thoughts, and one fought its way to the front. I crossed the street and walked toward

Vaughn, who stood by the drink station in front of the Broad-side Tavern, watching the crowd. He spotted me, and his face lit up, and I felt myself mirror his reaction.

He picked up a second flute of champagne and offered it to me. "To my favorite substitute teacher," he said. "Thanks for the A-plus."

"You earned it." I took it and clinked his glass, swallowed a sip, and asked the question on my mind. "Do you want to get married?"

"Is this a proposal?" he asked in reply, raising his eyebrows.

"Maybe," I said playfully then gestured toward Carson and Beatriz with my flute, taking care not to spill champagne. "This whole thing made me look at my life differently. I told myself that I moved on when I moved here, but maybe I didn't."

"Are you sad that your ex married Beatriz?"

"I'm delighted that he married Beatriz. They're meant for each other. And that gives me hope for the future."

"Maybe that's the problem. Maybe you shouldn't think so much about the future, and you should focus on today."

I turned my back on the crowd and gave him my full attention. "And what is it about today that makes it any different from yesterday or tomorrow?"

"We're both here. Together," Vaughn said. "No exes, no murder investigations, no outstanding loan balances, or inquisitive family members. Just you and me and"—he looked past me at the crowd of friends and neighbors and strangers who filled the street—"two hundred of our closest friends."

I glanced over my shoulder then back at Vaughn. "Do you want to get out of here?"

"I thought you'd never ask."

# ABOUT THE AUTHOR

National bestselling author Diane Vallere writes smart, funny, and fashionable character-based mysteries. After two decades working for a top luxury retailer, she traded fashion accessories for accessories to murder. A past president of Sisters in Crime, Diane started her own detective agency at age ten and has maintained a passion for shoes, clues, and clothes ever since. Find out more at dianevallere.com.

# ACKNOWLEDGMENTS

I wasn't sure how easy it would be to reconnect with Poly Monroe and company after a few years away from San Ladrón. Life has a way of not changing for just long enough to make us comfortable and then pelting us with curve balls, and this book emerged out of a few years of having been pelted. As it turned out, Poly, Charlie, Vaughn, and the rest of the Material Witness gang were ready for me to revisit them, and they made my job very easy by showing up every day and telling me the story you found here.

Thank you to Angela MacRae for your thorough work on this manuscript. I'm sure Poly would love for you to shop at Material Girl, too! To fellow writers Gigi Pandian, Lisa Q. Maxwell, and Ellen Byron, for your assistance in working through sticky plot points and the inspiration that led to me researching the world of ballet.

Thank you to my mom for exposing me to fabric at an early age and answering my questions about material to this day.

Thank you to the Polyester Posse, for helping spread word of this book to the world, and to subscribers to the Weekly DiVa for your interest in my books.

And lastly, thank you to the readers who continued to ask about Poly's return. Without you, this book would not exist.

# ALSO BY

The Pajama Frame

Lover Come Hack

Apprehend Me No Flowers

Teacher's Threat

The Kill of It All

Love Me or Grieve Me

Please Don't Push Up the Daisies

<u>Sylvia Stryker Outer Space Mysteries</u>

Murder on a Moon Trek

Scandal on a Moon Trek

Hijacked on a Moon Trek

Framed on a Moon Trek

<u>Material Witness Mysteries</u>

Suede to Rest

Crushed Velvet

Silk Stalkings

Tulle Death Do Us Part

<u>Costume Shop Mystery Series</u>

A Disguise to Die For

Masking for Trouble

Dressed to Confess

Made in the USA
Middletown, DE
03 November 2023

41840726R00175